FROM THE DARK WE RISE

BOOKS BY MARION KUMMEROW

A Light in the Window

Not Without My Sister

MARION KUMMEROW

FROM THE DARK WE RISE

bookouture

Published by Bookouture in 2021

An imprint of Storyfire Ltd.
Carmelite House
50 Victoria Embankment
London EC4Y 0DZ

www.bookouture.com

ISBN: 978-1-80019-288-1
eBook ISBN: 978-1-80019-287-4

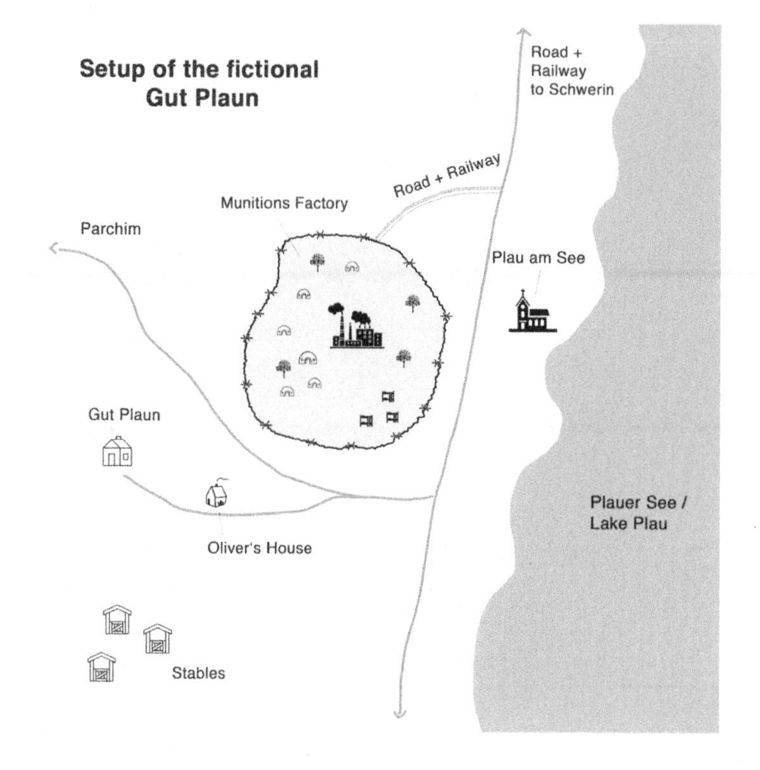
Setup of the fictional
Gut Plaun
Road +
Railway
to Schwerin
Road + Railway
Munitions Factory
Parchim
Plau am See
Gut Plaun
Plauer See /
Lake Plau
Oliver's House
Stables

1

Plau am See, Germany, Late Summer 1942

She marveled at the beautiful landscapes north of Berlin, as she sat beside Horst Richter, head of the Gestapo in Leipzig.

"I believe you will find the manor a welcome respite," he said affably as his black limousine emerged from the woods and a small town appeared before them.

"It's been a while since I've visited here." Despite being on friendly terms with the Gestapo officer, who had become something of a mentor and father figure, she was bathed in a cold sweat.

Horst, as she now called him, had been instrumental in making sure she inherited the vast Huber family fortune. He treated her as a doting father would treat his daughter, something he thought she was lacking since her parents—and then, several months later, both of her brothers—had died in a bombing.

There was only one problem: he wouldn't hesitate to send her to the Gestapo's torture dungeons if he ever suspected she wasn't really Annegret Huber, daughter of his late friend SS-Standartenführer Wolfgang Huber, but Margarete Rosenbaum, the Huber's former maid—and a Jew.

An imposter who'd taken on Annegret's identity after a devastating British air raid had sent the Hubers' house tumbling to the ground, leaving Margarete as the sole survivor. It had been a rash decision to grab Annegret's papers, who was only two years younger than herself, and pretend to be the high-ranking Nazi's daughter in order to save herself from suffering the same fate of her fellow Jews.

She shivered at the memory, not only because of her momentous decision, but even just thinking about the explosion itself. If she closed her eyes, she could still feel the low rumble of the earth when the bombs came nearer, the earsplitting screech of the impact and the bloodcurdling sound as the building collapsed. Something hit her and she was knocked unconscious. When she came to again, at first, she couldn't see, because the air was filled with dust and debris. Coughing and spluttering she finally realized the serendipity that had saved her: the staircase had broken into two, forming a triangle where she'd been trapped beneath and thus protected from the crumbling walls all around her.

Once she could see and breathe again, she crawled from her cave, crinkling her nose at the smell of burnt material and singed flesh. That's when she saw her, Annegret Huber, lying with twisted limbs and empty, staring eyes. When she was still alive, nobody would have confused the two girls for each other: the haughty, elegant, rich, confident daughter of a high-ranking Nazi and the downtrodden, dull, poor, cowed Jewish maid.

But after crawling from a building blasted to shreds, coated in dust, the two girls of similar age, both with brown shoulder-length hair and hazel eyes, would be interchangeable for any stranger. At least that was what Margarete had based her split-second decision on when she'd borrowed, or rather stolen, Annegret's identity papers.

And it had worked. Better than planned. In fact, she'd never once imagined she would keep Annegret's identity for longer than was needed to escape Berlin, and certainly never intended to inherit any part of the Huber family's fortune.

That day seemed like a lifetime ago, since so much had happened since. And today she would shed her skin once again, and become the mistress of the beautiful manor Gut Plaun, in the quaint village of Plau am See, about one and a half hours' drive north of Berlin.

She'd never been here before and had only seen the place in paintings and photographs. In reality the landscape was even more beautiful. The dark woods, the lonely roads, everything was so different from war-riddled Berlin. Here, it almost seemed as if Hitler hadn't thrown the country into a raging war years ago, both against its neighboring countries—and unbeloved parts of its own population.

"Such a lovely sleepy town," Margarete exclaimed as she admired the streets lined by houses in light-colored masonry with orange-red tiled roofs, red-framed windows, and red doors. When Horst gave her a puzzled glance, she quickly explained. "It doesn't sound like me, right? I always used to say the countryside was boring and stopped coming here altogether when I was ten, because I hated it so much." She giggled in Annegret's high-pitched manner, something she'd perfected through weeks of practice in front of the mirror. "After last year's horrible experiences, I've changed my mind and right now, peaceful and boring is what I need most."

"Your father liked coming here, because it gave him, too, a sense of peace that Berlin couldn't provide," Horst said.

No wonder, since Hitler tossed us into this awful war. Margarete nodded and turned her head. They had left the town behind and she looked at the passing green meadows, contrasted by the darker shades of the trees, and the blue water of the huge Plauer See.

She hadn't come unprepared. She had spent countless hours in the public library in Leipzig and read up on the history of Plau am See, a medieval town spread around the old castle and the gothic

Saint Mary's Church, featuring some of the most beautiful ancient half-timbered houses. The village had prospered in the last century due to the cloth mill and the iron foundry that had produced the state's first paddle steamer in 1845. Later, a brickwork factory had completed the town's industrialization.

Even though nowadays the area was mostly known for its beautiful location on one of the lakes in the Mecklenburg Lake District, it featured a wide array of industries—mostly ammunitions factories safely tucked away from the big cities and the threat of enemy air raids.

"We're here," Horst announced about ten minutes later as he pulled through the gates and parked in front of a stunning manor house whose walls were partly clad in ivy. It was a sight to behold and Margarete involuntarily gasped, reminding herself that she now owned this most impressive building.

"It looks smaller than I remember," she said, just to say something. In reality it was a lot bigger than it had appeared on the photos she'd seen.

"Because you were a child when you last came here."

"Of course."

As he exited the vehicle and walked around to help her out of the Mercedes, the manor's front door opened and a man stepped out to retrieve their luggage from the trunk. Margarete barely restrained herself from lending a hand. These ingrained habits still surfaced despite her best intentions and threatened to give her real identity away.

You're the lady of the manor. Never forget that. She put on a gracious smile and turned toward the house, where a woman in her fifties appeared. Despite wearing a uniform consisting of a blueish-beige dress with white collar and cuffs and an immaculate white apron, she exuded authority. Even without matching her appearance to the one picture she had seen of her, Margarete knew that this woman was Frau Mertens, the housekeeper.

"Welcome, Fräulein Annegret. Herr Reichskriminaldirektor," Frau Mertens greeted them, even as she ordered the servant to carry the luggage inside with nothing more than a flick of her wrist. "Please forgive me, Fräulein Annegret, I wasn't informed about your preferences and thus have prepared your old room for you. But if you want to reside in the main chambers, I will immediately take care of the arrangements."

"That'll be fine, Frau Mertens," Margarete answered, fighting the urge to bow her head.

"Thank you, Frau Mertens," Horst said.

"I have refreshments prepared in the small sitting room, but since we didn't know the exact time of your arrival, lunch will need another thirty minutes." Frau Mertens made it sound like an apology.

"That will be fine. We shall freshen up before coming downstairs," Richter answered. He turned to Margarete. "Would you like to take a stroll through the gardens? I don't know about you, but my legs could use a good stretch."

"That sounds like a fine idea," Margarete readily agreed.

"Good then. Shall we say, in ten minutes?"

"Ten minutes is perfect." Margarete looked at Frau Mertens, wondering how she could go about inquiring about the location of her room without giving her false identity away. "I trust everything is in order at the manor?" she asked, stalling for time.

"Everything is in the best condition, Fräulein Annegret. Would you be wanting to request anything special for dinner? We don't have our normal provisions, but I can try..."

Margarete shook her head. "Whatever you had planned will be fine. I'm not picky."

Frau Mertens raised a brow at that. "When did that happen, Fräulein Annegret? Even as a wee baby you had very strong likes and dislikes."

Margarete pressed her jaws together. Nine months pretending to be Annegret and she still made such unnecessary slips. Thinking quickly, she decided to use the opportunity to start with a clean slate, and make her version of Annegret more likeable than the real one had been. "I mostly dislike being compared to how I once was as a child. The war has changed all of us and I'm proud to have grown beyond my former selfish and self-absorbed ways."

"Well, that is a good thing then." Frau Mertens paused for a moment, side-glancing at Richter, seemingly pondering how best to continue. "My deepest condolences on the death of your brothers. It is deeply disturbing that they were killed in such a heinous way—murdered by the evil French Résistance—and I'm sure our great government has taken steps to avenge their deaths."

Richter's eyes became cold and distant as he answered in a clipped voice, "The dangerous criminals responsible for bombing the restaurant in Paris are being rounded up as we speak. No doubt they will face execution after we have found out everything we need to know."

Crushed by his words, which were news to her, Margarete pulled together all her strength and willpower to stay upright, putting on an expression of satisfaction. "It is balm for my soul to know those monsters will pay for the grief they caused, not only to me, but also to the families of the other victims." In total four Nazi officers, among them the two Huber brothers, Reiner and Wilhelm, had perished during the explosion.

When Horst didn't offer any further explanation, she decided to wait until a later time to ask him about the identity of the resisters, hoping her good friend Paulette wouldn't be amongst those captured.

Memories swamped her. Again, she had been the sole survivor of a vicious explosion, walking away from the destruction like a phoenix from the ashes. Her stomach tightened at the smell of burned material and singed flesh. A smell that had been imprinted onto her brain, making her wake up at night, bathed in sweat, gagging.

It had been the right thing to do—if killing someone could ever be correct—but she still suffered from nightmares. This time she had orchestrated the explosion, had lured the four men into the trap, had locked them inside without a chance to escape the catastrophe.

She still felt a twinge of guilt whenever she thought about it. That last moment, when Wilhelm, the man whose sister she was pretending to be, had looked at her with an abundance of love in his eyes, before he'd sacrificed himself to save her life. She gave a deep sigh.

"Are you alright, Fräulein Annegret?" Frau Mertens asked.

"I am just thinking of my brothers. I still can't believe they're gone."

Frau Mertens nodded. "You poor girl. Let's go inside." She turned around and they followed her into the house, where she waved at a thin girl who couldn't be much older than eighteen. "Come here, Dora."

Dora wore a similar uniform to the housekeeper, a black dress with a stiff collar. She had a pretty face with big brown eyes and high cheekbones. Her black hair was plaited into one long braid reaching all the way down to her hips. She approached them with her eyes cast downward, stopped a few feet away from Margarete and curtsied. "Fräulein Annegret. Herr Reichskriminaldirektor."

Herr Richter raised an eyebrow at hearing her strong accent and the girl visibly tensed under his scrutiny.

Frau Mertens hurried to explain, "Dora is Ukrainian. She was assigned to us by the labor office."

Everyone in the room relaxed. The Ukraine was an ally and, thus, Ukrainians were welcome to work in household positions. Margarete had long given up to seek rhyme or reason in those decisions, because how was a Ukrainian citizen different from a Russian or White Russian? It showed once more that the whole race theory was random and had more to do with politics than science.

"Fräulein Annegret, apart from her general household duties, Dora will be your personal maid while you stay with us," Frau Mertens explained.

This was the help she'd been looking for. Relieved, she told the maid, "I was just about to freshen up in my room. If you'll accompany me, you can hang up my clothing and I'll let you know what needs to be pressed for dinner."

Dora made another curtsy and nodded several times, before heading up the staircase. Margarete looked at Horst. "Will you find your way? Or should I send Dora back for you?"

Frau Mertens jumped in. "That won't be necessary. I'll show the Reichskriminaldirektor to his room myself." She paused for a moment and then added, "I'm so sorry, but we don't have the number of staff we used to have."

"No need to apologize, the war requires sacrifices from all of us," Margarete cut her short, and reached the top of the stairs just in time to see Dora enter the last door on the right down the left wing. She forced herself to walk sedately in that direction, making sure anyone observing her would believe her to be completely at ease in a once-favorite family getaway.

2

When Margarete entered the room, she involuntarily shuddered. She had already known that neither Annegret nor her brothers had been at Gut Plaun for close to a decade, but this room confirmed the fact. There was no way the fashionable, life-hungry, spoilt twenty-year-old she had known would stay in a room that looked like a little girl's dream.

Dora bustled around, opening Margarete's suitcase, hanging up clothes and placing shoes in the wardrobe. "Shall I take this to the bathroom?" Dora asked, holding up a bathrobe.

"Yes, please." Seemingly disinterested, she observed the maid with eagle-eyes, eager to familiarize herself with the new surroundings. Dora opened a hidden door in the wall, leading to a private bathroom.

The luxury in the manor was marvelous, and even the Hubers' former house in Berlin didn't measure up. Never in her life had she imagined that she'd go from being an exploited Jewish maid on the brink of deportation to a labor camp to the heir to the Huber estate and mistress over dozens of employees.

Margarete walked over to the window and looked out over the vast fields, the sculpted gardens, the stables and the nearby forest. She had no idea yet what exactly she would do with her fortune, but she was determined to fulfill Wilhelm's last wish, who'd urged her to use it for good.

Yearning filled her heart. Her relationship with Wilhelm had been a complicated one. He, the SS officer and she, the Jew. When he'd forced her to live with him in Paris pretending to be his sister, it had initially been a sinister plan for him to get his hands on the trust fund of his actual sister. And she'd hated him. But every day that passed, he'd shown her an unexpected kindness and she'd slowly fallen in love with him, despite every intention not to.

One day, he'd taken her out into the Bois de Boulogne to a concert organized by the German administration in honor of some thing or other; she didn't remember the occasion, what she remembered was the wonderful time she spent with Wilhelm.

He'd arranged for a picnic basket, complete with blanket, dishes, baguette, cheese, pâté de foie gras and other delicacies. Finally he'd even produced a bottle of expensive Bordeaux and two glasses. Long after the concert was over, they still sat surrounded by rose bushes, eating, drinking and talking. It was there that he'd told her about his dreams.

"I always wanted to work with art. A curator for a museum, a professor of art history, or even a wealthy philanthropist," Wilhelm said, his eyes glazing over with a dreamy expression.

She elbowed him. "Holding weekly meetings with artists. Especially the young and beautiful women."

He grinned at her. "I might. Although you know to whom my heart belongs. In my perfect world there would be no obstacles standing between us and you could be the hostess of my weekly circles, holding intelligent conversation, philosophizing about the essence of life."

"I know nothing about art or philosophy," she protested so as not to think about his prospect of getting married to him and living happily ever after, since it was not just impossible, it was illegal and a betrayal, especially to her people who suffered so much at the hands of the Nazis.

"I would teach you." He fed her another piece of cheese, which she washed down with the wine.

"Where did you learn about art and philosophy?"

"At my family's summer residence, Gut Plaun. Reiner and I used to have a private teacher, several actually. While Reiner was more interested in riding horses and all kinds of physical exercise, I took a liking to our literature teacher. When our teacher noticed how interested I was in the finer arts, he introduced me into a whole universe of fantastic things. Once he took me into Plau am See to visit the gothic Saint Mary's Church. It was incredible! This majestic building is more than seven hundred years old, and you can't imagine how impressed I was. What stayed in my mind most was the baptismal font made in 1570, which has inscriptions referencing Martin Luther's Reformation." He looked at her, his eyes full of excitement before he continued. "One day I should hope to show it to you and explain all the finer details that superficial visitors miss, like the wonderful combination of the old Marian piety with the modern Lutheran teachings." He stopped talking, shaking his head and looking utterly forlorn. Then he put a hand on hers and said, "Well, it was this visit that inspired my love for antiques and my curiosity to find out what is behind each piece of art. What did the artist think? Why did he choose this motif over another? What did he want to convey to the beholder?"

Margarete remembered how much her opinion of him had changed after that conversation. He wasn't the mindless Nazi she had believed him to be, and if the way of the world had turned out differently, the two of them might actually have had a chance to love each other.

But she'd fought her attraction for him tooth and nail, because despite his kind heart, he was still a cog in the Nazi machine—a machine that was intent on eradicating every member of the Jewish race from the face of the earth. As long as he didn't turn his back on Hitler, there could never been anything between him and her.

Margarete sighed. Wilhelm was the reason she had come to the country house with the attached lands and stud farm. He had implored her to do good with the inheritance, just before sacrificing his life for hers, and here was the place he'd been happiest, here he'd developed his love for the arts. Here, she hoped to feel close to him and find inspiration.

Because she needed to consider her next steps and how to best use all that money. The French Résistance asked her to finance weapons, dynamite, and other things to sabotage the Germans. But she loathed the idea that she would indirectly be used to kill people, even if the victims were Nazis. That was the main reason why she hadn't accepted their offer to stay in Paris and work with them. She still hoped to find a way to further the war effort, albeit not the German one, in a non-violent way. She'd given herself a deadline of two months, and if no opportunity presented itself by then, she'd return to Paris and find a way to support the Résistance.

Several minutes later Dora finished unpacking the suitcases and asked, "Shall I unpack your travel bag as well, Fräulein Annegret?"

"No, wait."

"Yes, Fräulein Annegret." The look on Dora's face was pure anxiety.

"How many people work on the estate?"

"You mean, you don't know?"

Margarete tilted her head. "I was a child the last time my parents brought me here."

"In the house we are four: Frau Mertens, Gustav Fischer, the estate manager, Nils, our handyman who picked up your suitcase, and me. In the stables you have Oliver, I mean, Herr Gundelmann, and maybe twenty grooms, and then there are the seasonal workers for the farmland, and the forest."

"Thank you." Margarete was amazed at the sheer quantity of people working for her. Her real father, a well-to-do owner of a haberdashery, had only ever employed two people—before the Nazis came to power and made life impossible.

"Shall I unpack your other suitcases?"

"Not right now. You can do so once I've freshened up."

"As you wish, Fräulein Annegret." Dora curtsied again and hurried from the room.

All the curtsying was getting on Margarete's nerves, but she decided not to mention anything until she had a better grasp on how things worked at the manor. For now she would use the brow-beaten maid as her main source of information, because, if truth be told, she was intimidated by Frau Mertens who had apparently known Annegret right from the cradle, and might see through her acting.

Dora, on the other hand, was new at the manor and had to stay on good terms with her employers, since Frau Mertens could simply send her back to the labor office, requesting a more suitable girl. And who knew what might happen to Dora if she was returned with a less than glowing reference. As a Ukrainian, she didn't have to fear deportation or labor camps, but there were certainly more arduous jobs than serving at the manor.

Once the door closed behind the maid, Margarete rushed to her travel bag and rummaged for her amulet. *It was a folly to take it with you*, she chided herself, as her fingers caressed the beautiful round pendant on a silver chain. It showed a Tree of Life, made of silver strings representing the branches, atop a shimmering blue-green opal-like background. It was her only reminder of her parents, who'd given it to her at her Bat Mitzvah many years ago. Back then, even though the warning signs had been written on the wall, nobody had been able to imagine the horrors that would await them.

She scanned the room with the dark pink walls and light pink drapes for a suitable hiding place, but came up empty. The canopy bed was flanked by two night tables, one with a lamp on it, and the other one with several exquisite porcelain dolls. On the other side of the room stood a wardrobe and a chest of drawers, and on the windowsill sat several stuffed animals, orderly in rank and file. There was nowhere to hide an amulet, not even an armchair with upholstery.

With a sigh she decided it was best to hide it in plain sight, since Dora would never dare to question her new mistress. So she put it back into her bag, together with an antique golden bracelet Wilhelm had given her.

She went into the attached bathroom to refresh herself, before she returned downstairs to meet Horst. He was already waiting in the foyer.

"Is your room to your satisfaction?" she asked.

"Very much. And I see you're already taking on the role of the lady of the manor. Your mother would be proud of you."

"I hope she would approve of what I'm doing." Although Margarete was pretty sure that neither Annegret's nor her own mother would approve of the charade she was playing. Her mother had always instilled in her that honesty and loyalty were the most important character traits in a person. And Frau Huber... it didn't bear contemplating what she would make of the imposter who was playing mistress in her daughter's place.

Horst opened the door for her and she walked through, adopting a leisurely pace as they headed for the corner of the house. The gardens were in full bloom, and Margarete had to control her urge to praise the various flowers and colors, as that was something Annegret would never even notice, let alone comment on. Horst probably wouldn't know, but it was better to stay as true to Annegret's character as possible.

While she mused over the best way to get more information about the manor and surroundings from Horst, he broached the subject himself.

"I think perhaps we should go into town together so that I can introduce you to all the important people there." He stopped to look at her. "It is most unusual that a woman should inherit a family estate of this size, and some might object to you having a say."

After dealing with him for several months now, she knew exactly how to please him. And she did, because she needed his support to pull off her plan to help those in need. She knew it was a fine line to walk, but endearing herself to him was crucial. "That's why I have you to help me oversee the estate. Nobody will dare to object to what you say."

Just like she had anticipated, he delighted in the flattery. "That's exactly the reason why I'm here, even though I'm sorely needed at the office in Leipzig."

"I know and I'm so very grateful for your guidance." Indeed she was. Having a high-ranking Gestapo officer as her mentor was the best thing that could happen to someone in her position.

But she admonished herself to be careful and not develop true feelings of fondness for him, since he was literally the enemy of her people, even though he'd been nothing but kind to her personally.

She realized the irony of the situation and found pleasure in imagining the expression on his face should he ever find out whom he'd been helping all these months. Although she hoped that would never happen.

"I'd forgotten just how large this estate is," Margarete murmured as they walked toward the stables.

"Well, that's understandable. Gut Plaun has grown considerably during the past years, especially since the war began."

They walked in silence for a while, admiring the landscape, as Margarete continued to ponder her relationship with Horst Richter for the umpteenth time. She needed him, more than she probably realized, not only because he'd helped her inherit the Huber fortune, but also because he was capable of ironing out any problems that might present themselves in the future.

She needed to stay on good terms with him, if she ever hoped to use her new riches to help those in need. Who was better suited to navigate her through possible pitfalls and bureaucratic obstacles than one of the heads of Gestapo himself, whose kindliness to her had been second to none?

On the other hand, she knew it was wrong to think positively of him, for he was exactly that: Head of the Gestapo. He was one of the men who was hounding her people and sending them to their deaths. It was confusing, to say the least. His despicable political opinions, his anti-Semitism and the infamous cruelty of the people he commanded, stood in stark contrast to the kindness he showed her, Annegret, on a personal level.

Swearing never to forget who he really was and to remember that being kind to one person didn't mean he was a good man, she sighed involuntarily.

"What has you so downcast?" he asked.

"Nothing really." She decided to use the chance to get some answers from him. "It's just... Honestly, I'm wondering how can someone like you, a good-hearted man, have such a merciless job?"

He stopped to look at her. "My wife used to ask me the same question when I first started out, but it's merely a matter of doing my duty for Führer and Fatherland."

She nodded.

"I know that the Gestapo has a bad reputation, and partly that is intentional, but you must always remember that those who fall into our hands aren't innocents. They deserve everything and more for the crimes they have committed against the people's community. Take the Jews, for example: they have conspired against Germany for decades, attempting to ruin our nation, and I daresay they almost succeeded. If it weren't for Hitler, they would have taken over by now, enslaving the Aryan race and running the economy into the ground."

"I see." Although she didn't see at all. To her that sounded exactly like what Hitler, the supposed savior, was doing.

"It is normal to have sympathy, especially since you are a woman. But your kindness is misguided when it is directed towards criminals, traitors and work-shy people. We cannot and must not allow our hearts to soften toward those whose only goal is to destroy our nation. This is why our Führer encouraged the Jews to leave Germany for so many years, but, sadly, they stubbornly refused, because like parasites they chose to cling to their host until they have killed it. Thus, more drastic measures had to be taken. Believe me, I don't take joy from sending them to work camps, but I take consolation in the fact that they aren't even humans. You wouldn't shed a tear for a rat who dies because you won't let it steal your food, now would you?"

"Of course not."

"It's the same with the Jews."

She shivered. His answer had made one thing clear: as nice as he was to her, she should never forget how he thought about her people. She'd use him for her purposes, but wouldn't allow herself to be fooled by his kindness on a personal level.

Just before they reached the stables, he took out his pocket watch and said, "We had better return, or our lunch will be cold."

"We wouldn't want Frau Mertens to get angry at us for being late."

He stopped in his tracks and looked at her with a gaze she couldn't decipher. "She is your servant. She cannot get angry at you."

Again, she had slipped from her role. As beneficial as it had been to have the Gestapo officer deal with all the red tape to inherit the Huber fortune, she had to do better or he'd become suspicious. "I'm sorry, Horst. This is all new to me, since my mother always took care of the household. And truth be told, Frau Mertens was very frightening when we were children."

Horst's expression softened and he patted her hand. "You're not a child anymore, and will grow into your role, no doubt. But... you should never let the servants know that you're scared of them, or even value their opinion, or they will soon steamroll over you and think they're the head of the house."

"As always, you're right."

"I do think maybe Frau Mertens has become a little too... how should I put it... comfortable in running the manor?"

Margarete pondered for a moment what his remark might mean, since it couldn't be a bad thing for Frau Mertens to run the house as efficiently as she seemed to. "Well, do you think I should sit down with her and let her know she has to run all major decisions past me?"

"Exactly!" He beamed with pride, as if Margarete was a

student who'd finally grasped a difficult concept. "Servants have to be kept on a short leash, or they will betray you. That said, while I encourage you to take over all decisions related to the manor itself, just like your mother did, I would advise you against meddling in the men's affairs."

"Men's affairs?"

"The stables, farmland and other things." For the briefest moment she wondered what those other things might entail, but he didn't leave her much time, and continued, "You can leave everything other than the manor itself to the estate manager, Gustav Fischer."

"I see."

"He's been in charge for a few years now and your father completely trusted him. These past months I did a background check on him and found he's a trusted party member, always willing to be the first in line to praise our Führer."

"That certainly makes him trustworthy." Margarete put on a pleased expression, despite her urge to vomit. She'd rather spend her time with a Ukrainian maid than a staunch Nazi. But this bit of information was worth gold, since it gave her an idea what kind of man Fischer was. Loyal to Führer and Fatherland until his death. She'd have to tread carefully with him and remember to pretend to be fervently enthusiastic about the Reich and Hitler's ideologies.

They reached the manor again, where Dora was waiting on the stairs for them.

"I've taken the liberty to arrange for you to meet Fischer and the other senior staff members this afternoon," Horst said.

"What would I do without you?" she said, knowing how much he liked the flattery.

"I'm sure you would manage sufficiently well on your own, but I'm glad to help you settle in. While I'm not your official guardian, I do like to help. Initially I felt an obligation to keep my late friend's estate afloat for the Reich, but, truth be told, you're almost like the daughter I never had."

3

"Oliver?" a voice called throughout the barn.

"Last stable on the left." Oliver was bending down to inspect the hoof of a beautiful black Oldenburger horse. Moments later he heard the sound of jackboots on the hard dirt floor of the stable and turned to see the estate manager, Gustav Fischer, looking over the doorway, which was rather unusual.

"Is there a problem?" Since Oliver had been appointed stud master at Gut Plaun about a year ago, he'd never seen Gustav set foot in the horse barn.

"Fräulein Annegret has summoned all of us to the manor one hour from now. You better get yourself into presentable shape," Gustav said with a pointed gaze at Oliver's smeared dungarees.

Oliver let the horse's hoof go, patted the mare on her neck and left the box to join Gustav, who looked immaculate as usual in his brown pinstripe suit, white checkered shirt and tie. His pant legs were stuffed inside the matching brown jackboots and he casually wore a short coat over it. The white hair was slicked back, not a single strand out of place, as opposed to Oliver's own tousled shock of dark blond hair that always seemed to look as if he'd just gotten out of bed. Not that he cared. And neither did the horses.

"What's she want?"

"Getting to know her employees it seems."

Oliver frowned and wiped his hands on his thighs. "I thought she'd be here for a few weeks at most."

"That's what we all thought, but judging by the amount of luggage she has brought with her, she's here for good."

"I see." Oliver wouldn't let the other man know how much he loathed Annegret Huber. He remembered all too well a time when she'd been seven or eight years of age. She and her brothers would arrive at the manor in a flurry of activity, sending maids and butlers scurrying around to meet their demands and make sure they were sufficiently entertained to avoid pestering their parents.

Only four years older than her, but son to a stableman, she'd treated him much like a personal servant and would complain to her father if he didn't dance attendance on her. He hadn't seen her since their childhood days and could only imagine how much more demanding and entitled the young Huber heiress had become over the years.

The hardships of this war seemed to have split people into two kinds: those who developed sympathy for their fellow humans and went out of their way to help others, and those who embraced the Nazi ideology with open arms and relished the power it gave them.

With Annegret the latter was definitely going to be true, since gossip about her disdainful behavior toward the more unfortunate had found its way back to Gut Plaun. There was no doubt that she was still the spoiled girl used to getting her own way.

"Make sure you're at the manor on time—clean, shaved and in appropriate clothes." With these words, Gustav turned around and left the barn. Oliver stayed behind, giving every horse a stroke on the muzzle on his way out. He loved his job. Gut Plaun had been a small stud for decades, but with the armament in the thirties and the beginning of the war, the demand for reliable cart horses for the military had exploded and they couldn't breed or train them fast enough. These days the stud had around two hundred horses and Oliver oversaw twenty men working, in one way or the other, in the horse breeding.

His favorite mare, Sabrina, nudged against his head, and he took a few seconds to cuddle with her. "Good girl. But I don't have time right now. Fräulein Annegret is back and apparently I must shave before she can be expected to set her eyes on me. You wouldn't know it, but this girl means trouble with a big T."

Sabrina whinnied in agreement, causing a smile to spread across his lips. Horses were so much more loyal than humans, and they never deceived or mistreated someone.

"I have plenty of work to do as it is, I have no time to cater to Annegret's whims. Why on earth would she come here anyway? Last I heard she was living it up in Paris, going to dances, and plays at the theatre... all things we don't have here."

He gave Sabrina a clap on her neck and limped down the aisle, mentally going over the horses currently within his care. While most of them were destined to be military cart horses, he had some who'd been trained with a rider. As much as he disliked Annegret as a person, she was the mistress of Gut Plaun and he'd better have a horse available for her, because as an avid horse lover, she would no doubt expect to ride every day the weather allowed. A dappled gray mare with a snow-white mane and tail caught his attention. The strands of her mane fell down her elegant neck.

"Hey, Snowfall, how's my girl?" he asked quietly, reaching into his pocket for a piece of carrot. The mare gently lipped it from his palm, snickering softly in response to his touch on her neck.

"Annegret's back. And you're just the perfect horse for her. Will you be on your best behavior?"

Snowfall nudged him for more carrots and he chuckled, running his hand down her shoulder. "Sorry, but no more treats. After your ride with Annegret, you can get more. I'm betting she comes by to meet you later this afternoon, or first thing in the morning. Be nice to her." He gave her one last caress and walked out of the barn, looking for one of the stable lads.

"Piet," he called out, "make sure Snowfall is ready for Fräulein Annegret at all times during her stay at the manor."

"Sure thing." Piet wasn't a man of many words, but Oliver

knew he could rely on him to get things done—correctly and on the first attempt.

Then he limped up to the gardener's house where he lived, located a few hundred yards from the manor. A Russian bullet had shattered his lower left leg and after the doctors had managed to put the bones back together, it was about an inch shorter than the right leg. He hated how the shorter leg made him limp, but on the other hand, he should be grateful, because it was the reason he'd been discharged from the Wehrmacht and could now work with his beloved horses once again.

At his house, which was never locked, he opened the door and broke out into a wide grin when he saw the apple that the maid Dora had left for him. He much appreciated her little treats, although he would have to tell her to be more careful, because Frau Mertens was very strict about morals. She would not approve of the relationship that had developed between Oliver and Dora.

He walked into the attached bathroom, took off his dungarees, washed and shaved, before he walked upstairs into the bedroom and took his Sunday suit out of the wardrobe. If Gustav and Annegret put so much importance on appearances, who was he to resist?

On the way out, he grabbed the apple and bit into it. He really was a lucky man, because he loved his job working with horses, had a roof over his head, and always enough to eat. Food on the estate was excellent, since Frau Mertens had a gift for making delicious meals out of the most basic things. And the good woman always took great care there was enough for the hard-working stable hands and even for the foreign workers who were assigned to Gut Plaun.

4

Eating a hearty venison goulash with potatoes, carrots and red cabbage, Margarete thanked Frau Mertens for the delicious treat. "It's been a long time since I ate with such pleasure."

The housekeeper was visibly proud and said, "All from our own land. It's hunting time for deer and we grow our own vegetables as well."

"That is the advantage of the countryside, it has more food. The very reason why the National Socialist People's Welfare has instigated the *Kinderlandverschickung*," Horst mentioned after asking for a second serving.

Margarete was aware of the program to evacuate children under the age of ten from the heavily bombed cities to the safer, more rural areas of the Reich. But she was also aware that most parents opposed the idea of sending their children away to stay with strangers, especially since it now seemed the final victory wouldn't come as fast as everyone had hoped.

Perhaps that was a direction she could take? Could she harbor Jewish children amongst the others to keep them safe under the guise of the *Kinderlandverschickung*?

"Yes, Herr Reichskriminaldirektor, when the Standartenführer was still alive he enlisted Gut Plaun in the program to accept mothers with toddlers, but the need was not high enough, so we never received anyone," Frau Mertens said, shattering Margarete's hopes.

"It is a shame really, those urban children would profit from being in the country and learning about the culture and dedication of our farmers." Horst finished his glass of wine, which Margarete assumed came from well-appointed cellars, and clapped his hands. "Time to meet the staff."

She folded her napkin and followed him into the impressive parlor with tapestries and old-school masters hanging on the walls, where five people including Frau Mertens were already waiting on her. That woman must possess supernatural abilities, because she stood there with the rest of the employees patiently waiting, as if she hadn't just served Margarete and Horst lunch in another room.

Horst took care of the introductions. "This is the new lady of the manor, Fräulein Annegret. She'll visit frequently and will oversee all matters of the household, together with Frau Mertens, who remains the housekeeper and head of household staff."

Margarete nodded at the older woman. "The house looks to be in marvelous shape. Thank you for looking after it."

Frau Mertens looked shocked by the compliment and Margarete realized too late that Annegret would never have offered someone such praise, let alone a person she considered beneath her social status. Mentally kicking herself, she decided now was the best time to take things into her own hands and show them that Annegret Huber had undergone a dramatic change of heart through the various ordeals she had suffered this past year.

"Thank you, Fräulein Annegret." Frau Mertens stepped ahead and proceeded to introduce the remaining staff. "You've already met Dora who will be your waiting maid, in addition to her general chores in the house and kitchen."

Margarete gave a measured nod at the skinny girl, wondering under what excuse she could later ask her for a tour through the house.

"I'm sure you remember Nils..." A bald man in his fifties with a weather-beaten face stepped forward. "He's our handyman. Nils can repair anything in the house, stables and gardens. He's been with the family for close to twenty years now."

Fear crept up her throat, as another person who knew Annegret from the past popped up. "Good to see you, Nils."

"If you need anything, Fräulein Annegret, you know where to find me," he said in a sonorous voice.

She nodded, despite not having the slightest idea, and he stepped back into the line. Next, Horst clapped his hands and shot a glance at Frau Mertens, who hurried to say, "Dora and I are needed in the kitchen. Will you please excuse us, Fräulein Annegret?"

"Certainly." Margarete looked after the retreating women, suddenly feeling abandoned with the three remaining male employees in the room. After another glance from Horst, Nils also excused himself and there were only two men left in the parlor. Both of them wore a dress suit, combined with jackboots, indicating they were more important than the dismissed employees.

Horst stepped forward. "These two men don't actually work in the house," he said. "Gustav Fischer, as I told you already, is the estate manager."

"Herr Fischer." She inclined her head.

"I'd like to give you and the Reichskriminaldirektor an overview of the estate in my office, after we're finished with the introductions, Fräulein Annegret," he said while holding out his hand to her. From the way he spoke it was crystal clear that he considered himself the most important person on the estate, which was refreshing to witness, because usually everyone kowtowed to Horst.

"That would be nice." She instantly liked Gustav Fischer for his willingness to give her a more thorough understanding of the inner workings of her estate. She almost didn't dare to think it, but his friendly demeanor emboldened her to hope that he was a Nazi only on paper and might even be open to her hidden agenda of helping those persecuted by the Reich.

"And this here is the stud master, Oliver Gundelmann, who's been back with us for about a year." Fischer's voice was clipped, giving Margarete the impression that the two men didn't particularly like each other, which made her not like the other man either.

"Welcome back, Annegret," Gundelmann said, but didn't offer her his hand. He looked to be in his mid-twenties and despite being clean-shaven and combed, as well as wearing a suit, his appearance was somehow that of a rebel.

Something about his stare was utterly unsettling. But what was even more unsettling was the fact that he seemed to know Annegret and was on first name terms with her. Before Margarete could decide how to react, Fischer stepped in and said, "Show some respect, it is Fräulein Annegret."

"We used to know each other when she wasn't much taller than that." Oliver Gundelmann put his hand about the height of his hip. "But if you insist, I'll certainly address you with *Fräulein* Annegret." He jutted his chin forward as if daring her to contradict him.

He made her extremely nervous, because she could feel the underlying aversion in his dealings with her. Something must have happened between him and Annegret when they were children. Knowing Annegret, it probably wasn't anything good. Since having an enemy on the estate would put her in grave danger, she cast him a conciliatory smile and said, "Don't worry, Oliver, things haven't changed."

His eyes blazed at her and again, she knew she'd said the wrong thing. So, indeed, Annegret and he had skeletons in the closet.

"My condolences on the loss of your family. I always enjoyed playing with your brothers when they came here."

"Thank you. That is so very kind of you." Unsure whether she should say anything else, she waited to see if he would take the initiative.

"I thought you'd be desperate to go for a ride as soon as time and weather permits? I have the perfect mount ready for you," Oliver added after a slight pause.

Breathing became difficult and she could only hope her face didn't show the panic creeping up her spine. *A horse? I've never been on a horse before. If I accept his offer, I'm going to make a fool of myself and everyone will know I'm not really her.*

She ducked her head to hide her eyes and then forced a cough. Horst immediately came to her aid, patting her on the back, asking, "Are you well, my dear? Perhaps something to drink would help soothe your throat?"

"Yes, thank you," she croaked.

"When shall I expect you at the stables?" Oliver's voice stopped her cold.

Margarete cleared her throat and looked at him, not liking the spark of hostility lurking behind his eyes. She could only imagine the insults he'd suffered at the hands of Annegret, especially if he'd known her as a child. She'd been demanding and a brat as a young woman, but according to the household gossip and her own brother Wilhelm, she'd been insufferable as a child.

"I'm sure Annegret will visit as soon as she gets her bearings," Horst Richter assured him and then, true to his Gestapo ways, probed into Oliver's background. "How come a young and strong man like you isn't in the Wehrmacht fighting for the Reich?"

Oliver's eyes darkened even more, but his voice was neutral as he spoke, "I was in the Wehrmacht, Herr Reichskriminaldirektor, fought in Poland and later in Russia, but was discharged in 1941 because a bullet shattered my lower leg."

"I see. Is it true that your father used to work in the stables at Gut Plaun?"

"Yes, sir, he was the stud master. But he retired several years ago after he injured his back in a riding accident and he couldn't do the hard work anymore. He now works as a janitor in the public school, but his heart remains with horses. He taught me everything I know."

Gustav Fischer had watched the exchange with hawk's eyes

and Margarete got the impression he didn't like the way this was going. Only moments later her suspicion was confirmed when he cut the conversation short. "I'm afraid Oliver has to attend to his duties in the stables, since we have obligations to fulfill."

"Certainly." Horst gave a slight nod. "Should we proceed to your office now? You must be a busy man and we are taking up enough of your time as it is."

"Oh no, I'm absolutely delighted to receive the new owner of the estate and give her an account of my work, since I have nothing to hide. Please, follow me," Fischer said.

Oliver took that opportunity to slip from the room, giving Margarete the impression he was happiest when he could be with the horses. On her part, she wouldn't mind if he stayed down at the stables, so she wouldn't have to cross paths with him ever again.

She and Horst followed Fischer through a long hallway until he stopped in front of the last door to the left and opened it for them. In the middle of the room stood a large wooden desk that looked very similar to the one Herr Huber had used in his house in Berlin.

Fischer settled behind the desk and pointed to two chairs in front of it. "Please have a seat." What followed was a lengthy, but superficial, run through the different parts of the estate, mainly the stud and the agricultural operation. He also mentioned industrial activities, but didn't go into detail.

Finally, he slid a sheet of paper across the desk. "I took the liberty to summarize the entire business into these key numbers, showing the estate's accounts, what is still to be paid out and what we anticipate the harvest will bring in over the next several months."

Margarete looked at the numbers, shifting slightly to the side as Horst leaned forward and took the sheet into his hands. "These numbers look very good," he commented.

"Gut Plaun has been doing very well, considering the state of the world right now." The pride in Fischer's voice was evident.

"Thank you, it seems everything is in perfect order," Margarete said. In fact she hadn't understood most of what he'd told her. Gut Plaun was such a vast estate with so many different operations, it didn't compare to the easy bookkeeping she'd helped her father do in his haberdashery, but she wouldn't let Fischer know any of that. He needed to believe she was able to keep up with his explanations.

"You can trust me, Fräulein Annegret, I've been doing this for a long time and your father—and latterly older brother Reiner during his tragically brief period as head of the family—always gave me a free hand to decide as I saw fit, because he was busy serving the Fatherland through his military duties."

"And I appreciate your kindness in explaining the operations to me. I wouldn't dare question your decisions as you have been taking such good care of Gut Plaun. Although, when you have a moment soon, I'd like to understand a bit more, and would love you to teach me."

His lip twisted slightly. "That is laudable, Fräulein Annegret, and I'm always at your disposition for any questions you should have. Although, and I'm sure Reichskriminaldirektor Richter will agree, a lovely young woman like you will find it much more rewarding to take charge of the manor as your mother did. Also, my wife is eager to meet you and introduce you to all the important ladies in town." He chuckled. "I have it on good account that they want to enlist you for charity work. So I think you won't have time for boring things like selling crops." Gustav Fischer was quite the handsome man with his white hair, well-trimmed beard and his pleasant, yet straightforward manner. She felt like she could trust him.

"Thank you. Reichskriminaldirektor Richter has already advised me to let you handle everything concerning the estate, which I fully support, seeing how well you have been running it in the absence of my family."

"And I will continue to work hard for the best of Gut Plaun, so there's no need for you to concern yourself with it. You've had to endure quite a few blows of fate this past year and I want you to know that during your time here you can dedicate yourself to the more pleasing activities in life."

Richter echoed his suggestion. "I concur with Herr Fischer, it's best to let things continue on as they have been, with the addition that he gives you, say, monthly updates on where the estate stands?"

"Monthly updates are very doable," Fischer agreed.

Margarete nodded, happy to let things stand as she didn't have the slightest idea of how to run a farm, or a manor house, or take care of crops and animals and workers. "I feel blessed to have someone like yourself here to manage things. Thank you."

For the moment she wanted to keep a low profile and survive the war, while finding a way to help other people. That was what Wilhelm had wanted, and why she'd come here. To think of ways to use her new fortune for good, which meant she needed Gut Plaun to keep producing. And who could be better suited than the same man who'd run the estate for years already?

The ringing telephone interrupted them and Fischer picked it up, only to hand the receiver to Richter. "For you, Herr Reichskriminaldirektor, from your office in Leipzig."

Horst talked a few sentences with the person on the other end of the line, hung up and said, "I'm so very sorry, but something of utmost importance has come up that requires my return to Leipzig on the morrow."

Margarete nodded. "Don't worry about me, I'll be fine here and Gut Plaun is in the competent hands of Herr Fischer."

"Good." Horst stood up and shook hands with Fischer. "I'll be leaving first thing in the morning so I'll bid you farewell here."

Fischer closed up the ledgers, placed them in one of the desk drawers, locked it, and pocketed the key. "I'll let you two go about the rest of your afternoon and see myself out. Fräulein Annegret, my wife and I live in town but I arrive here at my office for work most mornings at eight, should you need anything."

"Have a good evening," Margarete wished him. She covered a

yawn with her hand and Horst chuckled beside her. "I am more tired than I thought."

"Why don't you rest before dinner?" he suggested.

"I believe I will." Margarete hid another yawn as she left the office and headed up to her room. She lay on the bed, tired but not sleepy. Her mind couldn't seem to turn off. *One day at a time. That's all you can do, take it one day, even one minute at a time.*

5

Dora was busy cutting vegetables when a bell rang. Since she'd never heard that tone before, she looked up with surprise, her eyes seeking Frau Mertens who had her back turned on her, seasoning meat.

When the bell rang a second time, Frau Mertens turned around. "What are you waiting for? Go and get it!"

Usually Frau Mertens herself would open the door when someone rang, so this was quite surprising.

"The door?" Dora asked.

"Don't be silly. That is the bell in Fräulein Annegret's room."

"I'm terribly sorry, Frau Mertens, I didn't realize..."

"Now you do. Don't dawdle and run upstairs to ask what the Fräulein wants."

"On my way." Dora put down her knife, washed her hands and raced up the stairs. She knew she had been lucky with this job, because while Frau Mertens was very strict, she was a correct person and never beat or kicked her, which a number of the Ukrainian maids she sometimes met in town while running errands endured at the hands of their employers. Some even worse than that.

Dora reached the upper floor with its six bedrooms, each with their own private bathroom, which was a very unusual luxury not many families possessed, and hesitantly knocked on Fräulein Annegret's door. She'd imagined her to be very different. A lot older for one, but it had turned out Annegret was just a few years Dora's senior. More elegant, yes, and certainly more mature, but also... how could Dora explain this? Annegret seemed cowed... even anxious. It was as if she was constantly reminding herself about something. It didn't make sense, but Dora felt as if the other woman wasn't actually herself. She shrugged, the poor girl was probably shellshocked after losing her entire family in two separate bombings, while she'd walked out unscathed both times. Anyone would be anxious after such a frightful experience.

"Come in!"

"You rang the bell, Fräulein Annegret?" she said with a curtsy.

"Yes. I was wondering if you had some time to spare?"

"Of course. Frau Mertens has made it clear that my duties with you supersede everything else." For good measure she curtsied again.

"Can you please stop that curtsying?" Annegret hissed.

"But Frau Mertens said..."

Annegret smiled ruefully and answered in a much softer tone. "Could you at least stop doing it when we're alone? I'm not some princess."

"If you wish, Fräulein Annegret." Dora stood waiting to hear what her mistress would want from her, but no orders came. It was the most peculiar situation and she had the impression the other woman was searching for words.

"Would you..." Annegret hesitated. "Would you give me a tour through the house?"

Dora's eyes widened, since this was such an unexpected request.

"It's just... I haven't been here for such a long time and I would like to catch up with any changes that might have been made."

Dora kept herself from curtsying at the last second. "I wouldn't know anything about changes, Fräulein Annegret, since I've been working here for less than a year. You might better ask Frau Mertens—"

Annegret shook her head and lowered her voice. "To be honest, Frau Mertens sort of scares me. She's very stern..."

Dora had difficulties not to break out into giggles. It was refreshing to know that the new lady of the house was as scared by Frau Mertens as she was. "She can be very frightening indeed. I'll show you around, but I might not be able to answer all of your questions."

"That won't matter, I just want to get reacquainted with everything, and, frankly, find a more suitable room than this," she made a grand gesture around the room, "girlish dream."

Again, Dora felt sympathy for the other woman who seemed to work so hard to get everything right. Oliver had warned her that the new lady of the manor was a selfish, obnoxious and outright mean person, but his description didn't fit the woman in front of her in the slightest. "When shall we start?"

"Right now!" Annegret jumped up and rushed through the door, full of energy. "Left or right?"

"Let's start with the room opposite yours." Dora followed her mistress into the hallway and opened the door on the other side. "Nothing was changed in here as far as I know. It belonged to one of your brothers, but I don't know which one." She looked at Annegret expectantly, who frantically looked around the room, as if searching for something.

When Annegret's eye fell on the delicate antique nightlamp beside the bed, she seemed to relax and said, "I remember how Wills found this lamp in some dubious shop and fought with our father for days until he was allowed to buy this 'piece of junk'. Turns out it was rather valuable." Her face took on a dreamy expression.

A wave of compassion hit Dora and she fought the urge to pat her mistress on the arm. "You must miss your family so much."

"My family?" For a moment she looked puzzled, but then caught herself again. "I do. I often think they're still alive."

They continued through all the rooms on the upper floor, but when Dora offered to continue downstairs, Annegret politely declined. "I don't want to take up too much of your time, since you must have other chores to attend to."

Dora nodded, indeed she had. Frau Mertens had kept her busy even before Fräulein Annegret arrived. Cooking for several dozen farm workers and permanent employees wasn't a task done on the side. At least Horst Richter had left early that morning and no formal dinner had to be prepared, but she would still have to dust and sweep the big dining room for Fräulein Annegret to come down later.

"About dinner..."

"Yes, Fräulein Annegret?"

"As it will be just me, I will take my meals in the small sitting room."

"Are you sure? The dining room is so lovely..."

"But very large for just a solitary person, don't you agree?"

"As you wish. If that is all, I should perhaps return to the kitchen now."

"Yes, that will be all."

Dora hurried downstairs to find a very grumpy-looking Frau Mertens in the kitchen. "Where have you been all this time? The work doesn't do itself!"

"I'm so very sorry, Frau Mertens, but Fräulein Annegret held me up." She wondered whether she should tell her boss about the tour, but decided it wasn't necessary. "She asked all kinds of questions about the household."

"She should have asked me," Frau Mertens bristled.

"This is what I told her, but she insisted you would be much too busy to attend to such menial tasks."

The flattery showed the intended results and Frau Mertens' expression softened. "She's right with that, although I'd never had her down for being considerate."

"I believe she was a child when you last saw her, she has grown up and the experiences she has had must have changed her." Dora couldn't fathom why everyone was harping on about how bad a person Annegret was, when she'd been nothing but kind since arriving at Gut Plaun. "Oh... I almost forgot. She said she would prefer to take her meals in the small sitting room instead of the dining room."

Frau Mertens' eyebrows shot up. "Is that so?"

Dora nodded and returned to chopping vegetables. She couldn't wait to tell Oliver about everything that had transpired today. The two of them had been stepping out with each other for several months now, although they were both careful to hide their feelings in front of others, since Frau Mertens wouldn't approve of Dora getting involved with a man. She was very traditional in that respect and guarded Dora's honor as if she were her own daughter.

But ever since Dora had come to Gut Plaun all alone, thousands of miles away from her country, she'd found in Oliver a friendly soul, someone she could talk to and who would soothe her when she was homesick and yearning for her family.

6

"Delivery, sir." A young lad knocked on the door of the receiving office, situated at the rear of the garage next to the manor house.

"Come in." Gustav Fischer waved the lad forward. "What have you got?"

The lad handed over two pieces of paper, one for a delivery of potatoes from another local farm, the second sheet of paper for flour from the mill. Gustav withdrew his receiving ledger from the drawer and clearly and legibly recorded both deliveries, the date and the time, as well as the quantity that was received. He scrawled his signature on the bottom of both sheets of paper and returned them to the lad.

"Did Frau Mertens inspect the goods?" Gustav asked.

"She did, sir. I waited until she gave her nod of approval before bringing them papers to you."

"Well done. I just need you to countersign the ledger, right here." Gustav pointed at the column next to the two entries he'd made. After the lad signed, he waved him away. "Thanks and tell your boss I'll be calling in for more."

"He'll be pleased. Always a pleasure to do business with you. Not everyone is so honest."

Gustav brimmed with joy. He prided himself on being on best

terms with the important merchants in the region. Which was the very reason why, despite the ever-increasing shortage of supplies, the workers on Gut Plaun—good German men and women who did their bit for the war effort—always had enough to eat. Together with his reputation as a strict, but fair estate manager it ensured he never lacked applicants who wanted to work for him.

The stud had very lucrative contracts with the Wehrmacht and could afford to employ only the best horsemen, which in turn helped to train more horses faster and sell them with a nice profit.

Yes, Gustav had a knack for business and under his tutelage Gut Plaun had become a money machine. But his best idea had been to construct a munitions factory from scratch, well concealed in the dense forests near the lake, and yet near enough to both the highway and the railroad for easy transport of supplies.

Herr Huber had immediately jumped on the plan when Gustav had presented it to him, shortly after the beginning of the war in 1939. It had become the main source of income for the Huber family—and Gustav.

Since Fräulein Annegret was just a woman, he'd agreed with Reichskriminaldirektor Richter not to burden her with too much knowledge about the factory. Women could be so emotional, especially when they found out about forced workers used for the backbreaking and dangerous tasks.

Even his wife Beate used to have qualms and felt sorry for the prisoners. It had taken him many nights of discussion to make her see that these abhorrent subjects weren't actual people. The criminals, the work-shy, the homosexuals, all of them had chosen to step outside the shepherding German people's community and turned against the hand that was feeding them. Sympathy with them was misplaced.

At least on the subject of Jews, Beate and he saw eye to eye. Even his kind-hearted wife understood that they were an evil that had to be exterminated from the face of the earth, much like she eradicated the weeds in her garden. Once a person saw them for what they actually were, it didn't tug any heartstrings.

From what he knew about Fräulein Annegret, she wasn't one prone to misplaced kindness, but he'd still agreed with Herr Richter that it was best for everyone involved that she only concerned herself with the manor and the women in town, while he kept the business side running.

While he, of course, would pay Fräulein Annegret the respect she deserved, as well as offer his guidance and friendship to her, his true boss was now her de facto guardian, Horst Richter. And Gustav intended to always stay on good terms with him, because truth be told, he was afraid of the powerful man.

After talking on the telephone with him for months, he'd met him for the first time during his recent visit to Gut Plaun, and judging by his sharp blue eyes that never missed the slightest detail, he would be a very unpleasant adversary to have.

No, Gustav would work hard to keep the estate producing riches not only for Annegret Huber and the Reich, but he'd do his very best to please the Reichskriminaldirektor along the way.

He closed his ledger and tucked it away in a drawer. The military clients might request an audit of the books whenever they wished, and Gustav made sure everything was in perfect order at all times. Nothing would derail his profitable business faster than a careless entry.

He stepped from the office and observed the delivery truck leave through the main gate, before he walked to the unloading area, where he instructed one of the farm hands to separate the flour and sacks of potatoes into two portions.

"Bring this part down into the storage cellar for the manor, and don't forget to ask Frau Mertens how much she needs in the pantry for immediate use," he said. When the farm hand walked away with a heavy sack of potatoes on his shoulders, Gustav returned to his office and called the factory manager on the telephone.

"Hello, Heinz, the food supplies just arrived. Come up and get them." Gustav waited for the factory manager, while he divided the portion destined for the factory into two parts.

"We came as fast as we could." Heinz, a burly man jumped

down from a horse-driven cart and shook Gustav's hand, before two men in striped uniforms crawled from the back of the cart. "Always plenty to do at the factory, never enough workers and those we have are lazy. They don't even deserve the food we're giving them."

"Such a shame. Looks like, once again, there won't be enough for them lazybones."

Heinz chuckled and asked, eyeing the sacks of potatoes and flour, "This is it?"

"Yes."

"Load the sacks onto the cart, and fast. Make sure to keep the two parts separate," Heinz shouted at the two scrawny men. Lighting a cigarette and offering one to Gustav, he walked a few steps away from the prisoners. "Same buyer as always?"

"Yes. You'll receive your share once everything's delivered to the customer's satisfaction." Gustav inhaled the smoke from his cigarette, watching the two men load the cart as he calculated his profit.

"Has the Huber girl arrived yet?" Heinz asked, puffing smoke circles into the air.

"Day before yesterday."

"And? Will she present a problem?"

"No need to worry. She's young and inexperienced, and seems happy to leave the business side to me. I assume she'll soon be too busy redecorating the rooms in the manor and participating in the ladies' coffee parties. Beate can't wait to take her under her wing."

"If you say so."

"She seems kind-hearted, but I don't think there's any love lost between her and the Jews. Even if she found out, she wouldn't mind, although she might want a share." He gave a short bark of laughter.

"I'd hate it if her presence derailed the profitable side of our business."

Gustav took another drag from his cigarette and puffed out the air, before he answered, "Don't you worry. Have I ever let you down?"

"No..."

"And I won't start now. The books are in perfect order and the only ones who might complain about not receiving the full amount of supplies are the filthy Jews, and who would even listen to them? Although..." Gustav looked pointedly at the two prisoners about to finish loading the sacks onto the cart "... you might want to get rid of those two. Better not to have any witnesses."

"Really? They have proven to be extremely useful—and it costs me virtually nothing." Heinz furrowed his brows.

"Trust me, better to be safe than sorry. Get rid of them tonight."

"Will do." Heinz took his cap, waved at the prisoners and shouted, "Hop on the cart, we're going back."

Gustav watched them drive away and grinned with satisfaction. Gut Plaun was indeed a money machine. Herr Huber had been too interested in his military career to give much thought to the running of the estate. And Gustav, astute as he was, had found the perfect way to line his own pockets. He took great care not to steal from his employer or the Reich, but only from the forced workers. By all means and standard, that wasn't even a punishable crime, because no judge in his right mind would convict him for "stealing from the Jews". He chuckled at the ludicrousness of the thought.

He was actually doing the Reich a service, because if the vermin starved faster than anticipated, he'd have to order new ones and the SS was always happy to "loan" them to him, at excruciatingly inflated prices, of course. There was an inextinguishable supply of cheap workers, at least until Hitler had finally managed to exterminate every last Jew in Europe, but until then... Gustav would have built his nest egg and could live like a king.

7

Margarete woke when someone entered her bedroom and she squeezed her eyes shut as that same person offered her a cheery, "Good morning," and pulled the curtains wide open.

She cracked open her eyes and glared at Dora. "Why are you waking me up so early and making so much noise?"

"I'm very sorry, Fräulein Annegret, but it's Sunday. If you don't rise now and get ready, you'll be late to morning Mass."

Mass? Lutheran Mass? Margarete quickly closed her eyes again and pulled the covers up over her head. Herr and Frau Huber had always attended church in Berlin and even made Annegret accompany them. A good and devout Lutheran family that never missed Sunday service, probably in an attempt to wash their souls of the ugly sins committed during the week. Abusing Margarete as a slave worker being the most benign one.

She gave a dismayed sound at the realization that in this small town the presence of the new mistress of Gut Plaun would be expected at Mass. Her absence would be considered an insult and tongues would start wagging. And drawing attention, or even worse, doubt, was absolutely the last thing she needed.

Although she was sure to mess up and draw attention either way, since she had never been to a Lutheran service before and had no idea what was expected of her. Even though her parents weren't particularly religious, they had always insisted it was forbidden for Jews to visit a Christian church.

She really should have questioned Aunt Heidi about customs and such when she had lived with her in Leipzig for several weeks after first adopting Annegret's identity. But who would have thought that one day she would have to attend Mass pretending to be the goy lady of the manor?

Heidi herself was Aryan but she had married Ernst Rosenbaum, Margarete's father's younger brother, way before the persecution of Jews began in earnest and interracial marriages became illegal. Still, the two of them had faced many obstacles because Heidi's family had been against her marrying a Jew, even an assimilated one. Margarete had been too young to understand, but apparently it had been quite the scandal when Heidi had disregarded conventions and forced her will through.

She only remembered the wedding with the beautiful bride, who soon became her favorite aunt, and her own princess-like dress as she walked down the aisle, strewing flowers for the bridal couple. Ernst and Heidi had been the happiest couple, despite the derision they endured due to the rising anti-Semitism. They had never had children of their own, and so Margarete and her siblings became their "adopted" children who'd visit them every summer vacation and spend weeks filled with fun in Leipzig.

But last year, the Gestapo had come to take Ernst away, and had left Heidi heartbroken. After desperately trying to find and liberate him, she'd finally been informed that he'd been transported to a labor camp. Completely broken, she had taken on her maiden name Berger again, in order to at least stop the constant harassment his last name caused her.

"What will you be wearing, Fräulein Annegret?" Dora's voice interrupted her thoughts.

Pushing down the covers, she sat up, eyeing Dora who stood in front of the open wardrobe, looking at her expectantly.

Right, what should I wear? She wracked her brain to remember what Frau Huber and Annegret had usually worn to church. Something smart, of course, but also modest. Maybe Dora could help to choose.

"Will you be going to church too?"

"Yes, Fräulein Annegret. Frau Mertens always insists that all of us servants attend."

That was good. "Maybe you could suggest what I wear? I want to fit in with the other ladies in town."

Dora looked surprised, but dutifully turned around to inspect the choice of outfits. "What about this gray muslin? It has that little hat with the veil and matching gloves. Since the sun is shining, you won't need a coat."

"Sounds perfect."

"The townsfolk will be delighted to see you, I think, since the family pews have been empty for such a long time."

Great! Family pews! Dread crawled up her spine, since Dora's words had slashed her hopes to slip quietly in and out of the church without being noticed. Knowing the Hubers, those pews would be front and center, so everyone's eyes could be on them as they attended Mass. Appearances had always taken priority over actual devotion in this family, or how else could one explain that Herr Huber knelt on Sundays before God with his head bowed and his hands folded, only to return to his office on Mondays to send thousands of Jews to the camps—and their deaths—with a stroke of those same hands.

Another frightening thought came up, since she couldn't afford to choose the wrong pew. "Will I have to sit alone in the family pew?"

"Why would you say that?" Dora asked with big eyes.

"Well..." *because I have no idea about this whole Christian religion business* "... because my family..." She broke off, taking on a sorrowful expression.

"Oh. Fräulein Annegret, you must be so shaken with grief."

"I am."

"You won't have to be alone, Gustav Fischer and his wife will be there with you, since he's been representing the family all this time."

A heavy burden fell from her shoulders. Herr Fischer had been so kind and caring towards her. She'd feel safe by his side, and she could simply mimic all his actions.

Margarete dressed and arranged her hair before a commotion outside drew her attention. She walked over to the window and peered down. An involuntary gasp left her lungs when she saw what was happening. Not only had all the employees who lived at Gut Plaun assembled for the walk to church, but also a horse driven cart had appeared with Nils, the handyman, in the coachman's seat.

It was quite clear that he'd come to pick her up and no doubt, present her to the townsfolk. She wondered whether she was expected to wave from the coach like Hitler always did. Her stomach responded by tying into a solid knot. She'd thought coming to the country house would allow her to lead a low-key life away from Berlin. In fact, she hadn't set foot in the capital since assuming her new identity, for fear of meeting an acquaintance of hers or Annegret's, who might expose her.

Not least of all Erika, Reiner Huber's widow. Erika had been more than a little peeved, that thanks to his father's stipulations in his last will and testament, she'd not inherited the Huber fortune, and that everything—apart from Reiner's personal wealth and a trust fund of one hundred thousand Reichsmark—had gone to Annegret.

It had actually been Horst Richter who had suggested that Margarete might consider avoiding returning to Berlin, whilst Erika was still there, lest there be a nasty scene between the two grieving women. Once again, appearances mattered most, but this time she was grateful for it. Even for the formalities of meeting the family lawyer, she'd faked an illness and sent Horst Richter in her stead.

To quieten her bad conscience, she'd later sent Erika a note of condolence and a money transfer for a quarter million Reichsmark to support her and her three daughters. She'd never heard a word back, not even a thank you, but a few months later Horst had brought the news that Erika had sold the house in Berlin and moved back to the countryside to be with her parents.

Margarete sighed. Today she would be like a goldfish in a bowl, as the townsfolk scrutinized her every move. It dawned on her that coming to Gut Plaun might not have been such a good idea, and she should have stayed in Paris instead, working with the French Résistance.

But it was too late. She steeled her spine, penciled her eyebrows the way Annegret had always done and hoped for the best. None of these villagers had seen her in at least a decade, and nobody would suspect the woman who'd returned to Gut Plaun wasn't the same person as the scrawny girl they'd known.

Margarete picked up the hat, carefully pinned it on her hair and dropped the short veil over her face. The light gauzy material came down to her chin and provided just enough cover to obscure her features and hide the fear.

She looked at herself in the tall standup mirror in the corner and her reflection gave her renewed confidence. This woman wearing the latest Parisian fashion and hairstyle looked exactly like the haughty heiress she pretended to be.

Pulling on the matching gloves, she inhaled deeply one last time and exited her room to meet whatever fate had in store for her. For the moment it was Frau Mertens impatiently waiting in the small dining room with Margarete's breakfast.

"You look lovely, Fräulein Annegret. The coach is waiting outside, so whenever you have finished your breakfast, we can leave."

The knot in her stomach tightened and her hunger was completely blown away. But it wouldn't do any good to show signs of nerves, so she settled at the table, ate a slice of bread with butter and drank a cup of *Ersatzkaffee*, before she got up and announced, "I'm ready to go."

Nils jumped from the coach seat the moment she stepped out

of the front door and handed her up into the carriage. Frau Mertens and Dora settled in the back of the carriage, and they left for town.

Margarete had already seen Saint Mary's Church with its tall steeple and bell tower from afar when she'd arrived at Gut Plaun mere days ago in Horst's limousine, but as the coach stopped in front of the church, it seemed even more impressive, oppressive even. She didn't subscribe to the belief that Jews shouldn't be allowed to visit Christian churches, like some of the more orthodox people, but she still had an eerie feeling creeping up her spine. Today would be the first time she'd actually stepped inside a church during Mass, and it felt entirely wrong.

In an attempt not to give away how lost she felt, she smiled at the townsfolk left and right, walking down the aisle, subconsciously waiting for something truly awful to happen. She imagined a hundred pairs of eyes riveted on her, waiting for the slightest misstep and the mounting tension made her short of breath. With a sigh of relief, she spotted the back of Gustav Fischer's head in the first pew on the right, next to an elegantly dressed woman. Their presence gave her strength.

She wanted to slip in beside him, when the priest, dressed in a black gown with white Geneva bands, descended from the raised platform to greet her.

"Fräulein Annegret, it is such a pleasure to have you back in Plau am See." He took both of her hands and bowed his head over them momentarily. "We were so very saddened to hear of the passing of your parents, and again when word came about your brothers' untimely deaths. We thank God for sparing you and even more so for sending you here to us. May your soul heal soon from its grief."

"Thank you," she murmured, sensing everyone behind her taking their seats. She peered to her right where Herr Fischer was seated, wishing for his comforting presence. Even though the priest was clearly kind and well-meaning, he certainly unnerved her, since she had no idea about the protocols to follow when interacting with a clergyman.

The priest followed her gaze and said, "Please take your seat, we can chat some more after the Mass."

Margarete inclined her head and stepped into the pew. Herr Fischer jumped up and shook her hand. "Fräulein Annegret, you look very elegant this morning. May I introduce you to my wife, Beate Fischer."

Beate gave a friendly smile and shook her hand. "I'm so sorry for your loss."

"Thank you very much, Frau Fischer."

"If you ever need anything, don't hesitate to ask. My husband and I will be pleased to help. Your late mother and I were good friends."

"I will." Margarete sat down, wondering why she'd never heard Frau Fischer's name mentioned in the Huber household, if the two women had been such good friends. Was she angling for favors? Margarete pushed the thought away, since it wouldn't do any good to suspect anyone and everyone to have ulterior motives.

A few minutes later, the priest stepped up to the pedestal and everyone rose to their feet, including Margarete, who kept one eye trained on the Fischers, mimicking their actions. Nevertheless, she was caught completely off guard a bit later, when the parish responded to the priest's words with an auditory reply. Not knowing the required words, she resorted to moving her lips and humming the word *Rote Beete,* beetroot, in the same rhythm as everyone else, while wracking her brain where she could later look up the prayers and learn them by heart.

As the service drew to a close, the priest and the altar boys retrieved a cup and a plate of small wafers. He invited the parishioners to come forward and receive the Lord's Communion and everyone stood to their feet. When Margarete made no effort to leave the pew, Frau Fischer gestured for her to precede her.

"I need another moment or two," Margarete said and let the other woman pass, while she sat back down and ducked her head, pretending to be in deep prayer before receiving the Holy Communion, when in fact she fought a war with herself, whether to commit such a sacrilegious deed or not. Because even she knew that only Christians who'd received the sacrament of confirmation were allowed to eat the body of Christ and drink the wine that represented his blood.

Then she shrugged. What did she care for the Protestants' sacred traditions if these so-called Christians murdered her people in the thousands every day? She stood with defiance and stepped into the line, closely observing those in front of her as how to behave.

But the closer she got to the priest, the more her confidence dwindled. Once she stood before him, she felt like a mortal sinner, but still opened her mouth and allowed him to place one of the wafers on her tongue with the words, "The body of Christ."

"Amen," she answered like those in front of her had done, and did the same when he offered her to drink from the chalice. Then she stepped aside hoping she wasn't angering their God to the point that he would strike her dead with a lightning bolt.

Riddled with guilt and defiance at the same time, she barely followed the rest of the service and heaved a sigh when it was finally over. Rushing from the church she yearned to hop into the carriage and be taken back to the manor, where she intended to hide from the world for the rest of her life. But that plan was thwarted by a large man standing next to the coach and patting the horse.

"Oliver, what a pleasure to see you," she said.

He looked up and glared at her. Whatever had occurred between him and Annegret all those years ago, it had clearly left a lasting dislike in him. She opened her mouth to take exception to his manners, but he didn't give her the chance.

"When shall I expect you at the stables? I have made a horse available for you at all time."

"Uhm... thank you... I've been so busy getting a handle on things at the manor... there has been no time for pleasure yet."

He raised an eyebrow, obviously not believing that Annegret might be busy with actual work. "Well, if you have a brief respite, please know that you're most welcome to take Snowfall for a ride."

"That is so very kind of you, but I might not be able to ride in the near future."

"Whyever not?" He seemed flabbergasted.

Because I have no idea how to ride a horse, in fact have never been near one. Since she couldn't tell him the truth, she stumbled to find a believable excuse. "It's just... I hurt my back in the explosion."

"Oh, I didn't know..." There was something unnerving in his stare, as if he was dissecting her, trying to get beyond her pretty face and find out the dark secret she was hiding. Of course that was only her imagination, since he couldn't possibly know.

"I didn't want to shout it from the rooftops and seem ungrateful to still be alive." The real Annegret would have made a big show about her suffering, reaping all the attention she could get, but Oliver had the decency not to mention that, although he did raise an eyebrow.

"Hopefully you will recover soon. As I said, whenever you wish, there'll be a horse ready for you."

"I'm anxious to get back into the saddle, but the doctor advised me to take it easy." With these words, she inclined her head and turned toward Frau Fischer, who beckoned her to greet some of the townswomen. Although she'd been anxious about being introduced around, right now, nothing scared her more than having to spend more time with Oliver, who somehow seemed to see through her disguise.

8

Oliver observed the two horses moving in unison around the corral, his left hand on the lead of the closest animal and a light whip in the other hand. The horses were two of the dozen the Wehrmacht were coming to fetch in the next few weeks, to be employed as draft horses in battle areas, especially in the campaign to conquer Russia.

Secretly he thought Hitler was committing a mistake in turning on his former ally, Stalin, but who was he to offer an opinion? After the disastrous experiences in the Battle of Moscow, where Jack Frost had rendered the automobiles useless, the Wehrmacht had upped their usage of horses.

While technologically outdated, horses offered many advantages, including that they could work in much lower temperatures when the fuel had long frozen solid. They also offered warmth to the soldiers during the night, and—he pressed his lips into a tight line—could be eaten if all else failed.

It filled him with sadness to think about the fate of his beloved horses, but in a time when humans didn't show compassion for other humans, what could be expected for animals? Breeding and training horses for the Wehrmacht provided a livelihood for him and dozens of grooms, and he always hoped that his charges were well equipped to survive the slaughter, even if statistics proved otherwise.

Normally, it took about a year to properly train a horse to withstand the sounds and smells they might encounter on the battlefield, but with the need for battle horses increasing, the Wehrmacht constantly badgered him to produce more animals in less time. As if he could just miraculously train them in a few months.

While Oliver constantly argued and bargained with the Wehrmacht on this point, Gustav Fischer kept stabbing him in the back. That lout couldn't care less about the animals, because his only worry was money. Gustav had probably cut a deal to receive a provision for every horse sold. That might explain his eagerness to comply with the Wehrmacht's demands, despite better knowledge. Perhaps as estate manager he had to do this, but it still rankled Oliver, who had the reputation for caring more about horses than humans.

He stopped his musings when he saw Piet saddling Snowfall and called out to the lad. "Hey, Piet? Has Fräulein Annegret finally decided to deign us with her presence?"

"No, boss, but the mare's impatient to get some exercise. I thought I'd ride her myself and check up on the fences of the paddock by the forest."

"Want me to come with you?" Oliver needed to get away from the depressing thoughts of handing over his horses to active duty.

"Sure, boss. Or you could go alone if you wanted? I've more than enough to do around here." Piet handed him the reins.

"Thanks. I owe you one." Oliver climbed onto the mare and put her straight into a trot, feeling lighter already. He prided himself on being on friendly terms with the stable hands, since he believed people who were taken seriously and treated kindly worked much harder than those in fear of their bosses. Which was the exact opposite of the late Herr Huber, Gustav, and Annegret. They demanded absolute obedience from people working for them, and none of them had ever shown compassion to subordinates.

Snowfall whinnied with delight at getting out, and he allowed her to gallop toward the fringe of the estate, although his thoughts remained with the woman whom he despised for her cruelty.

Nevertheless he couldn't help but feel the tiniest bit sorry for her, because she'd looked completely out of her element when he'd seen her at church the day before. She'd even seemed afraid of riding, which was a peculiar reaction from a woman who'd spent most of her childhood in the stables and on the backs of horses. If he didn't know better, Oliver could have sworn the woman who'd come to Gut Plaun wasn't Annegret at all. He shook his head at the silly thought. People could change, couldn't they?

Not her, a voice in his head whispered. *She's a devil through and through.* He remembered one occasion when she'd dared to take her father's stallion out, despite his strict forbiddance. Herr Huber had been furious and unbuckled his belt, but Annegret had convinced him that Oliver was the one to blame, so he'd received the beating in her stead. He hadn't been able to sit for an entire week.

He pressed his heels into Snowfall's stomach to make her go even faster in the hope to run away from the disturbing memories. He shook his head, wanting to shake off the past, but he couldn't. A twinge of guilt remained for thinking she'd not changed, when in fact, she had changed very much. Gone was the spoiled, spiteful girl, and in her place was a woman who showed kindness naturally and seemed to be scared of riding a horse. Something awful must have happened to put that fear in her eyes.

He reached the far end of the paddock, jumped down and let the mare graze while he inspected the fence posts. Deeply inhaling the fresh air that smelled of the upcoming colder season, he determined that Annegret was none of his business. His life would be much simpler if she stayed away from the stables and he certainly wouldn't go to the manor to seek her out.

Snowfall sidled up to him and he patted her neck. "We better get back, I have to check up on the deliveries and then there's a few cart horses to train."

The sensitive horse put her ears up on alert, as if she actually understood his words.

The ride back home was pure joy, devoid of any unpleasant thoughts about the odious girl who had returned to occupy the manor. Back at his house a pleasant surprise waited for him.

"Hello, Dora, has your mistress let you go early?" he teased her.

"She's really not bad at all. Nothing like you said she was. People grow up and change, you know?" Dora followed him inside. "Anyway, Frau Mertens sent me up here to change your bed linen for the laundry."

Despite living in his own house a few hundred yards from the manor, Oliver received the same services as the men who lived in the servants' quarters, because Gustav insisted Oliver's time was better spent caring for the horses than preparing meals and doing laundry. Oliver secretly believed the real reason was that Gustav didn't consider him capable of looking after himself and wanted to make sure he was properly fed and clothed. Gustav was a very complex person, and while Oliver disliked his way of doing business, he could be very generous to those he considered friends. Either way, he enjoyed the comfort—and Dora's frequent visits.

He usually wasn't prone to falling for women, especially not with a colleague, but Dora had captured his heart from the first day she arrived at Gut Plaun. She looked so young and innocent at just eighteen years old, but at the same time she seemed so strong and resilient. He admired her for having the courage to leave her home country all alone to pursue a better life thousands of miles away. He appreciated her serenity and her intelligence—while she wasn't educated in a traditional way, she had mastered the German language at an amazing speed.

But what had completely done him in was her kindness to humans and animals alike. While she didn't know how to ride a horse, she loved to pat and groom them in her scarce leisure time.

He kissed her passionately and they canoodled for as long as they dared without raising suspicions with Frau Mertens, before Dora smoothed the wrinkles from her dress. "I need to hurry up, because Fräulein Annegret wants to change bedrooms and Frau Mertens has put me to the task of preparing the master suite for her to move into."

"It makes sense that she wouldn't want to stay in that nightmare of plush." Oliver had been in there once, helping Nils to fix a window, and he still shivered at the sight. While the room might be acceptable for a small girl, it certainly wasn't anything a grown woman would want to live in.

"Right? It's outright awful... although I sure would have liked something similar when I was a little girl."

Dora's face took on a dreamy look and he traced her cheek with his finger, intent on kissing her, but she moved her head away and gave him a cheeky gaze. "The master suite includes a dressing room and a parlor in addition to the large private bathroom, which means more work for me keeping everything spotless, but it does come with its perks."

"Does it now?" His feelings for Dora grew bigger every day and if it weren't forbidden, he'd propose marriage to her in the blink of an eye.

"Yes." She jumped up and down with excitement. "It has a separate staircase that connects it to the back patio, which will allow me to leave her room and come to your place without having to pass under Frau Mertens' curious nose."

"Now that is indeed a perk." He grinned, but moments later, his face fell. "Although we shouldn't have to hide our love for each other. There's nothing bad or wrong about it."

She sighed. "Let's hope this war will soon be over and then we will go someplace where we can live together."

9

Margarete stepped into the forest, a light prickle crawling down her back. It was the first time she had ventured so far on her daily walks, and being a city girl, she found the forest eerie.

But Frau Mertens had said it was the time of year for finding ripe blackberries and she wanted to pick some for herself, since it was such a rare treat in the rationed daily routine. She paused before walking further, regretting that she hadn't asked Dora to accompany her, but the poor girl was swamped with chores. On the other hand, Margarete needed time away from the watchful eyes of Frau Mertens and the other employees, a respite from having to be on alert at all times and carefully consider every word she said.

It was exhausting. In the nine months she'd been pretending to be Annegret, she'd never felt such scrutiny. In Paris the only person who'd known the real Annegret was her brother Wilhelm, and he was in on the ruse. None of his friends or acquaintances had met his sister before, and so didn't constantly compare her previous behavior to her ways of acting now, like they did here.

Unlike Oliver. She'd been carefully probing Frau Mertens, and even Nils, to find out what had transpired between the two of them as children, but apart from generalities about fighting over trifles, she'd gotten no information and stopped asking altogether so as not to raise suspicions.

But deep inside she just knew there was hidden history between Oliver and Annegret, an awful incident, perhaps, one he'd never forgiven her for, thus ensuing the deep-rooted antipathy he still harbored for her. It was a dangerous situation, because if she was right, she believed he'd be all too willing to harm Annegret as a chance to savor revenge.

The tingle on her back increased as if Oliver were in the forest, observing her. Perhaps she should tell him her true identity? Since he hated Annegret so much, he might even be sympathetic to the impostor in place.

She quickly shrugged off the thought. It was ridiculous at best and outright dangerous at worst. Despite Dora's attempts to act aloof, she'd seen how the girl's eyes brightened whenever he was around. If the two were indeed a couple, he might tell her... and then Frau Mertens and Herr Fischer might get wind of the truth and neither of them would be benevolent. On the contrary, they'd gladly hang her on the lamppost by the entry gate.

As nice as Herr Fischer had been to her, she'd sensed his deep-rooted anti-Semitism. In that aspect he was much like Horst Richter, kind to those inside his circle, cold-hearted and perhaps even cruel to those outside. She would never understand how men like them could compartmentalize humans into strict categories: worthy, unworthy to live... and Jews.

Jews were a category by themselves, ranked even lower than the disabled, soft-minded, or otherwise sick. They stood beneath the asocials, homosexuals, work-shy, and criminals. In fact, according to what Wilhelm had told her, murderers and rapists were appreciated for their brutality and elevated to the highest ranks in the camp hierarchy, encouraging them to legally torment their fellow prisoners to keep them in line and lighten the workload for the Nazi guards.

Deep in thought, she walked much farther than she had intended, forgetting all about looking for blackberries. When she looked up again, she was surrounded by trees with barely any light filtering through the canopy of leaves and needles. The rare rays of light shining through scattered to and fro. Margarete sensed how much cooler the air had become. The earth smelled damp and she heard the scuffling of small animals as they hid from her. Birds called from the trees. It was such a peaceful atmosphere, but still the eerie feeling increased.

Behind a moss-covered log she glimpsed a movement and kept still, hoping to see a rabbit or a squirrel scamper forward, while at the same time fearing it might be a boar or even a wolf ready to attack her. Frozen into place she barely dared to breathe, cursing herself for venturing too far into the forest without taking a strong stick with her.

A whimpering sound came from behind the log and terror gripped her heart. The forest was full of wild animals and oftentimes Herr Fischer would invite friends to go hunting. For them, it was pure pleasure, but Frau Mertens welcomed the animals they shot to enrich the meagre meat rations. She should have asked one of the male employees to accompany her, preferably with a rifle in his hand.

Once more the pitiful whimpering cut through the air and froze her blood. What if the animal was hurt? Maybe one of the horses had jumped the fence? *A horse is much too big to hide behind that log*, she scolded herself. She took a hesitant step toward the sound and the muffled whimpers stopped as if whatever was there, was as scared as she was and didn't want to attract attention to itself.

"Hello?" Margarete called out. "Is anyone there?"

No answer came. She stood completely still, listening with bated breath, but heard nothing. Slightly scared, she turned around to walk back the way she'd come, when suddenly a screeching sound cut through the air, followed by a curse. That definitely sounded human.

She was torn between having a look for herself and racing to the manor for help. The person could be anyone from a harmless child looking for blackberries to a member of the resistance. She shook her head. This was Germany, not France, and there weren't resistance fighters hiding in the woods. Most likely the person was an innocent wanderer who'd injured himself.

Seconds later she heard another heart-stopping whimper and gathered up all her courage to walk in the direction where the sound came from. Just in case, she picked up a sturdy stick on the way to the log.

"Please, don't be afraid, I won't do you harm," she said, more to assure herself than the other person.

The sounds stopped and so did Margarete. She stood perfectly still, her eyes staring into the shadows to pick up a movement. Her patience was rewarded when a slight figure moved haltingly away from her. She was tempted to let the other person get away, but then noticed the tottering gait. He was definitely injured, but obviously too afraid to let Margarete help him.

"Please, stop. I can help you. I promise, I won't harm you," she shouted once more and her feet put themselves into motion, following the fleeing person, even before her brain ordered them to.

She was gaining on him, when he stumbled and fell to the ground. Seconds later Margarete was beside him and stared aghast at the emaciated person with a shaved head and hollow eyes, dressed in a threadbare striped dress. With horror she realized that the person lying in front of her was a woman, more dead than alive.

Even though she had never seen an actual concentration camp inmate, it was crystal clear that the woman must be an escaped prisoner. As far as she knew, there were no camps close by, but then, the locations of those weren't exactly advertised in the newspapers.

"Please, let me help. I won't tell on you." It was a folly to help an escaped prisoner, but how could Margarete not? If it weren't for a lucky strike of fate, she might be the woman on the ground shivering with fear. A light of hope entered the prisoner's eyes, instantly followed by suspicion.

"What's your name?" Margarete asked.

"No. Go away..." the woman mumbled, trying to push herself up to a standing position, seemingly intent on escaping.

Margarete moved around the woman and crouched down in front of her. "I promise, you are safe with me. I don't know your story, but I can help."

"No, they will punish both of us..."

"There is no one here but me and I certainly won't send you back to whoever has so badly mistreated you," Margarete assured her. "Here, let me help you up and we will find someplace other than the ground to sit."

She reached for the woman, unable to avoid noticing the bruises that covered her arms, the tops of her shoulders, and even her neck. This woman had been badly abused, and Margarete's heart filled with righteous anger at whoever had done this. As she helped the escapee to return to the log, it dawned on her that the woman wouldn't survive the night if she stayed in the forest. Night temperatures had been falling to freezing point this past week.

"I'm Annegret. What's your name?"

"Lena."

"Don't be afraid of me."

Lena seemed unsure what to say, but at last she nodded and the arm she'd held the entire time defensively over her chest slipped slightly downward to expose the edge of something yellow.

Margarete recognized it instantaneously. The shock rumbled through her body.

When Lena noticed, she slumped back and her arm unblocked the sight of the yellow star sewn onto her prisoner's dress. "Now you know. You can turn me in."

"I will do no such thing. Jewish or not, I'll take you to my house and tend to your wounds."

"No... you can't... it's too dangerous... If he finds out... he'll kill me. And you, too."

"Nobody will get killed," Margarete said, despite not being so sure. Her brain was going a mile a minute figuring out how she could get Lena into her rooms. Passing the main gate unseen wouldn't be too difficult, and once they reached the back patio she could get her up the private staircase, which nobody used, to her suite. The difficult part was to cross from the main gate to the back patio without raising suspicions.

They'd have to wait until the employees were in the kitchen for dinner—and Lena could under no circumstances wear her prisoner garb.

"You'll have to get rid of your uniform," she said.

Lena stared at her with big eyes.

"If someone sees you in that striped dress, they'll know immediately." Margarete thought for a moment. "I'll give you my coat and we'll bury your dress." She took off her coat and handed it to Lena, who was still standing motionless, staring at her with blank eyes.

"Why are you doing this?"

Margarete bit on her tongue, before she was tempted to tell Lena the truth. If—God forbid—they got caught, it would only do harm. "Let's just say I don't like to see mistreated women."

The wary expression in Lena's eyes stayed, but at least she nodded, apparently realizing that putting her fate in Margarete's hands was her best option in this instant. She turned around to undress and Margarete's hand flew to her mouth when she saw the angry red scars and burns on her back. What kind of monster had done this to the poor woman?

When they reached the perimeter of the manor with the main gate Margarete instructed her. "I'll go first. You watch me closely, wait a minute or so and then take exactly the same route. I'll meet you around the corner at the bottom of the staircase. Everyone else should be in the kitchen for dinner, but if anyone happens to come across you, they'll assume you are me."

She stepped back, took off her hat and put it on Lena's bald head, nudging it into a fashionable twisted angle. "Don't talk to anyone. If you're caught I won't be able to help you and will have to pretend you stole my things."

Lena nodded. "Understood."

With a hammering heart, Margarete walked away with measured steps, attempting to look as if she'd just returned from her daily walk and wasn't conspiring to hide an escaped Jewish prisoner in her quarters. Only when she reached the back patio, did she let out a breath as she grabbed the handrail to steady herself.

Now came the most crucial part. If Lena was discovered on her way through the premises, Margarete could still claim ignorance, but if someone saw them together on the staircase, all defense was lost.

Barely able to breathe, she waited for the other woman. Seconds drew into minutes and the knot in her stomach grew exponentially. Lena still didn't show up. She perked up her ears, but heard nothing, except for the chirping of the birds. Had Lena lost her nerve and run away to chance her luck?

Undecided whether to walk up to her suite or return to the front patio to find out what had happened, she stood for what seemed an eternity, hearing nothing but the rushing blood in her ears. Pebbles rolled. And then... Lena rounded the corner. Margarete wanted to weep.

"Hurry." She took the other woman by the shoulders and shoved her up the stairs. At the top, she carefully opened the door to her private suite, peeking inside to make sure Dora wasn't there cleaning one thing or the other. Finding the room empty, she nudged Lena inside and lead her into the bathroom.

"I'll clean your wounds and find you a nightgown to wear." Margarete dampened a washcloth under the faucet, but when she turned around, Lena leaned against the wall with her eyes closed.

"Are you sleeping?"

"No," Lena whispered. She seemed to have used up all her energy and didn't even flinch, when Margarete helped her out of the coat and began to move her limbs up and down to gently dab at her wounds. Every time she wrung out the cloth, dark muddy water, tinged with a trace of dried blood came out.

"Ready," Margarete finally said, but Lena didn't move. She had her eyes closed and seemed to have fallen asleep standing up. Sighing, Margarete retrieved a nightgown from her drawer and pulled it over Lena's head and arms, before she nudged the woman into bed and tucked her in.

"Please... you won't turn me in? They'll kill me for sure and..."

Looking at the skeletal figure with the shorn head, Margarete felt guilty. Here she was, living a privileged life as lady of the manor when so many of her people were harassed, mistreated and even killed. She vowed to stop dawdling this very instant and begin her search for ways how to help those persecuted by the Nazis in earnest. There might not be an organized resistance in Germany like there was in France, but there must be people who opposed the regime and helped the Jews. And if there wasn't, she'd start her own movement, with Lena being the first person she'd rescue from the Nazis' clutches. So help her, God!

A knock on the door announced Dora's arrival, and Margarete raced out into the anteroom to prevent the maid from coming into her bedroom.

"Hello, Dora." She stepped directly into her way.

"Fräulein Annegret, Frau Mertens was asking whether you'd like to come down for dinner."

Damn. She'd completely forgotten dinner over the commotion with Lena. Quickly concocting a plan, she answered with a feeble voice, "I have a terrible headache, so bad it is making me feel nauseous and I was about to lie down."

"Can I get you anything?"

"No, no... although I think I'll take my dinner here. Would you be so kind as to bring it upstairs?"

"Certainly. Shall I serve it in your bedroom?"

"No!" Margarete snapped, before she continued in a neutral voice. "That won't be necessary. I would much prefer you to put it on the table in the anteroom."

Dora disappeared and Margarete waited in the parlor to make sure the maid wouldn't set foot into her bedroom.

After Dora served dinner, she told her, "I'll retire after my meal and don't want to be disturbed under any circumstances. Do you understand?"

"Yes, Fräulein Annegret."

"And don't wake me in the morning, not even for breakfast."

"Yes, Fräulein Annegret."

When Dora closed the door behind herself, Margarete let out a deep sigh. She returned to her bedroom, where Lena was staring at the door like a frightened mouse.

"No need to worry, that was just my maid. Are you hungry?"

"That would be an understatement. I ran away four nights ago, and haven't eaten much since."

How she'd survived so long without food when her body was already depleted was a testimony to her will to live. Margarete pondered whether she should suggest Lena eat at the table in the parlor, but decided against it. Dora, or worse, Frau Mertens might return to ask about the dinner, but they'd never dare to enter her bedroom against her explicit wishes. "I'll bring you something."

She skipped back to the parlor, taking a slice of bread and a knife. But just as she was about to coat the bread with liverwurst, her hand stopped midway. Since posing as Annegret she'd had to get rid of behavior that might identify her as Jewish, eating kosher food being a most obvious one.

But that didn't mean she had to force Lena to do the same. So she wiped the liverwurst from the knife and buttered the bread instead. Her gaze fell on the thick broth with blobs of grease. She knew it contained potatoes, carrots and chunks of meat, but she'd never given thought about what kind of meat. This business of hiding a Jew was getting more complicated than she'd expected.

Grabbing the slice of bread, she entered the bedroom. "Here you go."

Lena greedily shoved the bread into her mouth and devoured it in a few seconds. It broke Margarete's heart to see her so famished. Gathering her courage, she asked, "There's soup... but I'm pretty sure it's not kosher."

"You're the first goy ever to mention this," Lena said with amazement in her voice.

That would be because I'm not a gentile. "We used to have Jewish neighbors," she explained.

For the first time since she'd found her, Lena smiled. "Thank you for asking, but at this point I've eaten anything from tree bark to earthworms. So I'd certainly welcome a non-kosher soup with actual meat."

Margarete stared at her open-mouthed, because the discrepancy between Lena's downtrodden vagrant looks and her sophisticated speech couldn't be starker. It took her a few moments to recover and she went to fetch a bowl of soup from the parlor.

She turned the armchair to face the bed and settled on it to watch Lena eat. The other woman was so emaciated, the bones protruded sharply through the parched skin, and yet, she had the most beautiful features.

"Thank you for your kindness." Lena wiped her mouth after finishing the soup. "Now I need to leave."

"You can't. Where would you go?"

"Back to the forest, I was hiding in some cave."

"It's much too cold at night. You'll freeze to death. And what will you eat?"

"I've eaten now. That should be sufficient for a few days."

"Don't be ridiculous." Margarete was getting impatient with the woman who seemed hell-bent on leaving the safety of the manor. "You're severely injured and undernourished. No one knows you are here. Let me at least keep you hidden until you've recovered from your injuries."

"He'll find me. I know he will."

"Who is he?"

Lena's eyes clouded over with raw horror. "He's a powerful man. A beast. We have to call him Master."

"He's not going to find you here." Margarete put her palm on Lena's hand and all but recoiled at feeling nothing but bones. "I'll get you some aspirin for the pain, that'll let you sleep."

"I've been too afraid to fall asleep ever since I escaped."

"Well, I'll be watching over you, so rest easy."

"You'll get in trouble if they find out you helped me," Lena warned her.

"Let that be of my concern." Margarete took the bowl from her and returned it to the parlor. Then she rummaged in the bathroom for aspirin and gave it to Lena with a cup of water. "Will you tell me where you escaped from?"

It seemed to cost Lena a lot of effort to open up, but after a long silence she finally talked. "I was in Ravensbrück for quite some time, until they transferred me here to an ammunitions factory. It..." she seemed to hesitate "...it's not far away. This place is so much worse than the camp, because the men who run the factory are sadists. They don't just keep us toiling with barely any food for sixteen hours a day, but they also like to have private nightly sessions with some of the younger, prettier women."

Margarete swallowed hard, because judging by her beautiful face, Lena must have been abused in such a horrible way.

When Lena fell asleep, she got up and ate the rest of her dinner in the parlor, before preparing herself to retire. For tonight she'd sleep on the couch, but she had to find a better arrangement, especially since Dora came in every morning to wake her. Fearing that the maid might not remember the order not to disturb her in the morning, she moved the heavy armchair in front of the door.

But sleep didn't come, too great was her anxiety. Since Lena had mentioned the factory using prisoners for slave work was nearby, she decided to find out exactly where it was and to whom it belonged. Maybe she could talk to the owner into stopping his employees from violating the women. If he wasn't open to reason she might insinuate that it was a crime to have sexual intercourse with Jews. She snickered. What a twisted way to use the Nazis' own racial laws to protect Jewish women from them.

Her mind traveled back to her time in Paris, and to Wilhelm. She missed him so much. He would know how to go about finding the factory and its owner; he might even be able to use his position in the SS to force the foremen into treating their workers, if not well, at least humanely.

But Wilhelm was dead. His sacrifice had given her the wealth she possessed and she owed it to him to do good with the money. And now she knew exactly how.

10

Oliver was sitting in his living room, listening to the sounds outside. It was getting late and Dora should have arrived a while ago. He hated that she had to sneak in and out of the manor under the cover of night to visit him and was always worried something might happen to her.

Finally he heard the tip-tap of shoes on the cobblestones leading to his house. He jumped up and tore the door open to wrap her in his arms. "What held you up?"

"Fräulein Annegret, she's not feeling well, so I had to bring her dinner upstairs and then retrieve the dishes when she was done."

"What a spoilt woman!"

"Don't judge her so harshly, she is quite nice. At least to me."

Oliver couldn't understand why Dora was so fond of Annegret. Didn't she see that Annegret wrapped them all around her finger? Like she'd done with him when they were children, before showing her true colors.

Once upon a time, the two of them had been, if not friends, at least playmates. Until that fatal day, when he'd seen behind her pretty face and gotten a glimpse at her deep-rooted cruelty directed toward those she deemed unworthy.

Her two brothers, he, and Annegret had been out on an adventure trip down to the lake, when her brothers, fourteen and sixteen years old back then, had met some town girls and had disappeared with them, leaving Oliver to babysit ten-year-old Annegret. She had been raging with fury and to appease her, he'd suggested they return to Gut Plaun, where he'd show her the newborn foals.

But they had never arrived at the stables, because they came upon Albert, the blind guy, walking in the opposite direction.

"I hate him, he's always so clumsy," Annegret said.

"That's because he's blind."

"But why does he have to come to the manor? Why can't he stay at home where I don't have to see him?"

Oliver shook his head. Annegret always assumed the world revolved around her; she couldn't fathom that Albert came to the manor because he sold vegetables he cultivated in his garden.

"Let's play a trick on him," she said.

"Wait. No."

But she had already rushed forward, grabbed Albert's walking stick, and threw it into the underbrush. "That'll teach you to stay home where you belong!" she shouted.

Albert, who was normally a very kind man, shouted back at her in panic, "Give my stick back, you miserable brat! Straightaway!"

But Annegret only danced around him, giggling. "You'll have to find it yourself. Tee-hee."

Oliver couldn't watch this any longer and hurried to the location where she'd thrown the stick. He rummaged in the bushes until he found it, but when he returned, both Albert and Annegret were gone.

Unsure what to do, he looked around, until he heard a moan and followed the sound. He found Albert lying in the ditch, where he'd probably stumbled into while trying to find his stick.

"I have your walking stick," Oliver said, putting it into his hand.

"I'll teach you nasty youngsters how to behave," the man shouted and swung the stick in Oliver's direction.

He jumped away, so as not to get hit. Glancing back, he saw

that Albert had managed to stand up, still shouting and swinging the stick, so he took to his heels and ran away.

Back at the manor, Herr Huber was waiting for him. Before Oliver could say anything in his defense, Herr Huber unbuckled his belt and gave him a severe beating for abandoning his sweet little daughter alone in the woods.

Annegret stood by and watched.

"She's a two-faced snake!" he spat out to Dora. "I can see right through her and I tell you, something is off with that woman, trying to be friendly and all."

"People change."

Oliver couldn't contain the scoffing sound that burst from his lips. "Not Annegret Huber. Her mission in life is to make it miserable for everyone else."

"Give her a chance."

"I'd rather say we keep an eye on her. She's hiding something and knowing her it can't be anything good. But this time I'll be prepared and she'll pay for all the evil she has done."

Dora pressed a kiss on his calloused hand. "Let's not talk about her."

He was instantly mollified, playing with a loose strand of her hair. "What would you like to talk about?" He didn't wait for an answer, but proceeded to undo her long braid until her thick and soft hair fell freely down to her waist like the lushest of waterfalls. She was even more gorgeous like that and the fact that no one in the household had seen her with her hair down stoked his desire and he felt the passion rising in his loins. "Come to bed with me. Please."

She nodded and followed him upstairs into the tiny bedroom, where he loved her tenderly. In the early hours of the morning he woke and rolled over to look at Dora's face. Every day he loved her more and couldn't bear the thought of not being able to shout their happiness from the rooftops.

"You're so beautiful," he murmured as he stroked her shoulders to wake her up.

"What time is it?" she asked, turning on her side and snuggling into his arms.

"Just after four in the morning." Oliver slid his hand to the back of her head and pulled her in for a long kiss. When he finally released her, they were both out of breath and her cheeks were flushed a delightful pink. "When are you going to make an honest man out of me? I hate this sneaking around."

"We've been over this before. The Ukraine is an ally to Germany, but we're still considered Slavs. They'll never give us permission to marry. Worse, if we file the paperwork, Frau Mertens will find out." Dora had such a frightened look on her face, it tore his heart apart. "She would never permit a married woman to work as a maid and might even get me deported."

"I would never let that happen, my darling. I love you so much." He propped himself up on his elbows. "I wish I could find a way to marry you..."

"One day the war will end and that will happen, but for now... we have to be patient." She kissed him once more and then slid from his grasp and pulled her clothing back on.

"Let me at least walk you back to the house, I'm always worried about you," he begged her.

"That would be so much more suspicious than me going alone. Besides, what could happen to me? It's only a few hundred yards, and the main gate is locked at night."

Oliver sighed. Rationally, he knew it was unlikely for her to come upon a danger on the short way to the manor, but deep in his heart he remained worried. She was a pretty, young girl and one of the farmhands living on the site might get a bit too enthusiastic if he saw her alone at night. "Take care, my love."

He closed the door behind her and opened the blackout curtain ajar to watch over her until he saw her lithe figure slipping into the side entrance. Only then did he relax and walked up to his bedroom again, where he slept for another hour, before he rose and got ready to face the day.

11

Margarete was in the bathroom running a bath for Lena, when she heard a knock on the bedroom door.

"Shush. Stay here and make no noise," she hissed at Lena, before she pulled a bathrobe over her dress and tousled her hair to make it seem like she'd just gotten out of bed. Then she walked into her bedroom and called, "Come in."

"You're up, Fräulein Annegret. Are you feeling better?" Dora asked, walking over to the window to open the curtains.

"No! Don't!" Margarete said, because in bright daylight Dora would surely notice that someone had slept on the couch. "I'm still getting nauseous from the sunlight."

The maid waivered and turned around. "Would you like me to bring your breakfast upstairs, then?"

"Yes, please." Margarete made her voice sound feeble and held a hand to her temple. "And perhaps aspirin if Frau Mertens has some."

"I'll ask her and if we're out, she can send one of the lads into town. Should she ask the doctor to come and see you?"

A doctor would definitely help, but since he couldn't know about Lena's presence, she declined. "No, thank you, I'm sure it'll pass."

"Very well, Fräulein Annegret. I'll bring your breakfast right away and serve it in the parlor. Then I can clean your bedroom while you're eating."

Oh no! She couldn't let Dora venture into her bedroom. "I'm going to take a hot bath, so please set it on the parlor table and leave it there for me, will you?"

The maid gave her a puzzled look, but didn't ask further questions. As soon as she left, Margarete knocked on the bathroom door. "It's me. Annegret."

"Come in."

Lena was sitting in the bathtub, scrubbing the grime from her body. With a clean face she was even more beautiful.

"Here are towels. But stay in here until I come to get you."

"Don't worry. I know how to hide."

Margarete left Lena alone and walked through the bedroom, making sure nothing betrayed the presence of a second person in case Dora came in.

Only moments later she heard the clatter of dishes and assumed the maid was setting up the breakfast table. She preferred not to step into the parlor, but listened intently until she heard the door to the hallway being closed again. *Thank God, she's gone.*

She really had to find a better place to hide Lena, since her rooms didn't provide enough privacy. She considered telling Dora the truth, but immediately squashed the idea. It wasn't clear how the maid felt about Jews, and, even if she was sympathetic to the escaped woman's plight, it would put her in an impossible situation.

Sitting at the table in the parlor, she meticulously divided the breakfast into two portions, setting the bigger one aside for Lena. Just when she finished eating her part, a knock sounded on the door.

"Yes?" she called out, striding toward the door to stave off anyone wanting to enter.

"I'm sorry for disturbing you, but Reichskriminaldirektor

Richter is on the telephone," Frau Mertens informed her through the closed door.

"Please tell him to call back later, I'm not feeling well."

"He said it's important."

Margarete sighed. She wouldn't want to anger or worry him. "I'll take it up here."

"Very well. I'll hang up the downstairs phone once I hear you come on the line."

Margarete walked toward the elegant writing table that had no doubt belonged to Frau Huber and picked up the extension line.

"Horst, I trust you got home without incident?"

He chuckled into the line jovially. "Leipzig is much too far east to be within reach of those bloody British bombers, so there's nothing to fear. How is the countryside treating you?"

"Hold on just a minute, Frau Mertens went to hang up the downstairs phone." They both waited until they heard the telltale click signaling the other phone had been hung up.

"I have a favor to ask," Horst said, just when Lena came out of the bathroom, a towel wrapped around her body and another one around her head. She looked so small and vulnerable, it plucked at Margarete's heartstrings. The next second, the feeling morphed into pure panic, when Lena strode toward the breakfast table and tripped over something, making quite the noise. Margarete shook her head and put a finger in front of her lips.

"What was that noise?" Horst asked.

"I... don't know. It was outside, probably one of the lads slamming down on something. I'll go and close the window." She beckoned for Lena to return to the bedroom and made a show of loudly closing the door, before picking up the receiver again. "I'm so sorry for the disturbance. Please, how can I help you?"

"A group of colleagues are headed to your area for business reasons and it seems there's no suitable guesthouse to accommodate all of them."

Suddenly the room seemed to be getting very hot and she fanned herself. "How many men?"

"Eight."

She couldn't afford to turn him down, because she needed his, albeit involuntary, support for her resistance work and he'd certainly resent it if she didn't grant him this favor. She took a deep breath before answering. "We have only five empty bedrooms in the manor. Won't they mind having to share a room?"

"Not at all. The lesser ranks are used to that."

"Then, I'd be most pleased to welcome your colleagues into my house. Will you be joining them?"

"I'm afraid not. I just arrived back and you can't imagine how much work the relocation of the Jews is giving us."

She grimaced into the phone, once more being reminded how precarious her own situation was. Horst Richter wouldn't hesitate for a second to put her on one of the deportation trains if he found out who she truly was.

"For when shall I advise Frau Mertens to have everything prepared?"

"The day after tomorrow. I'll phone in the exact names and ranks for the distribution of rooms. My colleagues shouldn't inconvenience you for more than a few days."

"It's no inconvenience at all. On the contrary, I'm delighted to do my bit for the Reich and to entertain your colleagues." Her stomach lurched as she realized she'd actually have to stay under the same roof with not one, but eight Gestapo officers. The queasy feeling spread across her entire body, while her head was spinning in ten different directions. The rooms needed to be readied, provisions secured, and she had to make sure there was no trace of Lena for the men to find while they were at Gut Plaun.

"I must warn you, they are not just Gestapo. A few SS men will also be with them."

She gave a light giggle, knowing how much rivalry there was between Gestapo and SS. Herr Huber, SS himself, had often spoken with disdain of the Gestapo and it was a miracle that he and Horst had remained such close friends. "I will make sure the best rooms are given to the right people."

Horst guffawed, before he said, "You really take after your father."

"Well, if that isn't a compliment..." *to my acting*. He obviously hadn't meant it that way but she felt pride swell in her heart. If she could fool an observant Gestapo detective like Horst, who'd known Annegret's father, then she didn't have to worry about eight complete strangers.

"So, how are you getting along?" he asked.

"Very well. I've been taking long daily walks and I still haven't managed to see all of the estate."

"I should hope not. If your desire is to see the entire estate, use a horse, not your feet."

"Yes, I have planned to do that," Margarete assured him, not mentioning that she'd yet to visit the stables. "Actually, I'm glad you called as I wanted to ask you about something."

"I'll be glad to help."

"I heard a rumor about a secret munitions factory in the woods nearby."

"Oh, Annegret. There's nothing secret about this factory. In fact, it belongs to you."

"To me?" she blurted out.

"Yes. It was constructed under the guidance of the Dynamit Nobel AG, but for reasons I can't disclose, your father took up the ownership. I believe they currently produce an explosive called Nitropenta."

Margarete leaned back into the chair, grasping to comprehend the implications of his revelation. If she was the owner of that factory... then Lena was running from... her? She cast a worried glance at the connecting door, behind which the woman was hiding. "So where is it?"

"Between Gut Plaun and the lake, next to the railroad. Your father was quite the prescient businessman and had a train station constructed exclusively for the factory to more efficiently transport supplies and workers."

Workers transported by train. That could only mean one

thing... concentration camp inmates forced into slave labor. The evidence thickened and with it the queasy feeling in Margarete's stomach. She did not only benefit personally from exploiting Jews, no, she actually was the reason for their plight.

"Why was I never told about this factory?" she said, trying her best to keep the horror out of her voice.

"Oh, you were. Don't you remember the list the lawyer sent you? It included all the assets you inherited."

Much to her chagrin Margarete had to admit that she'd received and signed the list, but never made the effort to actually read through all the details it contained. "Now that you should mention it... it must have slipped my mind."

"You're a woman and there's no need to burden yourself with war production. The factory is in good hands with Herr Fischer and the factory manager. Both of them report on a monthly basis to the *Wirtschafts- und Rüstungsamt*, the department in the High Command of the Armed Forces to coordinate supplies needed for the Wehrmacht."

Remembering his advice to concern herself only with the manor and leave everything else to the men, she said sweetly, "And that is such a relief. I just was caught unawares when someone mentioned it to me. I don't want to appear dumb."

"You're not dumb, Annegret. And people understand that as a woman there are certain aspects of your possessions that are way above your head. That's why estates generally are handed down to the eldest son, except in unfortunate cases like yours."

Margarete clenched her free hand into a fist, sick and tired of hearing how inferior she was. As a Jew, she'd been treated like scum, but apparently even a goy woman was only slightly above that level. Good enough to keep the house and the children at their best, but too much beneath the men to actually matter. Everyone expected her to nod her head, smile, and be a good little girl, while ignoring the travesties happening all around her.

She ended the conversation with Horst, promising to ensure his colleagues were well fed and had a comfortable stay. But his revelations wouldn't let her get back to business as usual. If Fischer knew about the factory, he most probably knew about the appalling conditions, too. The Nazi propaganda was probably too ingrained in him to acknowledge that Jews were actual humans, worthy of being treated as such. But she would still talk to him to find out whether he'd be open to implement some improvements.

She took a few moments to gather herself, before she walked into the bedroom to look after Lena. "Feeling better?"

"A lot."

"It's best if you stay in my bedroom. I'll bring you something to eat."

"You're too kind."

Margarete smiled as she served Lena the food in bed. She had done this so many times for Frau Huber, when she herself had been a maid, but now she actually enjoyed it. Moving the armchair next to the bed, she sat down and watched the emaciated woman eat. Her heart broke at the sight, but even more disturbing was the feeling of guilt creeping up her spine. She was responsible for Lena's suffering, because she owned the factory.

"Can you tell me more about the factory? Where it is? What it does?" Secretly she clung to the possibility that Lena had escaped from some other place.

"I don't know exactly where it is. We came here in cattle carts and the train stopped in the middle of the forest in some kind of makeshift station without a name or a village next to it. From there we were marched to our barracks, less than five minutes walk away."

That sounded very much like Horst's description of the factory's location and the weight pressing down on her chest increased.

"We have to produce several chemicals, mostly an explosive called Nitropenta." Margarete hissed in a breath, since that couldn't be a coincidence. "It's dangerous work because we have to handle nitric acid all day without any kind of protection. Most women develop ugly coughs after a while and if you get a drop on your skin, it'll burn right through to the bone."

Margarete cocked her head and peered at the round burns on Lena's arms. "Is that how you got those?"

Lena followed her gaze, her face suddenly pale. "No, these are from cigarette stubs."

Bile rose in Margarete's throat as she pictured how one of the Nazi guards used the young woman as his ashtray. She'd rather not know what else these vile monsters did, but she still asked, "Was this some kind of cruel punishment?"

"Not really. He does it for his enjoyment, when he summons a woman to his office for the night." Lena averted her eyes and her skinny shoulders began to quiver.

"You're safe now." But she knew without the shadow of a doubt that some other unfortunate woman had become the new playmate of whoever had done this to Lena. And she, Margarete Rosenbaum, had a duty to put a stop to that practice. It was her factory. She might not be able to defy the Nazis and free the slave workers, but she could at least stop the abuse.

Yes, she'd visit the factory and make it clear that under her ownership she wouldn't tolerate any kind of mistreatment.

"I'll find you something to wear," Margarete said and rummaged in her wardrobe for a dress, woolen stockings, and shoes. "Put these on, while I take the dishes to the parlor."

When she stepped through the door, her gaze fell on Dora who had just entered from the hallway, holding feather duster and broom in her hand.

Quickly pushing the door closed with her foot, she said cheerily, "Hello, Dora."

"Are you feeling better, Fräulein Annegret?"

"Not entirely. I think I'm going to lie down again and try to get some sleep. If you'd come back and clean later."

"Let me at least make your bed..."

"There's really no need. I'd rather you take the dishes down, the smell of food gives me nausea." She shoved the tray into Dora's hands, who took it with surprise, somehow managing not to let the broom and duster fall in the process.

Dora eyed her and looked around the room with a puzzled look upon her face. "Is someone else up here? I heard you talking..."

"Don't be silly. I was on the phone with Reichskriminaldirektor Richter. We will have guests arriving later this week to stay with us for a few days. And now, would you please leave me alone, I need to lie down."

"As you wish, Fräulein Annegret. Do you want me to bring your lunch upstairs later?"

"No. I don't want to be disturbed. If I need anything, I'll ring the bell."

Dora nodded and left the suite, leaving a distressed Margarete behind. This would never work out. Up until today she'd not realized how little privacy she had in her own suite of rooms and how often her maid was around.

She really needed to find a better place for Lena to hide. But where?

12

"I can supply whatever you need," Gustav told the man on the other end of the phone, sitting in his office with his feet up on the desk.

"We're short of copper sheet. How many can you sell?"

Gustav made a quick calculation in his head. With the war effort in full swing, the metal was sold at a premium, and this new client would be willing to pay a considerable price to keep his own production running. "Copper sheets are hard to come by."

A groan came from the line. "Can you sell or not?"

"I can, but they won't be cheap." Gustav had secured priority contracts with the SS and supplies for the factory were delivered like clockwork to produce not only the Nitropenta explosive, but also the blasting caps. Unfortunately the Wehrmacht was rather stingy and didn't allow for much scrap.

"Price hiking already? I can go somewhere else," the prospective buyer said.

"Not at all. But I can't sell underprice either, I need to replenish my own supplies and extras are always hard to come by."

"You'll come up with a satisfactory solution. My contact told me you're very creative."

Gustav rubbed his hands, not only because of the compliment, but because he knew the other man was desperate for copper. Lighting a cigarette, he did another calculation. "Three tons. Double market price. No papers."

"Is tomorrow too early?"

"Definitely not. Send someone to the factory, tell him to talk to Heinz Strobel. He'll have everything arranged."

"If this turns out to my satisfaction, there will be more business down the line."

Gustav inhaled smoke before he answered, "I'm looking forward to a beneficial business relationship." After hanging up, he dialed the factory number and exchanged a few sweet words with the secretary, before asking for her boss.

"Gustav. What's new?"

"I have a new buyer."

"What's he need?"

"Three tons of copper sheets."

Heinz whistled. "That's a helluva lot. When does he need it?"

"Tomorrow." Gustav studied his fingernails. It was time to visit the factory urgently and get one of the prettier women to manicure them.

"We don't have that much surplus in stock."

"You'll have to take it from the production pile."

"How am I supposed to do that? You know as well as I do that the SS is a stickler for production goals."

"Heinz, I really thought you to be more creative. Use less material for our detonating caps."

"*Verfatzda!* It's my head on the line if they find out."

"You've been profiting nicely from our arrangement and this new client can earn us amounts of money you can only dream about." Gustav was getting impatient. Heinz was a good man, corrupt to the core. Greediness and cruelty only added to his usefulness and he'd turned out to be the perfect factory manager. But he also was a miserable coward and wet his pants every time SS officials came to audit the production process. "Make the detonating caps with thinner walls and nobody will notice."

Heinz huffed and mumbled some unintelligible words, before he cleared his throat. "All right. I'll talk to the foreman in the caps production line. We might have to slow down output for a week or so until we get new supplies."

"The workers will have to do overtime then, we can't afford to lag behind production goals."

"Better order new ones right now, since they'll drop like flies."

"Will do. Tell me when they have arrived, and keep your hands off the pretty ones." Gustav guffawed into the receiver, when he saw Annegret standing in the doorway. A hot wave trickled down his spine and he swallowed hard, wondering how much she'd overheard. "That will be all. Make sure our supplies arrive on time."

He hung up, removed his feet from the desk and walked toward Annegret, regaining his composure during the few steps. "What a nice surprise, Fräulein Annegret. How can I help you?"

She seemed hesitant to tell him and instead engaged in useless small talk about the falling temperatures, until he decided to cut her short. "As much as I love talking to you, I'm afraid I have to make a few more phone calls."

"I'm sorry..." She looked like a frightened rabbit, which was very reassuring. "I didn't mean to keep you from your work."

Gustav softened his voice to a paternal, benevolent tone. "Not at all, Fräulein Annegret. You know that I'm always at your disposal for any question you might have. I can only imagine how hard this must be for you."

"Thank you, you're so kind." She visibly relaxed. "It's probably a silly thing to ask..."

"There are no silly questions." Gustav beckoned her to come inside and take a seat, although his hands itched to pick up the phone and call the buyer to confirm the deal.

"Well, I would like to visit the munitions factory."

"Whyever would you wish to do that?" Gustav shook his head. "It is not a suitable place for a young woman."

She frowned. "I'm not a naïve little girl who thinks everyone lives in a manor."

"Fräulein Annegret, you must have misunderstood me. You certainly are a well-educated woman who knows about the harsh realities of war, but some of the workers in the factory use rather salacious language, comparable to that of a sailor. I would like to spare you the possible embarrassment."

"If that is so..." She shyly looked downward and he knew he'd chosen the correct words. No daughter of a good family wished to hear the words a sailor might use.

"Believe me, the factory is in the best hands with its manager, Heinz Strobel. Perhaps you would like to go over the books with me instead? I can explain to you how it works and how much profit it makes. What do you think?"

"That's a great idea and I appreciate your willingness to explain the details to me, but..." she pushed out her lower lip, giving him a bad feeling "...I'd still like to visit the factory in person."

He pressed his jaws together, trying to come up with a valid reason to refuse her request, but came up empty. It would be better to just comply and make sure Heinz was prepared ahead of time for their visit. Or... knowing how often women changed their minds, she'd probably forget about the whole silly endeavor soon enough. "As you wish, Fräulein Annegret. I will arrange a visit, but it will take several days to get it set up, since we need to follow safety protocols and request visitor permissions."

"Thank you very much. It's not urgent, but I'd still like to visit by the end of the week."

What a pigheaded woman. If she weren't his employer, he'd show her where exactly her place was in this world. "Everything will be arranged to your satisfaction, Fräulein Annegret, just leave it to me."

She nodded, biting her lip.

"Is there anything else?"

"Actually there is. Do you... I mean... I heard rumors about female workers being abused..." Her face clearly showed what kind of abuse she was talking about and how appalled she was even by the thought of it. It was a great opportunity to endear himself to her even more.

"That's a grave accusation and I should hope this cannot be true, nevertheless I will talk to Strobel about this. Rest assured that no such behavior will be tolerated on our premises."

She gave a relieved sigh. "That is so very kind of you. I'd better leave you to do your work now, since I've taken enough of your time already."

She was on her way out the door, when he had an excellent idea. "Fräulein Annegret, I was just thinking, would you like to accompany me on a ride around the premises?" If she was only half as besotted with horses as the long-term employees claimed, she'd soon spend most of her time in the stables and wouldn't have the time to snoop around.

But much to his surprise, she physically recoiled and barely stopped herself from taking a step back. The discomfort on her face changed into sadness as she said, "I wish I could join you, however, the explosion that took my brothers' lives also caused an injury to my back. It has been acting up these last few days and as much as I'd like to I probably shouldn't attempt anything as strenuous as riding a horse."

"I'm sorry to hear that, especially since I have heard you love horses so much. It must be a great grief for you."

"It is."

"Let me call the town doctor and ask him to come up..."

Annegret shook her head. "No need. The good doctor in Leipzig told me to take it easy. But if the pain gets any worse, I'll ask Frau Mertens to fetch the doctor for me."

Gustav thought she was acting peculiar, almost anxious, but shrugged it off. Women were like that, much too emotional. One had to keep them on a short lead.

"Oh, I almost forgot," she said, taking a tentative step nearer. "We will have guests arriving in a few days. In total eight men from the Gestapo and SS."

A burning sensation filled his veins. Was that the reason she had insisted on visiting the factory? Because the SS were on to him? They wouldn't care too much that he sold part of the food destined for the forced workers, since he paid them well for those damn prisoners, but he didn't want to imagine what they'd do to him if they found out about the copper deal.

For a moment he considered canceling it, but then pushed aside his fear. He dearly needed the money, because he wanted to gift his beloved wife an in-house bathroom just like those in the manor for her birthday. He'd already inquired with the craftsmen and it would cost him an arm and a leg. Without the extra profits from that new deal, he could never afford it.

"What is the reason for their visit?" he asked.

"I'm not privy to their business dealings. Reichskriminaldirektor Richter bid me to accommodate them and since we have the rooms, I was delighted to help out."

"A very noble thing to do."

"Not at all. It's the least I can do for our Fatherland. And I was thinking we should organize a formal welcome dinner for them. Maybe your lovely wife would like to attend?"

Keeping good relations with the people in the corridors of power was the best way to climb the Nazi hierarchy and what better opportunity than attending a dinner party where he didn't have to foot the bill. Therefore, he eagerly agreed. "That is an excellent idea, Fräulein Annegret. You do take after you late mother, if I may say so. I'm sure my wife would be pleased to attend, and also to help you out with the preparations in any way you see fit."

"Thank you, that would be wonderful. I've already spoken with Frau Mertens and she's having everything prepared for the guests. Although..." she smiled at him "...I wanted to invite a few important people in town as well and perhaps your wife could help me to entertain? Is there anyone in particular you'd suggest?"

He had to give her credit, the girl knew how to garner goodwill, which might prove beneficial later on. Herr Huber really had taught her well. Someone who regularly attended social functions at the manor was more likely to push a good deal in the host's direction. Perhaps he had misjudged her. She might even make a good ally for his side businesses.

"I do indeed. How many people were you thinking about?" he said with a genuine smile.

"Maybe four or five?"

"An excellent idea. Leave this to me. I'll go to work and find out the availability of the mayor, the priest, and two or three senior party members."

"Thank you so much. Please invite their wives, too. Our guests might appreciate the presence of well-refined ladies during dinner."

"I'm sure they will," Gustav said, although he was sure the guests would appreciate less-respectable women for their after-dinner entertainment even more and made a mental note to organize those, too. Nowhere did men bond better than in a room full of scantily dressed trollops.

Annegret left and Gustav sagged against his desk, running a desperate hand through his hair, while trying to tell himself that the Gestapo surely wouldn't announce their visit if they actually suspected him of any wrongdoings.

He pondered the situation and decided that attack was the best defense and prepared a trap for Heinz, just in case the SS had misgivings about the factory and Gustav needed to save his own skin.

13

Margarete returned to her suite. The visit with Herr Fischer had gone well. If she was honest with herself, she hadn't expected him to acquiesce so readily to her request to visit the factory, not after Horst Richter had been so adamant that she should stick to the female territory of house and church. This, and his genuine outrage at the rumors of abuse, only showed Fischer's kindness and how much he wanted to help her get her bearings. She'd been exceptionally lucky to have him as the estate manager and not the brooding, hostile, even rude Oliver.

She opened her door, somehow surprised to find the bedroom empty with the bed made, until she remembered that she'd locked Lena in a tiny cubbyhole—an empty storage cupboard below the window dormer in her room—barely big enough to hold one crouched person, before leaving to speak with Frau Mertens and Herr Fischer.

It seemed Dora had used her absence to clean, dust and even to change the bedsheets. Locking the door behind her, she pushed the heavy armchair from the entrance to the cubbyhole, opened it and said, "Lena, it's me Annegret. You can come out now."

Lena crawled out and took her sweet time to stretch, before she said, "I thought my limbs would fall off anytime now."

"I'm so sorry. Perhaps with a cushion next time?" Margarete was filled with remorse.

"Don't worry. I'm beyond grateful for what you're doing. There was someone in the room for quite a while, at first I thought it was you."

"That must have been Dora, the maid. She seized the opportunity to clean the room while I was gone. I don't think there's any way I can keep her from scrubbing, dusting and washing the entire suite every single day."

Lena cocked her head. "What a strange thing to say."

"Why?" Margarete furrowed her brows. Someone like Lena who had the vocabulary of an intellectual, but none of the airs and graces of a rich person, should understand her.

"Because I would assume you're used to having a maid look after you."

Ouch! Margarete really had to be more careful. Not that she believed Lena would betray her, but she absolutely needed to be above any suspicion by anyone. "You're very perceptive. I have lived such a long time in Paris, keeping house for my brother, it feels odd."

"Paris? How exciting." Lena's eyes lit up and a dreamy expression crossed her face. "I lived there, before..."

Before the Jews were considered subhumans. Margarete didn't speak out loud what they both knew to be true. "What did you do?"

"I'm a journalist. I covered French news for a radio station. Well, I did, before Goebbels decided that only pure Aryans have the power of word, fired me from my job and had me sent to a camp on the same day."

Margarete hissed in a breath. She did not want to imagine the conditions Lena had endured in whatever camp she'd been in. On a hunch, she put her hand on Lena's arm. "You're safe with me."

"But you're not safe with me."

The sadness in the other woman's eyes broke Margarete's heart. Both of them had a burden to carry, but when Margarete had thought hers was hard she realized with sudden clarity that it paled in comparison to what Lena and all the other forced workers in the factory had to endure. *I will make it up to them,* she promised herself.

"Can you tell me more about the factory?"

"I'm not sure you want to know."

"Believe me, I do. Maybe I can help."

Lena scoffed. "The factory manager and his cronies, they are sadistic, cruel men. Please don't take offense, but why should they even listen to you?"

Margarete shrugged. She wouldn't tell her that the real owner of the exploitive factory stood in front of her, and, at least in theory, the factory manager had to do her bidding. "You're probably right."

They sat a few moments in silence, before Lena began to speak of her time in Paris, and how she'd met famous artists like Edith Piaf during her work. Margarete became nostalgic listening to the familiar places and sighed. "I miss him so much!"

"Your husband?"

"No." Margarete shook her head. "My... brother. Actually my entire family. They were..." *deported* "...killed in a bombing."

"I'm so sorry for you. It must have been the only bombing ever in this rural area and your family had the misfortune to be caught in it."

"No, that was in Berlin. The one that killed my parents." The Allies didn't waste precious bombs to kill the fish in the lake and the deer in the woods, but focused their efforts on the big cities. "After the bombing I lived with my aunt in Leipzig for a while." Margarete smiled as memories of her time with Aunt Heidi filled her mind. "One day in December we were shopping for candles, and you can't imagine the horrid decorations for sale: Christmas ornaments with swastikas or Hitler's portrait." She shuddered.

"When I was a child I was often at my best friend's house, and they had the most beautiful Christmas tree ever. I begged my parents to have one too, but they refused, since we celebrate Hanukkah."

Lena's face lit up with the memories and Margarete encouraged her to continue. "Please, tell me."

"Hanukkah was my favorite holiday, probably every Jewish child loves it, just like you gentiles love Christmas. But I still thought it might be even more precious, if only we had such a beautiful tree." Lena laughed. "Such joyful times. All gone because of one mad man."

It felt good to meet someone who reflected her own emotions, so Margarete prodded, "Tell me how you celebrated the holiday."

Lena leaned back on the sofa, closed her eyes and began to recount, transporting both of them into better times, when they were children and their families gathered with relatives and friends for boisterous celebrations, filled with laughter, music, gifts and sweets.

Margarete licked her lips at the memory of the delicious *sufganiyot*, doughnuts, or *latkes*, potato pancakes, her mother had always baked. After lighting the candles her father had used to grab his guitar to accompany the traditional Hanukkah song Ma'oz Tzur'. She gave an involuntary sigh and opened her eyes to see that Lena was standing now.

"The *Shehecheyanu* blessing has always been my favorite. Even these days it gives me hope to live another day and one day leave all the evil behind. If you'll allow, I would like to recite it to you." Lena looked at her with expectant eyes.

"I would love to hear it."

"*Baruch atah Adonai Eloheinu, Melech haolam, shehecheyanu, v'kiyamanu, v'higiyanu laz'man hazeh.*" The words flowed from Lena's mouth recreating the festive atmosphere of many happy years in the family circle and without realizing it, Margarete finished the last few words along with the other woman, "... *v'kiyamanu, v'higiyanu laz'man hazeh.*"

Lena raised an eyebrow, but didn't comment. Instead she translated the Hebrew and once again Margarete found herself repeating the familiar words along with her, their two voices whispering in unison. "Blessed are You, O Lord Our God, Ruler of the

Universe, Who has kept us alive, sustained us, and brought us to this season."

"You're a Jew." It wasn't a question, but a statement.

A tear formed in Margarete's eye, and she blinked it away. Fighting with herself whether she should deny the obvious or be honest with Lena, she decided to come clean, at least with one person in her world. "I am, but everyone here believes I am Annegret Huber, the daughter of a high-ranking SS officer."

"How is that possible?"

"I was their maid. During a bombing raid in Berlin the house was damaged and everyone but me was killed. Since Annegret is—was—my age, and vaguely resembles me, having the same hair and eye color, I took on her identity."

"We all must do horrible things to stay alive."

"It was an impulse and I wanted to use her papers to flee from Berlin, but when I arrived at my Aunt Heidi's house in Leipzig, she convinced me that it would be so much safer for me to keep using Annegret's real identity papers instead of going into hiding at her place or trying to get fake papers."

"That does make sense, although it must be hard pretending to be someone else day in day out."

"It is. Sometimes I feel like I'm forgetting who I really am. But to make a long story short, I was almost found out. Until a Gestapo officer who was a friend of Annegret's father found me, and mistook me for her. It was him who helped me when I needed to disappear. He gave me travel permits and a recommendation for France and after several twists and turns I ended up in Paris with Annegret's brother, Wilhelm, who hid me for months, pretending I was his sister. Well, until Wilhelm died."

"I'm so sorry." Lena's voice was full of compassion.

"I'm afraid when all of this is over, I might have become too much her to ever be me again, if you understand."

Lena nodded.

Suddenly panic tugged at Margarete's heart. "Please, Lena, you have to promise that you won't say anything. To anyone. Ever."

"I know I said earlier that you're not safe with me, but rest assured that your secret is. Nobody will ever find out about your true identity from my lips. It's the least I can do for you. You saved my life. I don't think I would have lasted another night in the forest."

"Then, I'm glad I found you. Both for your sake and for mine. It's nice to be honest at least a few times a day." Margarete already felt lighter. She hadn't realized how much she'd missed having a true ally, a person like Aunt Heidi or Wilhelm, who knew who she really was. Without either of them, she wouldn't be alive today, but apart from saving her, they'd both done so much more: they'd given her a connection to her past, her true self.

Wilhelm was dead, but Aunt Heidi was alive. She'd seen her a few times in Leipzig after returning from Paris, but they both had agreed it was too dangerous to be seen together, since someone might recognize her as Heidi's Jewish niece.

With sadness she'd said goodbye to her aunt before leaving for Gut Plaun. They couldn't even write letters to each other, although they had come up with several code phrases, scribbled on a postcard without sender, to let each other know they were well.

14

Oliver eyed the arriving guests with narrowed eyes. It was late in the afternoon and Frau Mertens had sent word that canapés were going to be served in an hour. He hated being invited to formal dinners and couldn't think of anything more tedious than entertaining a bunch of Gestapo and SS officials.

To add insult to injury, Frau Mertens, who knew him well, had ordered him to wear his best suit and the only good thing coming from this stupid dinner was that Dora had been sent to his house for several hours this morning to iron his things. She hadn't been able to do much ironing, though, until she'd kicked him out.

Gustav and his wife Beate were also invited, along with the priest, the mayor and his wife, as well as several other important party members. That was so typical of Annegret, flaunting her riches and rubbing shoulders with powerful people.

Grudgingly he patted the horse on her back and walked up to his house to get himself into "presentable shape" as Frau Mertens had ordered. He just hoped those Gestapo men wouldn't want to ride some of the horses while they were here, since he had no time to babysit a bunch of city dwellers.

He found a note on his bed in Dora's neat handwriting. She

knew how much he hated these social events and offered him an excuse to leave the party early.

Oliver,

Don't despair. Just ask for "more sauce" and I'll spill food over your suit while serving.

Love Dora

His heart warmed with unconditional love. It was such a selfless thing to say, because she'd get in trouble with Frau Mertens for her clumsiness. Obviously he wouldn't take her up on the generous offer, but he already felt better. With a woman like Dora loving him, what more could he wish for?

Freshly bathed, shaved, and in his meticulously pressed Sunday suit, complete with a white shirt and a tie that threatened to strangle him, he walked up to the manor, wondering why Annegret had invited him.

Gustav, sure, for he was the estate manager and would know to answer all questions about the business side, but himself? He was only the stud master. *Perhaps her motive is simply to see me in agony.* He scolded himself for the thought, since she couldn't know how much he hated these formal occasions.

He sauntered into the house through the kitchen door and greeted Frau Mertens, while his eyes searched for Dora. She came in from the parlor with a tray full of empty champagne flutes and he winked at her, waiting for her to pass him by.

"Thanks for the offer, love you," he whispered.

"Will you be having champagne?" she asked, all business.

"Yes, please." He clandestinely brushed her fingers as she handed him a glass.

"Dora, hurry up, we need more canapés," Frau Mertens called from the other side of the kitchen.

Oliver formed a kiss with his lips and walked into his personal doom next door. All the other guests were already in attendance and a lively chatter filled the big room. Several townswomen stood next to their husbands, all of them decked out in evening gowns and sparkling jewelry. But his jaw dropped open when he noticed Annegret. She was strikingly beautiful in an emerald green satin gown, and a pearl necklace that he faintly remembered having seen on Frau Huber.

Despite looking very much like the lady of the manor, she also seemed eerily out of place and when their eyes caught, he believed he saw anxiety in them. The expression was so unlike her, for a moment he felt that this woman was a complete stranger.

Nobody else seemed to have noticed, because six men in uniform surrounded her in a semi-circle, captivated. Oliver secretly rolled his eyes at the show she was putting on. Did she really enjoy entertaining these uniformed puppets who would gladly sacrifice their own mothers for Führer and Fatherland?

The most senior officer harrumphed and clinked something against his glass. Waiting until the chatter had died down, he straightened his back, and raised his glass toward Annegret.

"Fräulein Annegret, I think I speak for all of us when I say we are delighted to be your guests. We had our reservations, since we didn't want to inconvenience you, but your exceedingly warm welcome has made us feel right at home, from the moment we stepped on your grounds. Your estate is beautiful, the manor an example of dignified German culture, and my only regret is that our business here will not allow us time to enjoy the local pastimes. But above all else, you, our hostess, are the epitome of everything an Aryan woman stands for. Beauty, elegance, attention to detail and a firm knowledge in keeping house and entertaining guests. The Führer himself would be delighted by your poise."

Oliver kept his eyes trained on Annegret, whom he fully expected to glow with the praise, but much to his surprise he noticed a barely visible flinch in her at the mention of an Aryan woman. It lasted less than a second, before an endearing smile brightened her face and she thanked the speaker for his kind words, before she said, "Dinner will be served in the dining room any minute. If you'd like to follow me, please."

Oliver was seated next to an SS man called Kallfass, a young lad in his twenties, dandified and eager to please. Despite the first bad impression, Unterscharführer Kallfass turned out to be a pleasant conversation partner and soon enough he and Oliver talked shop about horses. Since Oliver wasn't above seizing an opportunity when it presented itself, he said, "Herr Unterscharführer, I know you're here for business reasons, but if you should have some leisure time, I'd be happy to give you a tour through the stables."

"That would be fantastic!"

"And if you wish, I can arrange for you to attend a training session with one of the recently broken in cart horses."

"Oh, I would love that. In the city, I don't get to ride often. But, please, enough with formalities, call me Thomas." The Unterscharführer raised his glass—they'd switched from champagne to beer—and Oliver clinked with him. It was true, he didn't like the ruling Nazi party, but he'd long stopped fretting over things he couldn't change and stayed out of politics as much as possible. Thomas was a decent man, though, and one never knew when a friend in the SS might come in handy.

Opposite him sat Gustav Fischer with his wife. Gustav had been strangely silent throughout the meal, but now he asked the Gestapo man to his right, "What business brings you to our remote area?"

The other man, an Untersturmführer, had already been drinking enough alcohol to make his nose glow and his tongue loose. "Top secret, Herr Fischer. I can only tell you this much: there are serious issues with traitors to the Fatherland."

"By God, I should hope not in Plau am See?" Frau Fischer responded, her hand flying to her necklace. Oliver couldn't distinguish whether she was upset anyone would suspect people from her hometown, or afraid the criminals might harm her.

"We don't know, but I can assure you, if there are sympathizers in the surrounding towns and villages, helping to hide this scum, we will find out." He stood up, raised his glass and shouted, "No crime against the Reich will remain unpunished. Every traitor, helping others leave the country, will be found and hung!"

"After due interrogation," one of the Gestapo men said with a cruel smile, until he caught a warning gaze from the senior officer who'd earlier given the toast. "But let's not talk about business in the company of ladies."

Annegret clinked a spoon against her glass. "Esteemed gentlemen, I, and with me the townsfolk of Plau am See, couldn't be happier to receive you here. Please feel at home and don't hesitate to ask me, or the housekeeper, Frau Mertens, if there's anything not to your absolute satisfaction.

"Ladies and gentlemen from Plau am See, please receive my heartfelt thanks for accepting my invitation on such short notice. I sincerely hope everyone will have a most pleasant evening."

He had to give her credit, she had the situation under control and was the perfect hostess. Amicable, considerate, polite. It made him hate her all the more.

The conversation turned to mundane matters, but Oliver listened only with one ear, wondering who smuggled escapees out of Germany, and more importantly, how? Stralsund, a harbor on the Baltic Sea was less than hundred miles north of Plau am See, and from there he'd assume via ship to neutral Sweden.

The idea enthused him, not because he'd ever thought about actively resisting the regime, but knowing there were courageous people risking their lives to help others gave him a strange satisfaction. He was secretly sympathetic with the Jews, figuring if the Nazis could target an entire race of people, they could target and eliminate anyone. He itched to find out more, but was wise enough not to touch the topic again, so as not to raise suspicions.

After the second course, Thomas returned to the topic of breaking in horses, and Oliver was only too happy to explain. It was an innocuous topic where he was an expert and didn't have to be on his guard, always afraid to say something politically incorrect. He took the opportunity to explain the process and how the training was done with utmost respect for the animal, giving them enough time to adapt to the new reality.

He couldn't resist slipping in a backhanded complaint at the military buyers for wanting to rush the training, when just a few weeks extra would make the horse so much better equipped to resist the hardships on the battlefield.

Once in a while, Annegret's laughter caused him to look over to the head of the table, where she presided. Something about the sound of her laughter seemed odd. It was soft and warm, and didn't quite match up to her usual high-pitched tone of voice. Once again he had the odd feeling he was looking at a stranger.

He shrugged it off, since he shouldn't torture himself thinking about the cruel girl he'd known so many years ago, and whether she had changed or not. With any luck, she'd get bored playing hostess and would swoosh off to Berlin, her dozen suitcases in tow.

The senior officer complimented Annegret on something, and then Thomas asked her, "Is it true you are quite the accomplished equestrian?"

"I think that is a stark exaggeration." She flushed slightly, apparently shy at receiving the compliment.

"Don't be so modest. In my room is a newspaper article with a photograph pinned to the wall, showing you at an equestrian competition where you won, even though all the other competitors were much older." Thomas looked at her expectantly, and with him the gaze of everyone around the dinner table was on her, as the conversations died down.

Annegret smiled graciously, but she couldn't fool Oliver. Abject fear had crept into her eyes. "Oh... I won so many competitions. But, please, let's not talk about me, I'm sure all of you gentlemen have done so many more important things for the Reich." She turned to wave at Frau Mertens, who nodded and moments later sent Dora in with a huge cream cake.

Oliver's attention was diverted, as his gaze followed his girlfriend who gracefully put the cake on the table and then cut pieces and served everyone in the order of their status. Oliver came last, which gave him time to observe her. Unfortunately he wasn't the only one to admire her beauty and his blood boiled hot as he noticed how more than one of the men gave her an appreciative slap on her behind. If they weren't functionaries of the Reich, he'd have jumped up to give them a much less appreciative slap against their jaws.

Still glaring daggers, he witnessed how Gustav licked his lips as he leered at Dora when she had to bend over to serve his piece of cake. Despite his wife sitting right next to him, Gustav still managed to accidentally brush Dora's bosom with his elbow.

After dinner, he joined the men for brandy and cigars, but soon excused himself on the pretext of having to get up early in the morning to tend to the horses. Still fuming over the liberties these randy devils had taken with Dora, he needed to walk off his steam and decided to round the manor and go down to the stable before returning to his house. On the back patio he passed the private staircase to Annegret's rooms, Dora had mentioned. Instinctively he looked up and in the moonlight noticed a shadow moving behind one of the windows. A huge grin broke out on his face and he fought the sudden urge to race up the stairs and tell Dora, who must be up there fluffing the pillows for her mistress, how much he loved her.

After checking the horses, he had just settled into bed, when he heard a knock downstairs. Moments later the door opened and soft steps came inside.

"Dora?" he called out.

"Yes." She closed and locked the door, something he never did, and climbed the stairs.

"I didn't expect you to come tonight. Has the dinner party ended already?"

"No." Dora unbuttoned her dress to slip in bed beside him. "Frau Mertens sent me away, because some of the guests were getting a bit too handsy."

Again the rage caused his blood to boil. If he were allowed to marry her, this wouldn't happen. Damn Nazis and their stupid racial laws! "Thanks to Frau Mertens for taking such good care of you, although it should be me doing that."

She snuggled her cold body against him.

"Come, let me warm you up, darling. Did I tell you how much I loved your note? Although I would never want to get you into trouble with Frau Mertens, it was a relief to know I had a way out."

"That's why I wrote it. Could you read it well?"

He knew she was self-conscious about her writing, because while she spoke the German language almost flawlessly, she sometimes didn't remember the letters and used the Cyrillic ones instead.

"Actually I didn't notice. I was overwhelmed by the sweetness of your offer. And I realized how much I love you. More than I have ever loved anyone else in the world."

"I love you too, Oliver." She pressed her body tighter against him, and he stroked her back with his hands. When he moved down to her behind, the memory of the Gestapo officer slapping her bubbled up and his blood boiled once more. Then he made love to her, wildly and furiously. When they lay spent, her head against his shoulder, his thoughts returned to Annegret and her peculiar behavior.

"Didn't you think it was peculiar that Annegret couldn't remember that competition she won?"

"She said she'd won too many competitions to remember."

"As far as I know it was the only one."

"But you haven't seen her in a decade. How do you know she didn't continue with her riding?"

"Herr Huber always complained that he couldn't keep horses

in Berlin. That was one of the reasons why he came here so often. So if she didn't have a horse in Berlin, how would she compete?"

Dora sighed. "Why are you so obsessed with her?"

"Because she leaves trouble in her wake everywhere she goes. I tell you, something is off with her. Today I saw fear in her eyes when that man mentioned riding."

"Maybe she had an accident?"

"What if she isn't who she's pretending to be?"

"What?" Dora propped herself up on her elbows.

"Everyone tells me how kind, warm, and generous she is."

"Which you always insist isn't true." She let her fingers play with his chest hair. Normally he'd let her continue and love her once more, but not today.

"Today, I noticed the same. Either she has completely changed, or... that woman is not who she's pretending to be."

"You're plain crazy. Who else could she be? And don't you think people would notice? This Reichskriminaldirektor Richter, who came here with her. He was a good friend of her father's since serving together during the last war. He would surely notice if she really was an impostor?"

"Not if he's in on it." Oliver shivered with the revelation. "What if the whole thing is a ploy? She could be working undercover for the Gestapo. Didn't this other man say they were about to infiltrate a resistance network smuggling people out of Germany?"

"Oh, Oliver, you shouldn't listen to all those radio espionage plays." She giggled, but suddenly became silent. Even her hand on his chest stopped moving. "Although... now that you should mention it. A few days ago, I went into her room to clean up, but she met me at the door and refused to let me enter. She said she had a terrible headache, but ever since, she's been keeping the door locked a lot, which she never did before."

"I'm telling you, something sinister is going on."

"Maybe." Dora shrugged. "Let's get some sleep, I have to get up extra early because of all the guests."

Around three in the morning the alarm woke them. Dora gave

him a sleepy kiss, slid from the bed and began to dress in the dark. He sat up, scrubbed a hand over his face and swung his legs over the side of the bed.

"What are you doing?" she asked quietly.

"I'll take you back," he replied as he switched on the night-lamp, after making sure the blackout curtains were drawn. So far the Allied bombers had never threatened Plau am See, but one could never be too careful.

"You'd better not risk it. What if some of the guests see you and me? You know what will happen if Frau Mertens finds out about us."

"The handsy guests are the very reason why I'll deliver you safely to your room."

"They'll all be fast asleep by now." She shoved him back onto the bed. "Don't worry so much. I'll see you tonight."

"Let me at least show you to the door." He stood up again and observed how she dressed herself, a warm feeling spreading from his heart all over his body. "I love you so much!"

He escorted her downstairs, kissed her one last time and watched from the doorway until she disappeared into the manor, before he returned to his bed for another couple of hours sleep.

15

Margarete listened to Lena's regular breathing. The dinner had been a success, but the tension deep inside her simply wouldn't resolve. Again and again her thoughts returned to the moment when the young officer had asked about her equestrian prizes. Even now in the safety of her own bed, her heart beat faster as she relived the terror of the moment. Her entire cover story could have been derailed in that one instant.

A seemingly harmless question she couldn't answer—and four Gestapo agents in the room who were trained in interrogating people and reading between the lines. Fortunately for her, they all had been in a jolly mood with too much alcohol in their system to pick up her lapse.

Lena snorted from the other side of the bed and reminded Margarete of her other, more pressing problem. She absolutely needed to find a better place to hide the woman. Even if the Gestapo wasn't suspicious, Dora soon would be. She might be an uneducated maid, but she was no fool.

She slipped from the bed, and into the anteroom, where she checked the blackout curtains before she switched on the light. It was already two thirty in the morning, and she really had to get some sleep. Perhaps a glass of warm milk would help to ease her anxiety. Yes, that was a good idea. She returned to her bedroom, slipped her robe over her nightgown and walked downstairs into the kitchen.

Traipsing down the long hallway and the staircase in absolute silence so as not to wake anyone, she felt like a thief in her own home. *Except this isn't really my home.* The eerie feeling increased as she stepped into the kitchen, which was arguably Frau Mertens' realm. No doubt, she would notice the missing milk and possibly inquire who of the employees had been stealing provisions. She'd tell Frau Mertens in the morning, because she didn't want anyone to get into hot water on her account.

Fortunately the kitchen was similarly organized as the one in Berlin and it didn't take her long to find a pot, cup, spoon, milk and even a glass of honey. After lighting the gas stove, she heated the milk, stirring it around so that it would warm and not curdle. She tested it with her fingertip, turned off the stove and poured the milk into a cup.

Sitting down at the kitchen table she laughed as she pictured herself, dressing up in elegant clothes, pretending to be the lady of the house, while her real place in the Huber household had always been in the kitchen, serving the family. Strange things had happened in her life, and she wondered what might come next.

The warm milk helped to calm down her anxiety and she returned to her room. But just as she put a foot on the stairs, muffled noises from the other side of the hallway captured her attention. She paused, listened, and there it was again. A scratching coming from the servants' wing. It was the middle of the night and truth be told, she was scared. But then, someone might be in need. *You're the lady of this house, you must have a look,* Margarete encouraged herself and walked toward the sound into the hallway where she'd been only once before.

It was pitch-dark and she struggled to find the light switch. Her hand fumbled along the wall, until her fingers finally sensed the smooth plastic material and the protruding switch. She flicked it and ceiling bulbs bathed the hallway in light. Her mouth opened into a silent cry when she saw one of the SS men leaning against the wall. Only on second glance did she realize there was another person, pressed against the wall, mostly hidden by his huge body.

"What are you doing?" Margarete demanded in as cold a voice as she could muster.

His head jerked around, the face heated, as he stared at her. The hand tugging at the woman in front of him stilled, but he continued to press his other hand over her mouth, and pushed her into the wall with his weight, while she very clearly struggled against him. "Please return to bed, Fräulein Annegret. I'll take this girl someplace else where we won't disturb you."

Margarete recognized the lewd gaze. It had happened to her, too. Fighting against the nausea bubbling up from bad memories, she finally identified the small person in his grasp.

"You will let go of my maid. In this very instant!"

He made a scoffing sound and shook his head. "Why do you even care? I already said I'll take her to my room and make sure she doesn't breathe a peep."

"It is my house and she is my employee. And I will not tolerate such immoral behavior." She trembled with fury and fear, but she was banking on the fact that no self-respecting SS man would attack a well-bred German woman.

He straightened and put a few inches of space between him and Dora, but without uncovering her mouth. "Look, Fräulein Annegret, I'm sorry if I disturbed you, but she's just a maid, and a Ukrainian one at that. These savages don't know any better and like to be done wild. She has probably slept with a hundred men right beneath your nose."

"I know nothing of the sort. Unhand her." She held her breath, noticing the spark of defiance flickering in his eyes and already considered what threat to use to make him do her bidding, when he dropped his hands and took a step back, stuffing his shirt back into his trousers and buckling his belt.

"No harm meant! We were just having fun. Weren't we?" He

looked pointedly at Dora who slumped against the wall shivering like a leaf.

Margarete wondered how Frau Mertens might handle a situation like this one, since she always took utmost care to protect the decency of the unmarried female employees, even the day laborers. Slipping into Frau Mertens' role, she immediately sensed authority, and imitating the housekeeper's resolute demeanor, she said, "Under my roof, I don't tolerate this sort of thing. If you wish to have sex with a woman, I suggest you marry her first. This is a good Christian household," she almost choked on that, "where sinful behavior is not welcome. I trust I have made myself perfectly clear?"

"Very clear, Fräulein Annegret."

"And I trust you will inform your colleagues about our rules, so that we do not have a repeat of this performance?"

"I'll make sure everyone gets the word. Goodnight." He suddenly was in a hurry to leave and skirted around Margarete to make his way up the stairs.

She stood still for several breaths, before she turned toward Dora, who was still shaking uncontrollably. Putting her arm around Dora's waist, she decided to bring her into her own suite, but as soon as she'd set a foot on the stairs, she remembered that Lena was sleeping soundly in her bed.

"Let's sit for a while," she said and pulled Dora with her into the kitchen, where she put the young girl in a chair, and picked up the used pot and spoon to warm another cup of milk with a generous dollop of honey.

Dora was pale as a ghost, but at least the shaking subsided as she sat motionless, staring into the empty grate.

"Here, drink this." She handed her maid the cup of warm milk, adding, "You're safe now." Watching her silently for a while, she finally asked, "Do you feel better?"

"Yes, Fräulein Annegret. Thank... Thank you."

"No need to thank me. It was the least I could do."

"I was so scared."

"Anyone would be." Margarete was reminded of the repulsive experiences she had had with Reiner when she was still the Hubers' maid, and a Jewish one at that.

"Please, you won't tell anyone? If Frau Mertens finds out..."

Margarete wanted to give a sharp retort, since life was so cruel and unjust. Dora had just been attacked and all she worried about was how Frau Mertens might react? "I won't. But even though I told this man off, you should probably be more careful and not leave your room at night while the guests are staying here."

Dora nodded.

"Why were you even out in the hallway? I thought Frau Mertens sent you to bed hours ago?"

"I... couldn't sleep... and..." Dora's face flashed bright red "... I needed to pee." As opposed to the upper floors, in the servants' quarters there was only one shared bathroom for everyone. "Thank you for the milk. I should get back to my room now." She was suddenly in a hurry to get away.

"I'll deliver you to your doorstep."

"That's really not necessary, Fräulein Annegret. I'm fine now," Dora insisted, so they parted at the bottom of the stairs, but Margarete stood there watching until Dora disappeared behind her door, before she switched off the light in the hallway and climbed the stairs to retire to her own room.

16

A knock on the door interrupted Gustav's calculations. He scowled, because now he would have to do the entire sum again, and said, "Enter."

Following his prompt to enter, the door opened and two SS men stepped into his office. One of them was the young, overzealous lad who'd become fast friends with Oliver, talking about horses last night. "Heil Hitler, gentlemen," he greeted them. "What can I do for you?"

"You're in charge of the Nitropenta factory?" Unterscharführer Thomas Kallfass asked.

"That would be correct. Did you have a question?"

"We wish to visit the production."

Gustav suppressed a groan. Didn't they have anything better to do than harass hard-working men like him? "I would have to arrange a visit with the factory manager, Heinz Strobel, since he's the one to oversee the technical details and the workers. I'm only responsible for logistics and accounting." He pointed to his ledgers.

"Well, then, what are you waiting for? Give him a phone call," Kallfass demanded.

"With pleasure." Gustav picked up the receiver and dialed the factory number. When Heinz picked up on the other side, he said,

"Herr Strobel, I told you about our esteemed SS guests at the manor, didn't I? There are two of them in my office right now, wishing to get a tour through the facilities."

"Not a tour," Kallfass interrupted. "We are here to investigate possible sabotage, because we've received too many defective goods."

Hot and cold shivers ran down Gustav's spine. He'd always taken great care to only skim the food intended for the workers, never the material that was needed for production... until the last shipment. No, that couldn't be, since the end products hadn't even been shipped. Another thought burned through his veins. What if they wanted to check up on the inventory and found several tons of copper missing? He wracked his brain on how to best lay the blame on Heinz, or anyone for that matter, while he nodded and said into the phone, "You heard it, arrange everything for a thorough investigation this afternoon."

Again that insolent SS Unterscharführer interrupted him. "I'd rather start right now."

Inwardly fuming, Gustav inclined his head. "As you wish, gentlemen." Then he barked into the phone, "We'll be arriving in half an hour. See that you get those lazybones to have everything in order. We won't tolerate treasonous sabotage against the war effort in the Huber factory and whoever should be found guilty, will be hanged." He hung up and modulated his voice into a pleasant tone, "Gentlemen, if you'll follow me. If it's alright with you we'll take our truck, because the road down to the factory will be a bit rough after the heavy rainfalls we've had." He smiled apologetically. "Most supplies arrive via train, so the road is not a main priority."

"That will be fine," Kallfass said and the SS officers watched as Gustav put on his hat and coat, and took the keys for the office truck.

"Please, if you would follow me."

"Herr Fischer, do you have a moment?" Annegret appeared out of nowhere just as he opened the door to the truck.

"Fräulein Annegret, if it isn't too urgent, may I attend to your query this afternoon?"

She looked at the two SS men in his wake, and gave both of them a friendly smile. "Unterscharführer Kallfass, Sturmmann Heckel, did you sleep well?"

"Very well, Fräulein Annegret. Thank you again for your hospitality."

"No need to thank me, it's my duty as a good German to support the SS in their valuable service to the Reich every way I can. Is Herr Fischer giving you a tour of the estate?"

"No, Fräulein Annegret, we are actually on our way to inspect the ammunition factory," Kallfass said, who was at least twenty years younger than his underling.

"What serendipity." Annegret flashed her brightest smile at the young man. "Would you mind if I joined you?"

Dumbfounded by the flirtatious girl, he nodded eagerly. "Off course, Fräulein Annegret, we'd be delighted to have your company."

Gustav had neither the time nor the inclination to burden himself with Annegret, who would be better off finding herself a husband and beget children with him, instead of sticking her nose into men's business. "I'm afraid the factory is not a pleasant place for a woman."

"I can put on my boots and an overcoat."

"And there's only room for three in the front seat of the truck." He simply had to get rid of her, since he needed to focus all his energies on thwarting hard questions from the SS.

"Oh." She glanced between the two trim SS men and asked, "Would you gentlemen mind if I squeezed in between you? It will only be for a short time."

Obviously the two fools eagerly nodded and Gustav pressed his fist into a tight ball. If only he could show this woman her place... a good, hard spanking would serve her well.

"Then it's settled," Gustav said, putting a brave face on the matter before climbing behind the wheel. Once everyone was seated in the front row, he cranked up the motor.

During the fifteen-minute drive down to the factory, Annegret engaged in chit-chat with the two salivating SS fools, and Gustav began to think that maybe her presence wasn't all bad. With their eyes riveted on her luscious curves, the men might be too busy to take a closer look at the inventories.

The truck hobbled over roots and splashed through ankle-deep puddles on the dirt road through the forest, until suddenly the trees gave way to a cleared patch, where the factory stood.

"Here's the factory," he explained in an effort to gain goodwill with the SS men. Under no circumstances should they get the idea that he condoned or—God forbid—was involved in the alleged sabotage. "We have taken great care to conceal it from discovery of overflying Allied planes, although they are rarely, if ever, seen around here." He pointed at the biggest building. "This is the main hall, where the detonation caps are made. As you can see, we have left several trees standing and the roof is painted in an olive-green with a camouflage pattern similar to that of leaves."

He passed the gate and parked the truck next to the administrative building. As he stepped out, he sidled up to Annegret and whispered, "I haven't forgotten about the alleged abuse and started inquiries."

She gave him a grateful nod.

"But I think it better not to mention it to these men, since the SS has the reputation of being sadistic at times and it might give them ideas."

Her mouth formed a shocked "O", and he couldn't help but congratulate himself.

"Please, follow me, gentlemen," he prompted the two officers.

"What are these bunkers for?" Kallfass asked, pointing at several reinforced concrete buildings embedded in the ground of the forest.

"We call them penta-bullets, both for their shape and because it's in them where the explosive is cooked up."

"Very imaginative. But wouldn't it be easier to have the entire manufacture in the big hall?"

Gustav did his best not to show the other man how stupid that suggestion was. "From a purely practical point of view, you are absolutely right. But we have broken up the fabrication into several smaller units for security reasons. In the event of an explosion, the damage will be limited to the respective bunker, while the others continue to function normally. This way we have never had a production delay, because the other units can pick up the extra work."

Fräulein Annegret, for once, kept her mouth shut, seemingly overwhelmed by the sight of the concrete buildings, but the other SS man asked, "Do you often have explosions?"

Following an internal audit, any and all safety arrangements had been dismantled during the past year, which had resulted in more profit. "I can assure you, we have never had a German casualty, despite having several minor explosions every month."

"How so?" Heckel arched an eyebrow.

"We use exclusively concentration camp inmates for the dangerous work, which has led to considerable attrition among them. Therefore we have installed a standing order with the camp administration in Ravensbrück, who sends us regular replacements. In case of an unexpected need of labor, they provide us with the requested amount in a matter of days."

"What a clever idea. Killing two birds with one stone."

Gustav relaxed a bit, since the two SS men seemed to eat from his hand. But he was slightly worried about Fräulein Annegret, whose face had taken on a greenish hue. Women were just too emotional for this kind of business. If only she would accept she'd be better off entertaining the village nobility than getting her hands dirty with men's business.

Sturmmann Heckel pulled a cigarette from his case. Gustav became aware of what he was doing, just as the stupid man drew his lighter. "Stop!"

"What?"

"If you don't want to become our first German casualty you better extinguish that flame. As I explained, we're handling explosives on the grounds. One spark and the entire factory might go up in flames."

"Sorry." Heckel seemed honestly contrite, which was another point in favor of Gustav. He felt his self-confidence surging. The SS was no match for him. Nobody was. He was the most astute business man around.

The door opened and Heinz stepped out.

"Gentlemen, Fräulein Annegret, may I introduce the factory manager, Heinz Strobel, to you? He's responsible for everything that happens here. Production, usage of raw materials and oversight of workers." Gustav wondered what else he could include to make it one-hundred percent clear that any irregularities the SS men might find ought to be blamed on Heinz. "In addition he is responsible for hiring the German foremen, who train and supervise the prisoners."

Heinz wasn't the brightest cookie and beamed with pride. "Yes, yes. This is my realm, everything that happens in the factory goes past my desk."

"We'd like to have a look at the production," Kallfass said.

"For security reasons we can't go into the penta-bullets where the Nitro is cooked, but I can show you the fabrication of detonation caps."

Kallfass furrowed his brow and Gustav hurried to add, "I'm sure Herr Strobel can arrange for us to halt production in one of the bunkers, and, after sufficient airing, give you a tour. Would that be agreeable?"

Heinz Strobel glared daggers at Gustav, because it would take at least half a day of work to shut down the cooking and ramp it up again, but the SS man seemed satisfied with that solution.

"Why do you call it cooking?" Annegret asked.

Her question was once more proof that women belonged in the kitchen. But since she was the owner and, at least in theory, called the shots, he gave a slight laugh. "I'm sorry, I shouldn't have used slang words. We call the process cooking because crystalline alcohol is mixed with nitric acid in revolving boilers, much like a cook would stir dough."

She flinched as if she'd touched something acid. "What happens if a drop of that mixture gets on your skin?"

"It'll burn right through," Gustav said. "And this is the very reason why we need to ramp down production and air the place before anyone can go in."

"So how is this mixing done if nobody can go inside?"

He furrowed his brows. Was she really this dumb? "The workers do the mixing."

"Do they have special protective wear, gloves maybe?"

Gustav shot a desperate look at both of the SS men, meant to convey how hard he tried with a stupid boss like her. It would remind them who was the actual decision-maker on the Huber estate and with whom they had to talk. "As I explained previously, we use prisoners exclusively for this kind of work."

"Please if you'll follow me." Herr Strobel waved them forward. They entered the main hall through some kind of storage room. "For security reasons, every visitor has to wear protective gear." He handed them each overshoes, a coat, a helmet and goggles. Fräulein Annegret looked forlorn in her much too big things.

"I'm afraid we aren't prepared for female visitors. Would you rather wait outside? I would hate to inconvenience you too much."

"Oh no. I'm too curious." She grinned like a child on Christmas Eve and he wondered what on earth she expected to find inside.

Strobel led the group into the manufacturing hall and past several assembly stations, greeting the foremen and explaining the production process. Gustav always kept a few steps behind.

Annegret sidled up to him. "Herr Fischer, I know that you are only responsible for logistics and so on, but why doesn't the factory have protective gear for women?"

"You're our first female visitor ever. If I had known with some anticipation I would have arranged for better fitting gear for you."

"Thank you, that's so kind. But I didn't mean myself, I meant all the other women."

He gazed around the factory hall, wondering whether she was hallucinating. "Which women?"

"The workers."

"The workers?" Gustav hid his shock, acknowledging a group of decrepit creatures at the assembly station next to them. They had shorn heads, their hair in various stages of regrowth, were dressed in ill-fitting prisons shifts and wooden clogs, if they wore shoes at all. Their gaunt faces and hollowed-out eyes added to the abject appearance and made them resemble scarecrows instead of actual human beings. "But they're Jews. We don't squander money on them."

Annegret swerved slightly, and he grabbed her arm to support her. She clearly had too kind a heart, feeling compassion even for subhuman scum.

17

Seeing these lamentable women, Margarete became dizzy and she wondered how Herr Fischer could be so cavalier about it. With her, he'd been nothing but kind, but now it seemed as if he... didn't even consider these women to be humans.

The reminder hit her like a punch to her stomach and she buckled. To the Nazis, the Jews weren't human beings. They were vermin, equally unpleasant and annoying as cockroaches or mosquitoes. No need to show compassion for them, because who would feel bad crushing a cockroach under one's boot?

She wondered how and when Hitler had managed to change the perception of an entire nation to believe their fellow countrymen were actually a pest and deserved to be treated as such.

At least Margarete knew without a shadow of a doubt that Lena must have escaped from this specific factory, because the women assembling the detonation caps wore the same prison garb, and were equally emaciated. It dawned on her that maybe she had found her mission right here and now. So help her God, she would make a difference in the lives of these miserable people.

For the remainder of the tour she kept thinking about ways she could alleviate their pain. With a sigh of relief she returned her oversized protective gear and left the factory hall. Outside, the midday sunshine filtered through the leaves of the trees that shimmered in different yellow, orange and red hues.

The beauty of the landscape was a stark contrast to the horrors from hell she'd just seen inside the concrete walls. Fischer and Strobel conversed animatedly with the SS men, oblivious to Margarete's existence, for which she was grateful. She wouldn't be able to engage in polite chit-chat, when her heart had shattered into a million pieces at the plight of her fellow Jews.

Just as they returned to the truck, she saw a group of men dragging a mine car filled with shining metal across the yard. It must be exceptionally heavy, because the four men pushed and pulled to move it at snail's pace across the graveled yard.

A man in civilian clothes approached them, yelled something and swung his whip at them. In unison they threw themselves against the car to make it go faster. Then it was like Margarete's heart stopped beating, as one of the men turned his head. He locked eyes with her. Just for a split second. But it was long enough. Because his was a face she knew.

18

It couldn't possibly be true. She must be imagining things. Uncle Ernst had been deported to the East. But the man had recognized her too, because his eyes widened in shock. He looked away and then toward her again, with a half-smile that turned into a sad expression.

The entire exchange hadn't lasted more than two seconds, but it changed Margarete's entire life. None of her companions witnessed what had just happened, since they were absorbed in their conversation.

Just now, Herr Fischer realized that she'd stopped walking and called out to her, "Fräulein Annegret. Are you feeling unwell?"

"No, no." She shook her head. The group of prisoners had already continued pushing their burden toward the entrance to the factory hall, but the familiar face still lingered in her mind. *How can this be?*

Back at the manor, Frau Mertens met them in the foyer and announced that she had lunch prepared in the dining room whenever they wanted to eat. Margarete, though, had lost her appetite and excused herself. "*Meine Herren*, please go ahead with lunch and don't wait for me. I need to freshen up and will eat later."

They were either too polite or too hungry to protest and she climbed the stairs to the upper floor, so lost in her thoughts she bumped into one of the Gestapo officers stepping from the room next to hers.

"Excuse me," she said, even as he grabbed her elbow to keep her from falling. He was in his fifties with salt and pepper hair, and the man in charge of the group of guests.

"No, Fräulein Annegret, it was entirely my mistake, I should have looked before stepping out of my room. Are you hurt?"

"No, I'm fine," she said, but the next step belied her. Her ankle was on fire and she could barely put weight on it.

"Esteemed Fräulein, I can see that you're not fine. Let me at least help you to your room." Used to never having his authority questioned, he slung her arm around his shoulders and looped his arm around her waist to support her, while he marched her the few steps down the hallway

"Thank you so much," she said as soon as they reached her door. "I can manage on my own now."

But he didn't listen and swung the door wide open, exposing her anteroom, and a strip of her bedroom through the cracked open door, to his gaze. For the second time today her heart stood still, as she imagined what would happen if he discovered Lena. But a clicking sound seconds later indicated that Lena was securely hiding in the cubbyhole. Since she couldn't stay in there all day, they had found a way that she could open and close the latch from the inside and agreed she would quickly hide whenever she heard the outer door.

Fortunately the Gestapo officer was too occupied leading her to the armchair by the window to notice the sound. Just in case, Margarete said louder than necessary, "Thank you so much, Herr Kriminalkommissar. I can take it from here."

"Are you sure, you don't want me to call a doctor?" he asked with a sorrowful mien as he propped up her ankle on a stool.

"There's really no need. If it doesn't stop hurting in a few minutes, I can call my maid."

"If you're sure, then I should probably leave and let you rest."

"Again, thank you so much for your help," Margarete said and watched with increasing relief how he left the room and closed the door behind him with an audible thud.

"He's gone. I'm alone," she said and, moments later, Lena peeked her head through the doorway.

"What happened?"

"I stumbled and twisted my ankle."

"Let me have a look at it." Lena didn't wait for an answer, but knelt beside Margarete and touched her ankle with gentle fingers. "I believe it's not broken, but it might hurt for a few days. Let me make you a cold compress." She disappeared as quietly as she had come, leaving Margarete in a turmoil of emotions.

Today had been too close. If the Kriminalkommissar hadn't been preoccupied with helping her, he surely would have become suspicious at the clicking sound, and it didn't need a genius to find the door to the cubbyhole. Then, not only Lena's life was at stake.

She absolutely had to find a safer hiding space for her.

Lena returned with a soaked towel and wrapped it around her ankle. "You might want to call a doctor."

"No. I'd rather not have anyone come to my suite while you are here."

"I should leave, it's too dangerous."

While Lena was right, Margarete shook her head. "It's even more dangerous for you out there. Where would you even go?"

"I don't know. I'll manage somehow."

"It's foolish. You'll stay here until I have found another place for you, and that's my last word."

Lena laughed. "You're not only kind, but also determined. Perhaps some higher power has put you into this place to help others."

"That higher power would be Wilhelm," Margarete said with sadness.

"Your pretend-brother?"

"Yes. But he was so much more than that. At first I was afraid of him, even loathed him, but it turned out he was a kind man and I fell in love with him. Can you imagine? A Jew falling in love with a Nazi?"

"I can't." Lena sighed. "I have suffered too much at their hands, and none of them has ever shown the slightest kindness toward me. Not until I met you."

"But I'm not a Nazi!" Margarete protested.

"No, you just pretend to be one. But I was still deathly afraid when you found me."

"I'm sorry."

"There's no reason to be sorry, you rescued me."

Margarete took Lena's hand. "I'm sorry for everything that has happened to you, and that I didn't do anything to stop it."

"Well, there's nothing you could have done, since you're not one of Hitler's closest cronies and not the factory manager either."

But I'm the factory owner.

Just in that moment, Dora opened the door, the bucket of cleaning supplies in hand. When she saw that Margarete had a visitor, she curtsied several times and said, visibly distressed, "I'm so very sorry, Fräulein Annegret. Please forgive me for intruding, I should have knocked first. I will return at a more convenient time." But the next moment her gaze fell on Margarete's bandaged ankle and she exclaimed, "You're injured. Shall I ask Frau Mertens to call the doctor?"

The poor girl was a mess of anxiety.

"There's no need, really."

Now Dora took a closer look at Lena, who was still crouched by Margarete's side, and shrieked. To prevent things getting worse, Margarete jumped up, uttering a curse as she put weight on her hurt ankle. But she had no time for pain right now, she had to close and bolt the door to the hallway, lest one of the Gestapo men would venture inside, alarmed by the shriek and she could well do without further surprises.

Dora looked like a frightened mouse between her mistress and Lena, apparently unsure what to do. "Who's this?" She adopted an almost comical posture: standing only a few feet inside the room, the dustmop raised like a sword, ready to attack the intruder, while Lena crouched on the floor with her hands held up.

"There's no need to get upset," Margarete said in an effort to pour oil on troubled waters.

Dora half-turned to look at her, while at the same time pointing her dustmop at Lena to keep her in check. "We must call the police. She's stolen one of your dresses."

Before Dora could do anything rash, Margarete stepped between her and the exit to the private staircase. It was an untenable situation, and she didn't have the slightest idea how to get out of it.

"Please, Dora. This woman is not a thief. I found her injured in the woods and brought her here."

"But why didn't you call the..." Dora stopped mid-sentence, her eyes wide as saucers. "She's a prisoner... oh dear God!"

Margarete thought it best not to mention that apart from an escaped prisoner Lena was also a Jew, because one could never be too sure how people might react. Even the most outwardly kind women could release a tirade about the evilness of the World Jewry when prompted with the presence of one. "She's a foreign worker, just like you. She escaped because her employer abused her badly. If we call the police, they will surely send her back to him—or deport her to some camp for disobedience."

Dora's eyes jumped frenetically between her mistress and the intruder, the dustmop still raised in her hand, until she apparently decided that the emaciated woman posed no threat. Her hand sunk and she asked, "Where are you from?"

The breath caught in Margarete's lungs and while she wracked her brain for an answer, Lena preempted her. "I'm French."

"French?" Dora gasped, shaking her head vigorously.

"Yes, my name is Lena." Her voice was laced with a thick, and very authentic, French accent as she continued. "The work office in France promised me I could work for the Reich and earn enough money to support my family back home. I came here to work as a maid, just like you, but my employer had different ideas about what kind of services he expected from me. Please don't let them send me back to him!"

Dora seemed unsure, so Lena rolled up her sleeves and held out her bare arms covered with round burns and long red scars.

Pale as a bedsheet, Dora took a tumbling step backward. "I won't. I'm not..." She turned toward Margarete again, looking at her with pleading eyes. "Fräulein Annegret, I won't tell anyone, but she can't stay here. We have the house full of Gestapo and SS, and God only knows what will happen to you, to all of us, if they get a whiff of an escaped foreign worker hiding in your suite."

And if they find out she's a Jew, we'll all be hanged for treason. "I've been trying to come up with a better place to hide her, but since I've been here for such a short time..." It might be an error to make Dora privy, but the maid seemed genuinely good-hearted, and in reality, what choice did she have? Dora already knew about Lena, and making her an accomplice might actually prove beneficial. If she couldn't claim ignorance, she'd be more inclined to keep her mouth shut. "Maybe you know of somewhere?"

"Me?" Dora moved backward as though she wanted to disappear into the wall. "I'm just... I mean... I don't know anyone... or..."

"You know every nook and cranny of the manor and its outhouses. Perhaps there's a better place to hide somewhere?"

Lena who'd listened to their conversation silently, now stepped in. "Please, this is getting out of hand and I don't want to endanger the two of you. As soon as it is night, I'll disappear."

"No! We're heading into November and every night the temperatures are falling more. How will you survive when winter comes with frost and snow? What will you eat? How will you keep warm?"

"I'll chance my luck."

"You'll die. And, as God is my witness, I won't stand for it! I'll do everything in my power to keep you alive."

A heart-warming smile crossed Lena's beautiful features, as she nodded gratefully.

"To go anywhere she will need shoes," Dora said with a pointed gaze at Lena's bare feet.

"I know, but mine were much too small." Shoes were exceedingly difficult to come by, even with money and ration cards.

"And a hat, or her shorn hair will betray her from miles away."

Again, Margarete nodded, feeling resignation creep into her heart. Rescuing and hiding Lena was a lot more difficult than she had initially thought—like everything she'd done this past year. Every brilliant idea had been followed by a plethora of nasty details that had to be solved. It was tiresome, to say the least. And on days like today, her endurance was worn thin. Even with all her money and importance she had exactly zero power when it came to changing the world into a better place. She gave a deep sigh. *When will all of this finally end?*

"Please, don't despair, Fräulein Annegret. I'll see if I can find something in the clothing store for the farmhands. It might even help if she passes for a man, because nobody will suspect she's the escaped maid."

A stab pierced Margarete's heart, since there was no escaped maid, but a slave worker in the factory. Her factory. She shoved thoughts of the happenings this morning away, because she could focus only on one problem at a time. At least she had enlisted Dora's help in this one. Feeling the expectant gazes of two women on her, she pulled herself together. "Very well. Dora, you go and find clothes, but don't bring them here until nightfall. Meanwhile I'll go downstairs and entertain our guests. Later I will call for coffee in my room. Bring as much food as you possibly can without raising Frau Mertens' suspicions. And you, Lena, you better return to my bedroom and never venture into the parlor again, since we don't want to take a risk."

19

Margarete was on tenterhooks, counting the minutes until lunch was over. Despite being hungry, she couldn't force anything down her throat. It was a silly emotion, but she felt guilty for having all this food when Lena upstairs was starving—not to speak of her uncle whom she believed she'd seen in the factory.

"Fräulein Annegret, what would you recommend?" The question from one of the men returned her to the present.

"I'm so very sorry, what exactly are you looking for?"

"Things to do in town? An architectural work of especial beauty, perhaps?"

She gathered her wits, determined not to let herself get distracted again. "Well, Saint Mary's is obviously a very imposing structure and I'm sure the priest will gladly give you background information if you ask him to. Although," she felt she needed to give something more than platitudes, "my personal favorite thing to do is to stroll through the cobblestoned streets around the old castle. You may find the half-timbered houses very charming. And of course the lift bridge is a sight to behold."

"What about the lake? Any recommendation on a secluded spot to go bathing?" The salacious grin on his lips revealed the kind of bathing he had in mind, but Margarete chose not to acknowledge his behavior.

"At this time of year it would be rather cold, now, wouldn't it?" Out of the corner of her eye, she noticed how Kriminalkommissar Becker glared at him and gave a quick shake of his head.

The conversation turned to boring discussions about this campaign or that strategy in the war, until it settled on the Stalingrad campaign that whipped up feelings all around. She noted with amusement how each of the men tried to voice a qualified opinion without giving the impression he criticized the Führer even in the slightest way.

She would rather have listened in on them discussing the factory and what they'd seen there, but apparently that was much too irrelevant in the grand scheme of things. Forcing herself to keep smiling, she balled her hands into fists. For the workers it meant the difference between life and death.

After lunch she excused herself and went upstairs to look for Lena. She found her asleep in her cubbyhole. Once again, the sight of the emaciated woman with the scars on her arms broke her heart. Sometime later, a knock on the door indicated Dora's return.

She stepped into the parlor with a tray loaded with buttered bread and some cakes. "Fräulein Annegret, I brought tea, just as you said." Her face took on a conspiratorial expression. "Frau Mertens asked whether you didn't like your lunch?"

"Please tell her that my stomach was upset after visiting the factory and it has nothing to do with her food."

"You visited the factory?"

Margarete looked into Dora's thunderstruck face. "You knew about it?"

"Well, yes. It's not a secret. Herr Fischer has explained that they're producing explosives and made it very clear that we're strictly forbidden to go near the grounds because of the danger involved. He said one wrong step and we could cause a detonation that might burn down the entire area, including the manor and the stables." She looked outright panic-stricken.

Margarete sighed. It was commendable of Fischer to keep the employees away from harm, although he had laid it on too thick for her liking with the possible dangers, since he'd explained to her and the SS men that explosions were contained by using separate smaller bunkers for the manufacturing.

Possibly he feared the stable lads, mostly uneducated farm boys, might otherwise try to chase the thrill of witnessing how explosives were made. She thought of her two older brothers, who'd always done stupid and dangerous things during their adolescence. Kurt the eldest one, a veritable rabble-rouser, had rebelled against the increasing chicanery against the Jews from the very beginning and had been sent to the camp in Dachau after a violent brawl with several boys from the Hitler Youth.

Oswald, by contrast, had been the sensible one. But after his brother had been sent to a concentration camp, he'd completely lost his mind and taken out his rage on the brownshirts roaming the streets, which had not only led to a bloodied nose, but to a cruel torture during his stay in an unofficial prison and ultimately his deportation to a labor camp, even before her parents had been deported last year, shortly before she adopted Annegret's identity.

Her heart constricted painfully at the thought that they might suffer the same awful conditions she'd seen in her own factory. Once again, the familiar face of Uncle Ernst, her father's younger brother, and Aunt Heidi's husband, forced itself into her thoughts. She shook her head violently, since she refused to believe it could have been him whom she saw shoving that heavy mine car. He was much too old and frail for such hard work. No... her mind had been playing tricks on her.

"Are you alright, Fräulein Annegret?" Dora cut through her thoughts.

"Yes, yes. You can leave now. Come back this evening with any clothes for Lena you can find, but make sure nobody sees you."

"I already thought of an excuse. If you call down to Frau Mertens that you spilled coffee on your bed, she'll send me to get you fresh sheets. Then I can wrap the clothes in them and nobody will be any the wiser, even if they happen to see me."

"That is a very good idea. That's how we'll do it! When do you want me to call Frau Mertens?" Margarete was genuinely happy to have an accomplice and it seemed Dora was much more quick-witted than her humble upbringing might suggest.

A sheepish grin broke out on Dora's face. "Thank you, Fräulein Annegret. I already found the clothing and stashed them in the laundry room. If you call down after taking your coffee, it would be most believable, don't you think?"

Again, the suggestion made sense. "Then that's how we'll do it. Thank you so much." Margarete gazed into her maid's beautiful dark brown eyes. "You know that this is dangerous? And you don't have to do this, right?"

"But I want to help Lena. She must have suffered so much." Dora's eyes shaded over and Margarete got the impression that the other woman had experienced her own share of abuse by men who thought they could take from a woman whatever they wanted. *Welcome to the club*, she thought sadly.

"Just in case someone finds out, I want you to blame everything on me. Tell them I forced you to do it and threatened to send you away to a camp if you didn't do my bidding," Margarete instructed her and for once she was happy about Annegret's bad reputation, because nobody would doubt that she was able to issue such a heinous threat.

"I can't possibly do that... they will whip you... or worse..."

Fear prickled down Margarete's spine, but she courageously shook her head. "Then we better not get caught. But in case we do, you must save yourself, because who will take care of Lena if we're both sent away?"

Dora scrunched her nose in deep thought until she nodded. "I promise, I won't get caught. I'm very good at sneaking out unseen." She startled at her own words. "Not that I have ever done anything bad like stealing or such... I mean..."

"It's alright. You better return downstairs before Frau Mertens starts asking questions."

"Yes, Fräulein Annegret." Dora was so perturbed by her own words that she fell back into her annoying curtsying habit and basically curtsied backward through the room until she had reached the door.

Margarete locked the door behind her, returned to her bedroom and woke Lena, who crawled out of the cubbyhole.

"There's food for you in the parlor and Dora has found men's clothing, which will fit better with your short hair."

"Thank you." Lena stretched her long limbs and then followed her next door where she stared at the plate full of food. "I still can't believe that this is all for me. It's probably what I ate in a week in the factory."

"About that..." Margarete had determined she wouldn't tell Lena that the factory actually belonged to her, but she still needed to get as much information out of her as possible. "I was there this morning."

"You what?"

"Yes, our estate manager, Herr Fischer, gave a tour to some SS men and I invited myself to their party."

Lena recoiled, her eyes glazing over with panic. "Is he... are they here?"

"There's no need to worry. Herr Fischer manages this estate and the SS men are only here for a few days. But they're the reason why we have to be extra careful in hiding you."

"I had better leave then." Lena made to get up.

"No, you can't." Margarete put a hand on her arm. Lena was being completely irrational. "It's broad daylight and you'll be seen by at least a dozen people."

"You don't understand... if he finds me here, he'll punish me... and you. By the time he's done with you, you'll wish you were dead, only to find out that you're not. And then he does it again... and again..." Her entire body shivered. "I've seen women in agony for weeks before they finally succumbed to their injuries. He's worse than the devil himself."

"Who is he?"

Lena shook her head, trembling so hard, the slice of bread fell from her hand. "I don't know his name, but he's the boss of them all. He can do anything he wants."

For a moment, Margarete suspected that Fischer might be the man Lena was so afraid of, because who else could be Strobel's boss? But then she pushed the suspicion away. Hadn't Fischer himself been outraged at the allegation of abuse in the factory and had taken immediate actions to get to the bottom of it? Certainly, if he were guilty, he'd have reacted differently.

Margarete reached down to pick up the bread at the same time Lena did, and when she came eye to eye with her, the other woman was so full of panic, she thought it best to distract her and engaged her in a conversation about the differences between German bread and French baguettes, until Lena regained her composure.

From the first moment, she had disliked the factory manager, Heinz Strobel, a bullnecked man with hands big as bear paws, the kind of man who looked as if he preferred to sort out arguments in a brawl. Though she'd not have picked him out as a sadist, sexually torturing defenseless women.

After a while, she returned to the topic she needed clarity on. "In the factory, did you by any chance know a man called Ernst Rosenbaum?"

Lena shook her head. "Sorry, but mingling with the men was strictly forbidden. The only times I saw them was when they delivered raw materials and dispatched the detonation caps. We rarely exchanged words, let alone names." Lena paused for a while and asked, "Is he a friend?"

"I thought I recognized him, but I can't be sure." She hesitated, pondering whether she should entrust Lena with her secret. Finally she continued, "He's my father's younger brother. He married a goy—my aunt Heidi. But even that didn't help him, because he was rounded up and deported."

"It probably was someone who looked similar," Lena tried to cheer her up.

"I don't think so. He recognized me too. At least I believe he did."

"I'm so sorry."

Margarete nodded, deep in thought, and the words bubbled to the surface almost without her realizing it. "Aunt Heidi, she was the one who saved my life by taking me in and playing along with the ruse that I was indeed Annegret Huber. It was a great risk to her, but she loved me enough to do it. We even planned to get me away to a friend of hers in France, but then Wilhelm discovered me, and Horst Richter helped me escape." Her shoulders shivered. "I miss her so much. I thought she was my only relative left, and now... Uncle Ernst, he's here. In the factory."

"At least he's alive," Lena said and put a hand on Margarete's arm.

Margarete wasn't sure whether that was a good thing or not. Uncle Ernst had looked so excruciatingly miserable.

"We could light a candle for him?" Lena suggested, pointing at the beautiful candleholders on the windowsill.

Margarete smiled, reminiscing on how she and Wilhelm had bought them in Paris. Despite everything, she'd been happy in his company, and comparatively safe. They lit the candles and said a prayer for her uncle, before Lena ate her food.

After a long silence, Margarete asked, "If there were a way to make the conditions in the factory bearable, what would be the most urgent things you'd change?"

20

It had been a turbulent two days visiting potential clients and suppliers. Prices for food had gone up again, and Gustav had found many bidders on the surplus provisions he skimmed from the factory. Now, he walked into his office at the manor, ready to take it easy for a few days.

He was already looking forward to seeing the women who'd arrived with the latest transport and whom Heinz had raved about. The new ones were always so much better; they still had flesh on their bones and were more easily frightened than those night-marish scarecrows who'd turned into apathetic creatures long ago.

A smile crept up on his lips. His wife would be so pleased when he surprised her with the news that he had contracted a new bathroom for their house, complete with a tub and a shower. There would be running hot water provided by an electric boiler, a luxury only a few houses in the town possessed.

Beate was a good woman, who deserved to enjoy a good life, and he was eager to please her with everything she could possibly wish for. While he rarely found ecstasy and satiation in her arms, he still loved her with all his heart. She had been a wonderful mother to their three grown-up children, and was a perfect escort at any social event, as well as a talented cook. Their house was always spick and span, and she never complained about his long hours at work. What more could a man wish for?

But a nagging worry crept into his mind. Malevolent tongues might question how he afforded the luxurious lifestyle he and his wife led. Perhaps it was time to feed their neighbors and friends a story that a financial windfall had come their way, perhaps from inheriting a considerable sum of money from a distant relative, since his supposed wins at horse betting were beginning to shed a bad light on him.

Still thinking about his next steps, he didn't hear the knock on the door and startled when the door opened and Fräulein Annegret stepped inside.

"Herr Fischer, do you have a moment?"

"Fräulein Annegret, what a pleasure. Unfortunately, I'm very busy right now though. Can it wait until tomorrow?"

She looked momentarily crestfallen but then sat down on the chair in front of his desk. "No. It's very important."

"Well then, I'm at your service." He gazed at his wristwatch to convey that she better keep it short.

"I wanted to talk with you about the factory."

He inwardly groaned. It had been a mistake to let her piggyback on the visit. "If you have questions about the production process, Herr Strobel would be the one to consult, since he's the one who manages it." He hoped that would send her running, because he'd seen the instant antipathy in her eyes when meeting Heinz for the first time.

"I don't think that will be necessary." Gustav inwardly cheered, but her next words crushed his victorious feeling. "Because aren't you the person he reports to?"

"Well, yes."

"Then I want to come to an agreement with you first."

Her demeanor was unnerving. Never had a woman spoken to him like this. Not his wife who could be prickly at times, not Frau Mertens who managed the household with an iron hand, and certainly none of the many young women he used for pleasure. But with Fräulein Annegret he had to tread carefully, because out of some inexplicable caprice of fate this inexperienced female half his age had become his boss.

"Please tell me what's on your mind and I'll do my best to help." For good measure he gave her a kind and reassuring smile. It was a new experience for him, so different to his usual ways, but he began to enjoy this little game. Every woman wanted to be tamed, and this one was already eating out of his hand. Soon she'd be pliable enough to consider his suggestion to sign power of attorney over to him and then he'd be the one calling the shots again.

"From what I've seen, the working conditions in the factory are inhumane."

"Fräulein Annegret, please don't consider me disrespectful, but there's really no need for you to concern yourself with these unpleasant things."

"I disagree. I've never seen people more miserable in my life, and thinking they are working for me..." Her hands trembled slightly.

"Look, I know this is hard for someone as kind-hearted as you are, but these workers aren't normal people, they are prisoners. The scum of humanity: criminals, homosexuals, Jews. They are parasites of society with only one goal in mind: to destroy our great country. They can consider themselves lucky to get a chance at redemption and help rebuild what they have destroyed."

"But still..."

He could see she wasn't open to reason. "Perhaps now you understand why I wanted to spare you the sight. Some things may not be pleasurable, but they still have to be done. And for this, you have me, while you can pursue activities meant for good-hearted women like you."

She sighed and he perceived her inner struggle, as if she had to conjure up strength. He gave her a while to gather her thoughts and then said, "Is there anything else I can help you with?"

"No." Annegret made to stand up, but halfway changed her mind and sat down again. "Actually there is." She sat down again.

"Have you, I mean, do you—?" She seemed to struggle with her words, and he wondered what would come next. "Do you visit the factory often?"

What a strange question that was. He leaned back, scrutinizing her face, trying to find out her intention, before he answered, "Honestly, I probably should be more involved than I have been. Our visit together with the SS men was the first in several months. There's always so much to do around here and since I didn't have reason to distrust Herr Strobel, I thought it would suffice to have him come to my office instead of me going there."

She seemed to be relieved. "I completely understand. But I wanted to make sure, because I have reviewed the production numbers."

What gall! Would she stop at nothing? "Do you want me to explain them to you?"

"I do know how to interpret them." Her haughty expression all but left him speechless. "And I have come to the conclusion that productivity would soar if the workers would receive proper nourishment and enough breaks."

He was slowly losing his patience. Steepling his hands on the desk, he shook his head. "Fräulein Annegret, your concern is commendable, but you seem to not know what we're dealing with here. The subjects you call workers are work-shy individuals who exploit any kindness shown toward them. The only way to make them work at all is with strict discipline and draconian punishments. Giving them extra breaks will be seen as weakness and before you can turn on your heels, they'll have started a revolt. Is this want you want?"

"No, I don't. Rules need to be obeyed, but every human deserves to be fed properly, especially if you expect them to do hard labor all day."

"Again, they are not humans, they're deplorables, outlaws, subhumans, barbarians. Call them what you want, but don't make the mistake to think they are anymore similar to you and me than a horse resembles a pig."

"I don't care! I want the workers fed properly!" Annegret ran a hand through her hair and he thought how much more beautiful she'd be if she smiled instead of arguing with him like a petulant child.

"The rations for factory workers are allocated and supplied by the SS and unfortunately," he made a sad face. "There's nothing we can do to make them change their stipulations."

"Then we buy more food outside the allocated amount. It is my belief that people who are in better health will work better and more efficiently." She arched her brow as if it were the most natural thing to squander money on useless scum.

"If you don't like the state of the current staff, we can always ask for replacements," he suggested, hoping she'd see the ridiculousness of her demands.

"And do what? Starve a new set of workers until they are in the same deplorable shape as the current ones? That is not the answer I am looking for."

"Well, it's the only answer I have for you. I hate to be the bearer of bad news, but what you are asking is impossible. Food is at a premium, and where exactly should I find the money to feed the prisoners with gourmet food?"

"Herr Fischer, I have analyzed the statements you prepared for me. The factory makes more than enough profit to buy, not delicacies, but bread and potatoes for the people working there."

Gustav knew when a battle was lost, and seeing the militant glint in her eyes, he hurried to make the best of a bad situation. Buying more food with factory funds might actually turn out as a godsend. He could already feel the weight of banknotes lining his pockets after selling parts of the extra food on the black market. But then he had an even better idea.

He slumped into his seat, furrowing his brows. "I'm actually glad you voiced your suspicions that something is amiss with the food supplies. I've been worried about the very same thing but didn't want to bother you with a mere hunch."

"A hunch about what?" Her upper body moved closer to his

desk and her eyes sparked up with intrigue. He almost chuckled. Women were so easy to manipulate and this Annegret was about to witness a masterpiece of setting up a trap—such a shame, she'd never know and thus wouldn't be able to applaud him.

"It's just a feeling, but something doesn't add up. I receive the supplies when they arrive and separate them into a part for the manor with all its employees, farm and stables, and another part for the factory. And it should be enough to feed the workers decently. But somehow it seems supplies dwindle between here and there." He let the words hang in the air, knowing she would eventually take the bait.

"You mean someone has been stealing?" Her face was red with anger.

"I'm afraid so."

"You should have told me," she stared at him askance as she added, "or Herr Richter."

He made an effort to look contrite. "I know, I should have. But since I didn't have proof, I was unwilling to cast a possibly false suspicion on innocent persons, Fräulein Annegret. You know how overzealous the Gestapo can be to get to the bottom of things." She grimaced at the impact of his words and he congratulated himself for his knowledge of the female psyche.

"There you are right. Do you have a possible culprit in mind?"

"As I said, I'm wary to cast suspicion on anyone, but... and this must remain between the two of us." He regarded her intently.

"Most certainly. We don't want the Gestapo here chasing after rumors."

"There are only a handful of people at Gut Plaun who possess both the means and the audacity to repeatedly steal large quantities of food. But again, I hate to name anyone without hard proof."

"I am here to help you to research into this problem. Exactly who is it you suspect is behind this atrocity?"

Gustav wanted to rub his hands in victory, but he had to be careful when he launched into his final master stroke. One that would take care of two, possibly three, problems at the same time.

Oliver Gundelmann had come highly recommended, and he was exceptional with horses, but—actually there were two buts. First, this young man was infuriatingly incorruptible. Honest to the bone and clever—a dangerous combination. With him Gustav always feared the other man could see right through him, discovering all his little secrets. And second, Oliver had taken what Gustav wanted.

He knew all about the dalliance between the stud master and the perky maid, and it burned like acid in his stomach every time he caught a glimpse of them. Dora had rejected Gustav's advances in the past, but she would come running with open arms—and legs—if she believed he could help her beloved Oliver. It would be so rewarding.

"As I said, there are only a few men in a position to pull this off. One would be the factory manager, Heinz Strobel, although I believe he's not bright enough for such a clandestine purpose. Then there's Nils, the handyman—"

"Nils?" Annegret interrupted him. "I don't believe that, he's the kindest soul I've ever met."

Gustav nodded sagely. "I'm not denouncing anyone, I'm merely mentioning everyone who is in a position that would allow him to steal. And, of course you're right, Nils is above suspicion, he's been with your family for most of his life."

She nodded.

"You could also include me into the group of suspects."

"You?"

"In theory, since I would be able to access the supplies."

She cocked her head, examining him closely. He relaxed his facial muscles and endured her stare patiently. After a while she asked, "What would be your motive?"

Now it was time to play his trump card and show her that not only was he above suspicion, but also he didn't even need to work for her. "Usually the motive for crimes is money."

Annegret regarded his expensive suit, but said nothing.

"In my case, money is not an issue, because apart from my very generous salary..." he bowed his head in a gesture of gratitude "... I've also recently inherited a small fortune."

"Oh, I'm sorry for your loss. I had no idea," she stammered.

"It was a distant great-uncle I barely knew," he explained. "Beate and I decided to keep it private because people tend to be envious. Although we're fully aware that in time the townsfolk will find out. You know, wagging tongues."

She rolled her eyes. "Don't tell me. People in town know what dress I'm wearing even before I step out of the house."

He wondered whether this was his opportunity to discount the topic, but decided he couldn't pass up the opportunity to hang Oliver out to dry. "Back to our list of possible suspects. There is Frau Mertens, but she's also highly unlikely to ever do something forbidden, and as far as I know she's never stepped inside the factory." He made a pregnant pause. "And we have Oliver Gundelmann, the stud master."

"You believe he's the culprit?" Annegret asked, shock written on her face.

"As I said, I don't have proof, I'm merely listing potential perpetrators. But rest assured, I'll get to the bottom of this and put a stop to things."

"I'm so grateful to have your support on this, Herr Fischer, I truly couldn't have wished for a better estate manager by my side."

"Oh, I'm just doing my job," he said, inwardly glowing with the praise.

"Then let's move past this unpleasant topic and get to work on my suggestions for improvement."

What on earth was she talking about now? "About what?"

"About the working conditions in the factory." She pulled out a sheet of paper and began reading, "Starting today, we're doubling the workers' food rations, if necessary by buying extra supplies until the situation is clarified. Every person will be issued a blanket and a pillow. And those working on the production lines will be provided with the same protective gear visitors are required to wear."

He stared at her, his jaw slowly sliding open. Her demands were plain crazy. Next she'd ask him to give the prisoners free days and home leave. "I'm so very sorry, but we can't just buy a few hundred blankets, even if we had the money. Where should we procure them, when all material is sent east to help our valiant soldiers fighting against the Russians?"

Her eyes locked with his, and he did his best to appear caring and helpful. After several tense seconds, she relented. "Hmm... I hadn't thought about that. I'll try to think of a solution. Meanwhile, instruct the factory manager that no one is allowed to work more than a twelve-hour day and from today onward, there will be no physical punishment of the workers. Especially no beating or whipping."

He groaned, but that didn't stop her from reading more demands. "Each shift will have ten-minute breaks every two hours. And..." she looked at him expectantly "... I'm sure this will please you as it doesn't cost anything: all work stations will be provided with fresh water from the well at all times."

"I'm delighted."

She brimmed with energy. "I knew you'd appreciate my suggestions. I'll leave the list here, so you can see the measures will be implemented as soon as possible."

"With the greatest pleasure." He took the list and put it on his desk. After showing her to the door, he returned, grabbed the list and tore it into tiny scraps. He would not implement a single one of her outrageous demands.

21

Margarete was elated, that had gone a lot smoother than she could have hoped for. Too smooth, maybe? She shrugged off the doubt and hurried to return to her suite and tell Lena that she'd given Herr Fischer a list with the most urgent issues that had to be changed to make life at the factory more bearable for the inmates.

In addition, the Gestapo and SS officers had finally left her house that morning and she didn't have to live in fear that they'd somehow find the escaped prisoner in her rooms. Finally, the pieces were falling into place and she was making progress in her mission to do good. Best of all, she had Herr Fischer on her side. If she might have doubted him, his alacrity to include himself into the group of possible culprits made it clear he was above suspicion.

"Fräulein Annegret," Frau Mertens called from the dining hall.

"Yes, Frau Mertens, what is it you need?"

"I'm terribly sorry to inconvenience you, but the pest controller has announced he'll be here tomorrow. He was due to come before winter anyhow, but with the guests just gone, I thought now would be a good time."

Margarete didn't quite follow. "A good time for what?"

"For fumigation. With the stable hands going in and out of the manor it's a necessary precaution." Frau Mertens fought a losing battle with the hired workers to maintain a minimal personal hygiene and always groused at them for not cleaning their shoes, washing their hands and faces or dusting down the worst dirt from their clothing before entering the servants' hallway and especially the kitchen where they ate their meals.

"If you think it necessary, I certainly won't object." She was wondering why Frau Mertens made such a fuss, since she usually never consulted Annegret about day-to-day chores.

"I'm glad you see it that way. Your mother was always a bit squeamish and insisted it should only be done when she was in Berlin."

"I see." Margarete nodded, although she still didn't understand.

"The pest controller will arrive tomorrow at seven a.m. and I have instructed him to do your suite first, then you'll be able to return by nightfall."

"What?"

"It's completely safe. But if you prefer I can arrange a room for you in town for a night or two," Frau Mertens offered.

"Oh, no, that won't be necessary. Thank you for alerting me." With a pounding heart, she raced up the stairs, desperately trying to come up with a plan of where to hide Lena during the fumigation. It was clear that she couldn't stay hidden in the cubbyhole, not only out of a concern for her health, but also because the pest controller was likely to discover her.

When she arrived at her suite, she found Dora cleaning the bathroom.

"Where is Lena?"

Dora turned around. "Sitting on the windowsill. Don't worry, we've found a way to hide her behind the blackout curtain. There, she's much more comfortable than in the cubbyhole and can look outside."

Margarete beckoned Dora to follow her into the bathroom. She closed the door and said, "She has to leave tonight."

"Why?"

"Frau Mertens just informed me that the pest controller is coming tomorrow to fumigate the entire house, starting with my suite."

"Isn't it a bit early in the year for that?"

"It really doesn't matter. The man is coming and Lena can't be anywhere near the house. The risk of discovery is just too great."

"Yes." Dora wrinkled her forehead, before she said, "I'll take her to a safe place."

"You? But where?"

"I don't know yet, but I know good people, who will help."

"It has to be done tonight."

"That doesn't give us much time, but don't you worry, Fräulein Annegret. I'll figure something out. You make sure Lena is ready and has a warm coat. I'll return just after midnight and knock on the door leading to the private staircase. That way nobody will see us."

Margarete nodded, hoping things would work out. She didn't believe the maid would betray her, but so many things could go wrong and implicate all of them. "Are you sure you want to do this? You'll be risking your own life if someone sees you."

"Nobody will see me." Dora gave a knowing smile, making Margarete sense that she'd been sneaking out under the cover of night many times before. Suddenly she remembered several occasions where she'd seen Dora's eyes light up when Oliver walked into the manor. And him, seemingly accidentally, brushing her hand. While the two of them had been careful to hide their mutual attraction, now the pieces fell into place. What if... a wave of hot fright shook her. Oliver was the main suspect for stealing food from the prisoners. Would he cheer at the opportunity to capture an escapee? She decided to confront her maid.

"You can't tell anyone at the manor. Not even Oliver. I know you are sweet on him."

Dora flinched.

"Don't worry, I won't tell. But he may not be what he seems to be. He has a dark side to him and even if he won't betray you, he would be all too happy to cause damage to me," Margarete warned her.

"I should go now and arrange everything. Remember to stay up until midnight to let me inside."

"Thank you, Dora. I really appreciate your help."

Flushing, the maid mumbled, "I owe you. If it hadn't been for your intervention, that man..."

As soon as Dora had left, Margarete told Lena about the change in plans. She took it with surprising calm, but maybe when one had escaped the horrors she had suffered, one stopped worrying about petty things.

Margarete though, became sentimental. She felt as if she were losing her only friend. The one person who'd known her true identity and could somehow relate to what Margarete was going through every day, pretending to be someone else for the sake of staying alive.

22

Oliver was sound asleep when footsteps coming up to his house woke him up. He listened for a moment, got up and walked over to the window to look outside, only to see Dora at his door.

He hurried downstairs, worried, since she usually came over straight after dinner. Annegret had probably held her up once more with her unreasonable requests. He flung the door open and reached for her, intending to kiss her, but instead of falling into his embrace she shrank back and pointed behind her shoulder. There stood the most pitiful excuse for a human being Oliver had ever seen. "Who's this?"

"Can we come in first?"

He didn't like it, but nevertheless opened his door and ushered them inside. At second glance, the other person looked more like a woman with a shorn head than a man, despite wearing men's clothes beneath one of Annegret's fine coats. Without a shadow of a doubt he knew she must be an escaped prisoner of some sort and he groaned. "Really? Have you completely lost your mind?"

"It's only for a night or two at most."

"If you expect me to house a complete stranger in the middle of the night, you'll have to come up with a much better explanation."

"Please, Oliver." Dora put on her cute puppy face, the one she knew he couldn't resist, but he stayed firm.

"No. First I need the facts." He turned toward the woman. "What or who are you running from?"

She seemed to deflate a few inches and her voice wasn't much more than a whisper when she answered. "My name is Lena and I escaped from the ammunition factory. Please don't send me back, because they'll kill me."

Of course, he'd heard about the escaped worker. Gustav had been livid and raised hell, but to no avail. They'd combed the forest with hounds and found nothing, but that had been more than two weeks ago and he wondered if she was the same woman or not. In any case, it didn't matter.

"Do you know what will happen if they find her here? Gustav will gladly hang not only her, but also me on the next lamppost!"

"It won't come to that," Dora said. "Nobody ever goes into your house except me and anyway, she'll be gone by tomorrow night."

"And where to if I may ask?" He couldn't believe that his quiet, shy and hardworking girlfriend was actively engaging in such subversive activities.

"Somewhere." She worried her lower lip and he got the impression that despite putting on a brave face, she didn't have an actual plan.

"With a shorn head and a stolen coat?"

"It's not stolen! Fräulein Annegret gave it to her."

"Fräulein Annegret. The goodhearted angel of a woman residing at the manor?" His voice was dripping with sarcasm.

"You're such a stubborn buffoon! Just because you've held a grudge against Fräulein Annegret since you were both children, it doesn't make her a bad person now. She really is caring."

Oliver felt a violent outburst threatening to bubble over and turned away from Dora to take several deep breaths until he got a grip on himself. Then he faced the two women again and said in a calm voice, "She can't stay here."

Lena paled and said, "I'm sorry. I never wanted to cause

trouble to anyone, but you're right, my presence is a threat to both of you. I'd better leave and try my luck in the woods."

"Wait. I didn't mean it that way. I can't possibly send you into the forest." He ran a hand through his hair. "It's just... my house isn't a good place. It's much too small to hide someone and all the employees who live in town pass in front morning and evening. Even if it's just for a night, it's not safe here." He looked at Dora again. "Where will she go after this?"

She shrugged. "Fräulein Annegret said she could return to her rooms, once the fumigation is over."

"So Annegret sent you to my place?"

"No. I offered it."

He groaned again. What kind of ugly mess had Dora gotten herself, and him into? A horrible suspicion came over him. Dora might believe that Annegret had changed, but he knew deep down that she was still the same scheming, manipulative girl he'd known before. Could the entire story be a setup? Hadn't she invited the Gestapo to the manor? Perhaps Lena wasn't an escapee at all, but merely a plant, sent here to flush out the resistance and trap the people hiding escaped prisoners? He surely wouldn't put it past her.

Looking between the two women he knew he had to separate them. Lena had to disappear. If she indeed was a refugee, she'd welcome the hiding place he could offer and if she was a mole, then she couldn't wreak havoc from where he had in mind. In both cases, neither Dora nor himself would be implicated. It was the best solution.

"I know just the place."

"Where is it?" Dora asked.

"Not far from here and nobody ever goes there."

Both Lena and Dora followed him to the door, but he said, "No, Dora. You have to stay here. Just in case someone has seen you. The fewer people walking through the night, the less conspicuous we will be." *And if it's a trap, at least I'll be the only one caught, because I couldn't bear the knowledge of you being sent to some camp.*

"Thank you for doing this. I know how much you're risking... and for a stranger. I had lost my belief in humanity, but the past weeks have shown me there are still good people around," Lena said.

Oliver nodded, almost convinced she was indeed an innocent, or a very good actress. He'd heard rumors about Jews collaborating with the Gestapo to denounce other Jews in hiding. *Greifer*, catchers, they were called. They pretended to be helpers and then divulged the hiding places, so the Gestapo could catch and eventually murder the victims. It wasn't unthinkable that someone would do the opposite, pretending to be in need and handing over the helpers.

"Let's go." He took his greatcoat from the hook and slipped into his wellington boots. A short glance at Lena's feet told him Dora had raided the cloakroom for the farmhands. "No talking while we're outside. Not even a whisper."

At night the slightest noise carried far and wide, possibly attracting unwanted attention. The clammy night-air engulfed him the moment he stepped outside, settling into his bones and making his bad leg ache. But he didn't pay attention to the pain and focused entirely on listening for unusual sounds in the night.

One always believed the night was silent, which it was compared to the hustle of the day. But it had its own familiar sounds. An owl hooting, branches rustling in the breeze, horses snoring or moving about. He didn't hear anything out of the usual and beckoned Lena to follow him.

He knew the path from his house to the stables by heart, had walked it a million times and could find his way blindfolded, but for Lena it was the first time and he walked deliberately slowly in the darkness only lit by the stars in the sky.

The target was a small shed behind the stables. This particular shed was only used for a horse deemed contagious and in need of special medical care. It hadn't been used in months, because these days sick horses were shot, not nursed back to health. He shuddered, thankful that none of his charges had suffered this fate.

He unlocked the door, and waved Lena inside, before switching on his pocket light. The shed was little more than a box, covered with straw to make it a comfortable place for a horse, and now for a human, too. He took a rough blanket from a hook and gave it to her, before he switched off the light again. "It's not a great place, but it should do to keep you safe until we have found somewhere else."

"Don't worry about my comfort, this is a royal palace compared to the barracks at the factory." She said it matter-of-factly, without a hint of anger.

"Well, then. No one ever comes here. But you'll still have to be quiet during the day, as the stable hands often pass back and forth on the path we came along."

She nodded.

"Unfortunately I can't leave you the pocket light. The walls are not sealed and a glimmer might be seen. I'll come in the morning and bring you some food and I'll get the water system working so you can always get fresh water to drink." If it was good enough for the horses, she could drink it, too.

"I'll get along. Thank you again for everything you have done for me." Lena's soft voice hung in the air between them and it was so sincere, so genuinely grateful that he leaned toward the probability she wasn't a *Greifer*. Still, he decided better to be safe than sorry and didn't trust her just yet. As he left, he locked the door from the outside, both to keep her in and others out.

Returning to his house he mulled over the fact that Annegret had found the escapee. It was hilarious to say the least. The Annegret he knew would have delighted in returning this wretched woman to the factory for punishment.

But it was time he was honest with himself. The person who'd returned to Gut Plaun had little in common with the girl he once knew. Perhaps the blows of fate had indeed made her into a better person. The possibility couldn't be ruled out.

Back at his house he found Dora sitting at the table, worrying her lower lip. The instant he came inside, she jumped up. "Thank God you're back! Did everything work out? Is Lena safe?"

"Yes she is and as far as I know nobody saw us." He moved over to a cupboard where he kept a bottle of schnapps and poured two glasses. "Sit down. We need to get a few things straight." His heart burst at her fragility and innocence. He had to protect her at all costs, and thus it was vital to hammer the threat into her beautiful head. "She's down by the stables, but you can't ever go near there."

"Why not?"

"It would raise suspicions, since you don't normally go there."

She gave a reluctant nod. "But what about... who will bring her food?"

"I... I locked the place." He deliberately avoided giving her a clear location, just in case. "You just need to bring food to my house whenever you can and I'll take it down to her."

"I can do that." She smiled again.

"But don't be reckless. If Frau Mertens catches you stealing food..." He let the threat linger in the air.

"I'll ask Fräulein Annegret."

He shook his head. "I don't think that's a good idea."

"But she—"

Knowing how stubborn Dora could be, he decided to tackle the Annegret issue from a different angle. "The fewer people involved, the better for everyone. She may be sympathetic, but now that Lena is in my care, her job is done. Do you understand?"

She nodded with big eyes. "But... we can't hide her forever."

"I know." He'd had the same thought. "We need to get her to some safe place, but that will take time. We can't just go into town and ask around whether someone knows of people who smuggle escaped prisoners—and let's be honest, she's probably a Jew—out of the country."

Dora was near to tears. "All of this is so awful. Whyever did I have to come to this place?"

"To meet me." He grinned and his heart warmed at her sweet smile.

"That's the only good thing that has come out of this awful war."

"And when it is over, you and I will get married and live happily ever after. But for now, you better return to the manor and go to bed. Morning will be here before you know it."

She gave him a last desperate embrace before she ducked out the door. Oliver stood by the window and watched her disappear into the darkness, praying that this current course of events wouldn't drag them all into doom.

23

Margarete was restless. With the guests gone, and Lena, too, there wasn't much distraction. Not even her extended walks through the gardens and forest fulfilled her. From childhood onward she'd always been busy. First with school, then with home learning and helping her father in the haberdashery, and then as a maid working around the clock at the Huber household. Even in Paris with Wilhelm, she'd been busy keeping his household in perfect order.

But now... were rich women truly expected to sit around all day and do nothing but read, rest, and chat with equally bored society ladies? She decided a change was in order and, ignoring Herr Fischer's assurances that he would take care of everything, she resolved to do some of her own investigations into the alleged theft of supplies.

Her first stop was the kitchen. "Frau Mertens? A word, if I may?"

The older woman startled and wiped her hands on her apron. "Certainly, Fräulein Annegret. You should have rung the bell if you needed something, and I would have sent Dora to your suite."

"Oh no. In fact I was wondering if there was anything I could help with?"

Frau Mertens looked at her as if she'd made an indecent

proposal. "That won't be necessary, Fräulein Annegret. We are quite capable of managing the workload."

"I'm sorry, that wasn't what I meant. I just need something useful to do."

"Perhaps you might go to town and do some shopping? Or visit someone there? I'm sure Frau Fischer would be delighted to introduce you to the ladies in town."

Margarete recoiled at the idea of having to spend her afternoons at coffee parties with uppity women who were not only twice her age but mostly also diehard Nazis. How she missed her friend Paulette, the fun-loving, vivacious, cheerful Frenchwoman. With her here, everything would be so much easier. Apart from anything else, she'd know how to contact resistance organizations, if they existed. And she'd know how to get Herr Fischer to do her bidding. Margarete might not approve of the way how she obtained her information, but who was she to judge? Thinking about that gave her an idea.

"Thank you, Frau Mertens. That is good advice. Would you be so kind as to telephone Frau Fischer and ask if she's free to see me this afternoon?"

"It will do you good to have some company of your own kind. Is there anything else you'd like?"

She had another idea. "Who is providing the supplies for the factory?"

Frau Mertens pressed her lips together. "This is something I don't concern myself with. My obligation is to keep the manor in shape and cook for the farm and stable hands."

"I know, and you're doing a stellar job with that." Margarete felt a bit of flattery might help to loosen her tongue. "It's amazing how you feed this many people with the scarce rations we get and it always tastes so good."

"It isn't easy, but I do my best." Frau Mertens beamed with pride.

"So, who handles all the deliveries for the manor?"

"That would be Herr Fischer. I make a menu plan for the

following week and give him a list of the ingredients I need. Most of the time he manages to purchase what we need, but not always."

"Then you have to change the menu plan?"

"Sometimes I can do without one of the things. For example, a goulash soup: if he can't get carrots I use more potatoes, but sometimes I have to fall back on a different recipe. I do have a staple list of dishes to prepare with supplies we always have, like flour and potatoes."

"That makes sense. So who makes the menu plans for the factory?" Margarete hoped Frau Mertens wouldn't close up again. Her fears were unfounded.

"Menu plan? Please forgive my being frank, but you seem to not realize that the factory workers are mostly prisoners."

Margarete wondered what one thing had to do with the other. "Please, be as frank as you deem necessary, I want to learn how things are run around here."

"At the factory, inmates get the same food every day. Coffee, *Ersatzkaffee* that is, in the morning together with a slice of buttered bread. A hearty broth at noon, mostly with potatoes, but also smaller amounts of carrots, cabbage, onions and meat. And in the evening again bread with butter, jam, or cheese. Since they bake their own bread, the amount of flour they use each week is staggering."

"I can only imagine." Margarete tried to hide the amazement she was feeling, since Frau Mertens' enumeration didn't equate with what Lena had told her. According to her, breakfast consisted of just coffee, lunch a thin soup, where one could consider herself lucky if she found a chunk of potato. And dinner was a single slice of bread, normally without butter.

"Yes, Herr Fischer orders huge quantities of produce for them. I inspect the deliveries for quality and take away what I need for the manor, the rest is fetched by Herr Strobel, the factory manager."

"So after you inspect it, it goes directly to the factory?"

"I wouldn't know that, but I suppose it does."

Frau Mertens was getting impatient and Margarete hurried to get in one last question. "Just one more thing. Do you know who the kitchen manager at the factory is?"

She shook her head. "No, and I really should get on with my work now."

"Of course. Please don't forget to let Frau Fischer know that I will be in town this afternoon and would like to meet with her. And... please can you ask Nils to drive me there?"

"It will all be done. When would you like your lunch?"

"At noon would be perfect."

Margarete returned to her suite, settling at the window overlooking the gardens and entrance gate. Frau Mertens had seemed to be telling the truth, and if she were honest with herself, Margarete couldn't fathom the idea that such an upright woman might be a thief. Especially not if it meant letting people starve to death.

She would have loved to talk things over with Lena. How she missed her already! With her help she could have gotten a much clearer understanding of the workings in the factory, in particular everyone involved in handling the supplies. Somewhere there was a leak, a person bold and cruel enough to steal food from those who needed it most.

Anger snaked up her spine and she didn't hear the knock on the door until Dora stood next to her. "Fräulein Annegret, is everything alright? I knocked several times, but you didn't answer."

"No, no, I must have fallen asleep." She rubbed her eyes with her hands. It wouldn't do any good to make Dora privy to the theft, especially not when Oliver was one of the main suspects.

"You're not getting sick, are you? It's quite chilly outside and easy to catch a cold."

Especially if you don't even have a blanket to your name. "I'm fine. Really." She thought about Lena again. So far Dora had evaded all questions about the escapee. She tried again. "Please, just tell me whether Lena is safe and warm."

Dora curtsied, which she always did when she became nervous. "I'm sure she is, Fräulein Annegret."

"Why can't she return to my rooms? The fumigation is long over."

Another curtsy. "Because it's not safe for you or me. Please believe me, Fräulein Annegret, she's in good hands."

"Who helped you to hide her? And stop curtsying!"

Dora looked guilty and stood ramrod still. "I am not allowed to tell. Please don't ask me again. I promise. She's fine. She's getting enough water and food, and has a warm blanket against the chill."

"So she's somewhere outside?"

"I really don't know. He wouldn't tell me, because he said it was better if I knew nothing."

Margarete sighed, she knew this logic was correct, but it was still very frustrating. She wouldn't get any information out of the maid, but at least now she knew the savior was a man. Perhaps Nils, the kind handyman, or even Herr Fischer himself? Of course he couldn't openly show empathy with the prisoners, but since he'd so readily agreed to implement her suggestions to improve conditions at the factory, he might not be the diehard Nazi he pretended to be. *Just like me*. For everyone concerned she was the poster child of a good Aryan, despising the Jews, and yet... she sighed. If only people could show their true beliefs. It would make her mission to do good so much easier if she knew who was sympathetic to her cause and who wasn't.

Meanwhile, she would continue her inquiries regarding the theft. The next person on her list was Oliver, and despite her reluctance to meet him, she decided to pay a visit to the stables before lunch and see whether she'd get some information out of him.

Unfortunately, as she arrived, one of the stable hands told her that he had left for the day to negotiate the sale of a new batch of horses to the Wehrmacht.

With nothing else left to do for the time being, she advised Frau Mertens that she'd take her lunch early and would then leave for town.

"This is perfect," Frau Mertens said. "Because Frau Fischer advised me she'd be more than happy to accommodate you for coffee and cake this afternoon, since she has to attend a meeting with her women's group in the evening."

Frau Fischer wasn't the company Margarete yearned for, but she was better than nothing and perhaps she could glean some information from her. From her experience with the Huber men she knew that while they didn't share details about their work, they were only too willing to rant about the hardships of their day. Herr Fischer shouldn't be any different.

Frau Fischer, though, turned out to be a dead end, because all she talked about was the new bathroom her husband had ordered for her birthday, and the clothes she would buy from the recent inheritance he'd received.

"He's such a wonderful man. And he's working so hard to keep Gut Plaun producing. The poor man returns home late at night many days a week and is completely spent when he does."

Margarete thought her remark strange, because she had believed Herr Fischer always left on time, although of course she never checked up on him. Maybe he had to attend meetings at the factory or wherever else after finishing his work in the manor office?

Out of sheer desperation, she picked up the phone and called Horst Richter's number when she returned to her suite in the evening.

"Good evening, my dear. How did my colleagues behave? I hope they didn't give you reason for complaint?"

"Of course not, Horst. They were delightful company and I'm incredibly proud that I could help, even if only in the smallest way."

"That's good to hear. The SS men especially can be a rough crowd when not supervised well."

She imagined him sitting in his study smoking a cigar and shuffling papers. "May I ask you a question?"

"That's what I'm here for."

She knew she couldn't appeal to him about the plight of the forced workers, but when it came to the topic of stealing? That was an entirely different matter. "I've been having a look at the books for the manor and discovered a discrepancy in the supplies being recorded and set aside for the factory."

"A discrepancy?"

"I'm afraid to even suggest this, but it appears as if someone might be stealing from us. Mostly food meant for the factory workers, but it may also include materials needed for the production line."

"Have you talked to Gustav Fischer about this?"

"I have, and he had the same suspicion. He assured me he was already looking into it."

"Well then, you can leave it in his hands."

Margarete scrunched up her nose. This was the exact answer she'd expected. *Leave everything to Fischer. Don't concern yourself with men's business.* Just that she had no intention of following his advice. "I know, it is such a relief to have him investigate, although... the poor man is working so hard to keep Gut Plaun producing. I happened to meet with his wife today and she told me he returns home late at night many days a week and is completely spent when he does. I feel bad piling more work onto him and was wondering if I could somehow help."

"Such a shame you're only a woman. I'd employ you in the Gestapo in a heartbeat." Horst gave a full-belly laugh into the phone.

"Oh, I don't think I'd have what is needed to work for such an honorable institution, but with some tips from you, I might at least get to the bottom of the things happening at Gut Plaun." Margarete was quite proud of how she'd learned to handle the man, of whom she'd been deadly afraid when she'd first met him. She'd certainly come a long way from being the cowed Jewish maid to the lady of the manor.

"You're right, if somehow the quality of production is at stake, we have to act fast. I'll see if I can free up a man and send him over to interrogate everyone at the Gut and find out who the thief is," he offered.

Another Gestapo man was the last person she wanted. "I don't think that is necessary at this time, besides your people must be so busy and I certainly don't want to take precious resources from the Gestapo. If I can find out who the culprit is, I'll let you know, and then your men can swoop in to catch him red-handed." For once she didn't feel bad knowing what the Gestapo would do to whoever was stealing, because a person who caused so much suffering deserved everything that came his way.

"Hmm... you may have a point there. It would definitely make a good impression if we caught the thief in the act." Horst paused for several seconds. "Let me suggest the following: You take the next two weeks and see if you can uncover the culprit? If you haven't flushed them out by then, I'll get my men involved."

Margarete agreed, although the thought of a Gestapo man interrogating her employees and possibly torturing them was almost too much to stomach.

"Thank you so much. As always you know the best way to handle these things."

"Age and experience, my dear," he chuckled into the phone.

A few pleasantries later, she ended the call, thinking about the best way forward. Short of sounding out the rest of her employees, she definitely needed to inspect the factory again. Maybe she could find out something there.

24

Oliver stared at the Wehrmacht negotiator, his mood getting worse by the minute.

"We will need more than thirty horses within the next two months," the man said.

"I already told you, we just don't have them." Oliver felt as if he was talking to a brick wall. "Thirty is all we have."

"It shouldn't be so hard to breed more horses."

Oliver shook his head in frustration. "You don't seem to understand. It's not merely a matter of having a horse, there are other factors. First of all, the animal has to be at least three years old before it's ready to undergo the rigorous training needed to go into battle."

"They will learn on the job."

"No, they won't. They'll spook and either injure themselves or others." Oliver was growing impatient with this man's persistence. "Believe me, I have done this since I was a little boy and my father did it for decades before. If you start the training too young or do it half-assed, you'll do more harm than good. Each horse is different and you have to nurture the strengths and work against the weaknesses to make it a valuable battle horse."

"Now, *you* don't seem to understand." The man waved with

one hand. "The fact is, we need every last horse we can get for the campaign at Stalingrad before winter breaks in earnest. The situation is desperate and any horse is better than nothing. So, I expect thirty fully-trained ones, and at least twenty more we can use as replacements."

Oliver's heart broke at the cold demeanor of his counterpart, who saw his beloved horses as nothing more than cannon fodder needed to win a battle. "It's not that easy."

"The way I see it, it is very easy. We pay, you deliver. If you don't, we take our business elsewhere, and make a note that your stud is not in support of the Reich." Some of the stud owners around here were ruthless enough to sell everything with four legs that wasn't a foal anymore, but most of the horsemen were responsible enough to provide only properly trained animals to the Wehrmacht. Not only for the horses' sakes, but also for that of the soldiers. A mount crazed by gunfire might trample down an entire encampment and kill more soldiers than the enemy.

"There's no use in trying to blackmail me. At Gut Plaun we support the Reich and our soldiers, and that's the very reason why we don't want to sell you untrained animals."

"Then train them."

"They need to be mature enough to deal with the situations they will find themselves in."

The man stared at him. "How about this? Start training the two year olds right now. Choose the ten who have learned the fastest and sell them to me before the year is up? Then another ten, every month."

Oliver wasn't happy with this suggestion, but he knew it was the best he'd get out of the man, so he nodded. "It's a deal. I'll send the first batch over within the next two weeks and the others as soon as I feel they're sufficiently reliable."

"The sooner the better."

They discussed several more details, including remuneration. Despite the concession on the side of the Wehrmacht, Oliver was in a foul mood. He hated having to give away any horse, least of all one that wasn't fully equipped to stand a chance of survival.

When he finished the negotiations, he took the train and returned to Plau am See, where Nils was waiting for him at the station.

"How was the deal?" Nils asked.

"Unreasonable as always. They expect me to train the horses when they're too young, just so they have more cannon fodder. These people have no soul!"

"Easy, young lad. They're still the Wehrmacht and anything you say…" Nils cautioned him.

Oliver knew the consequences all too well, although Nils was a man he trusted, a kind soul who wouldn't harm a fly. He smirked. "Just like you, I fully and completely support this war, and I'm only opposing this because I want to give the Wehrmacht the best possible animals to win against the Russians."

"There's trouble at the manor," Nils said as they drove back.

"What's she up to now?"

"She has Frau Mertens in a frenzy because she asked all kinds of questions about the food supplies, implying there is foul play going on."

"Frau Mertens? Never. But it sounds just like Annegret to stir unfounded suspicions. I wonder what she's up to."

Nils clucked his tongue, to spur the horses into a faster trot. "Fräulein Annegret has changed so much though. She's not the mean, manipulative girl she used to be. But, yes, perhaps I wouldn't put it past her to play a nasty prank on us. Better watch your back."

Oliver wondered how much Nils knew about the incident with Annegret and the blind man, so many years ago. Probably everything, since gossip spread fast on Gut Plaun. The rest of the journey they rode in silence, but Oliver's mood turned even more sour the nearer they got.

"Thanks for picking me up," he said to Nils as he jumped off the coach box.

"No worries, I had errands to run in town anyway."

Oliver tipped his hat and walked down to the stables, needing the peace and acceptance he found only with the horses. They were his best friends and there was no place he'd rather be than with them. Except... maybe with Dora, but she was busy with her own work at the moment.

He strolled into the large barn and one of the stable hands called to him, "Fräulein Annegret was here looking for you earlier."

Annegret has finally come to the stables? He nodded and asked, "Which horse did she take out?"

The man shook his head. "None. She was looking for you and when she heard you were away on business, she left."

His favorite mare Sabrina stuck her head above the stall gates upon hearing his voice and whinnied. He walked over to pat her on the neck, and he wished for nothing more than to ignore the fact that Annegret was looking for him and take Sabrina for a ride.

Although, if he didn't go and find out what Annegret wanted, she might throw a fit and that could never end well. Sabrina would have to wait.

Halfway up to the manor, a lithe figure came walking toward him. *The devil's never far away.*

"Oh good, I found you, Oliver," Annegret said and hurried toward him.

"I just arrived from a business trip out of town, but I heard you came looking for me."

"I did." Her voice turned cold, even hostile. "I wanted to ask a few questions about our food supplies."

He groaned. So, after tormenting Frau Mertens, she'd now decided to implicate him in whatever sinister game she was playing?

"I wouldn't know anything about that."

"That's not entirely true, now is it?" She cast him what seemed to be a triumphant, yet somehow malicious, smile.

"What do you mean? Herr Fischer orders the supplies and

Frau Mertens inspects them before distributing it to several places."

"And you retrieve everything that's for the stables, isn't that so?"

"Yes, I do. Straw and hay are delivered directly to the stables, but the hard feed and the veggies go through the manor first." He could actually see how her brain was processing the information and something clicked, and he itched to know what sinister connection she'd made.

"And you simply take everything you see fit for your horses?"

"What a stupid question!" He could barely restrain himself from yelling at her. "Of course I take what they need. Do you want me to starve them?"

"So, you'd rather starve the factory workers just because your precious animals can't go out in the meadow and eat grass?"

The stupid woman seemed to have no idea that horses in training couldn't subsist on grass alone, especially during the cold season. "This has nothing to do with factory workers, and everything with caring for the animals under my charge."

"Aha. And that is your justification for stealing the food destined for the factory?" She stood with her arms crossed over her chest, seemingly wanting to browbeat him. But she was very much mistaken if she believed her antics impressed him. He'd long stopped being afraid of tantrum-throwing frumps.

He glared at her, and at the last moment stopped his hand from shooting up and flipping the bird at her. Just when he'd accepted that, maybe, Annegret had changed and wasn't the horrid person she used to be, she accused him of stealing.

"I've never stolen anything. I just retrieve what is assigned for the stables. That's all."

"Then, how do you explain that only a small portion of what is provisioned actually ends up in the factory kitchen to feed the workers?"

"What do I know? Why don't you ask Gustav?"

"I already did. And he isn't the thief."

Oliver clenched his fists, fighting the urge to wrap them around her neck and squeeze until she was no longer. He opened his mouth to defend himself, but he was at a loss for words, since she wouldn't believe him either way. Finally he spat out, "Well, I'm not the thief either."

He turned on his heel and stormed off, ignoring her calling his name and demanding he come back and finish their conversation. Angrier than he'd been in a long while, he headed straight for the barn, saddled Sabrina and galloped toward the forest. Annegret certainly hadn't changed one bit, no matter what anyone else said. She might be able to delude Dora, but not him. He knew her true character, and that was black to the core.

When he returned, it was already dark and a small voice reminded him that he should bring food for Lena, but he was still so angry with Annegret that he was convinced the other woman was a mole. For all he knew she was in cahoots with Annegret in some sinister game he didn't yet understand and deserved to rot in the quarantine box.

After dinner though, where he exchanged clandestine glimpses and a few accidental touches with Dora, he was in a much calmer mood. She had that effect on him, calming his temper and making him want to be a better man.

He felt guilty for having taking out his rage on a weak and injured woman. Therefore he passed by his house, where Dora had left food for Lena, and walked straight down to the stables, making sure nobody followed him.

During the day he could roam freely to any and all places at the stud, but going there after dark might raise suspicions, especially now that Annegret believed he was a thief.

He opened the padlock to which he held the only key and found Lena sitting in the straw, the horse blanket around her thin shoulders. Her emaciated figure tugged at his heartstrings and he wondered whether anyone would starve themselves into a walking skeleton to work as a mole. Or perhaps she was indeed an escaped prisoner, but had been recaptured and had agreed to sell out her helpers in exchange for her own life. People did a great many things to stay alive.

"Oliver," she greeted him with a soft voice.

"Lena. I'm sorry I'm so late..."

"Don't worry. You're here now and I truly am more grateful than I can ever express for what you're doing for me."

Her attitude humbled him. After what she must have endured, she was still soft-spoken and kind, instead of embittered. Even in her emaciated condition, she had fine features and he could see that she'd been beautiful once. Dark stubbles of hair grew on her head, but he only saw her infectious smile and wondered just what she would look like fattened up to a normal weight, without the bruises and scrapes, and with her hair grown back.

He spent much longer with her than he'd originally planned, talking with her about mundane things, until he heard the cry of an owl, reminding him it was getting late and that Dora would worry if she got to his house and he wasn't at home.

"I really have to go," he apologized. "Again, I'm sorry I was so late. I'll come earlier tomorrow."

"Whenever you can is fine. Truly."

Oliver nodded, but promised himself he would do better. Lena was so kind and unassuming... her attitude had convinced him that she was neither an impostor nor a snitch. She seemed honest to a fault and he knew deep in his soul that she was simply one of the unfortunate Jews caught up in Hitler's quest to eradicate them from the face of the earth.

25

Margarete watched Oliver, every sympathy she'd held for him evaporating. That impertinent man had not only flat-out denied her accusations, but he'd also ditched her in the middle of the conversation. She'd eat her hat if he wasn't the thief, because no innocent person reacted the way he just had.

Guilt had been written all over his face, despite him pretending to be outraged. She'd visit Herr Fischer and tell him about her findings, but first she had to do one more thing.

Nils was back from running errands in town and stood at the ready, waiting to drive her to the factory, where she wanted to make some further inquiries. She shuddered at the thought of having to deal with Heinz Strobel, the factory manager, but it had to be done.

As much as she wished for Herr Fischer to accompany her, his presence wouldn't help, because if Strobel was somehow involved in the theft, he'd not talk freely in the presence of the estate manager. But with a woman he considered stupid and beneath him, valuable information might slip from his lips, or he might even boast in front of her. Men often behaved like that, assuming that a woman didn't count.

"You sure you want to go to the factory?" Nils asked as he helped her up on the coach box. "It's not a pleasant place."

Once more she wondered how much everyone around here knew and why nobody seemed to care. She actually enjoyed the drive through the forest. It was so serene and peaceful, she all but forgot about her sorrows.

"Shall I wait for you here?" Nils asked as he stopped the horses in front of the gate.

"Yes, please. It won't take long." She steeled her spine and waited for Nils to round the coach to help her down.

"I'll be over there, letting the horses graze." He pointed to a clearing just outside the barbed wire fence, his eyes darting uncomfortably between the bunker-like buildings inside.

"That will be fine. I'll send someone to fetch you when I'm done."

The guard rushed from his porter's lodge, a rifle at the ready. "What is your business?"

"I'm Annegret Huber, the owner of this factory and I wish to speak to Herr Strobel."

He gave her a suspicious glance and said, "Wait here." Then he returned to the lodge and picked up a telephone. After a while he stepped in front of Margarete again and said, "He'll be here in a minute."

"Thank you."

As the guard had promised, Heinz Strobel walked toward them in long strides, his jackboots polished to a shine, his face decidedly unhappy about the unannounced visit.

"Fräulein Annegret, what brings you here?"

"Just a few questions." Since he made no move to let her inside, she added, "Can we talk in your office?"

His face darkened some more, but he nodded at the guard to open the gate. "Certainly. Please follow me."

They crossed the big yard, rounded a corner just as the same cart she'd seen last time came in sight, pushed and pulled by four skeletal men.

Strobel grabbed his baton and hit the nearest man on the back, shouting, "Hurry up, lazy rat!"

The man next to the beaten one looked up and his eyes locked with Margarete's. This time there was no mistaking him for anyone but her Uncle Ernst.

"Gretchen, my child," he muttered, using the nickname he'd often used when she was but a child sitting on his lap during her visits to his and Aunt Heidi's home.

A second later, Strobel's baton crashed down on his back with a loud thud. "Eyes down and no talking to Fräulein Annegret unless she speaks to you first."

"Yes, sir," Uncle Ernst pressed out, his face a grimace of pain.

Margarete had to force herself to keep still, because if she'd rushed to his aid, she'd have blown her cover.

"These Jews are brazen. He knows he's not supposed to talk to anyone, much less a lady like you," Strobel said, fastening the baton at his waist. "How do you even know such a despicable subject?"

"I don't remember ever seeing him." She felt like the worst of traitors, repudiating her own flesh and blood. "Maybe he worked for my parents in Berlin at some time." She hunched her shuddering shoulders, because she knew how hurt her uncle must be by her words.

Herr Strobel though, mistook her gesture and asked, "You want me to punish him for insolence?"

"No, please don't." She barely kept the bile down her throat as Strobel propelled the men forward, showering them with expletives of the worst kind.

When they arrived at his office, he offered her a seat and said, "Now what was it you wanted to discuss? As you can see I have my hands full getting these lazy pigs to work."

Margarete had all but forgotten her initial plan to interrogate him about the food supplies and who delivered them to the kitchen. Instead, she tackled another issue first. "Hasn't Herr Fischer told you that no physical punishment is allowed?"

Strobel guffawed long and loud. When he calmed down

enough to speak again, he said, "Why would Gustav issue such a stupid rule? He enjoys the beatings as much as anyone else."

She glared at him. "I beg your pardon, but this 'stupid rule' came from me and I instructed Herr Fischer to hand it over to you, along with a list of other improvements to be made to working conditions."

"Very funny, little lady. But I assure you, Gustav hasn't given me any kind of list. What else would be on there?"

Margarete drew her brows together, but right now wasn't the time to second-guess the veracity of Strobel's statement. "I'll tell you exactly, if you'd be so kind to give me paper and pen."

He looked dumbfounded, but obeyed and withdrew a notepad from a drawer, along with a pen. Margarete got to work and wrote down a list of five points:

- *All work shifts to last for a maximum of twelve hours*
- *Every worker is entitled to ten-minute breaks every two hours, and one longer break of thirty minutes*
- *All work stations are to be provided with fresh water from the well at all times*
- *Protective gear will be given to people cooking the explosives*
- *No physical punishment is allowed, ever*

She read through her list and added an exclamation mark to the last point, before handing it to Herr Strobel.

His face grew angrier with every word he read and by the time he was finished, it was beet-red. "You cannot be serious about that!"

"I am."

"If you insist on implementing even half of this, all hell will break loose. I'm sorry to say, but you don't have the slightest idea how to run a factory. The people we get are the scum of humanity. You have to beat them into submission or they'll soon start a revolt. And how would you like that?"

Margarete had known it would be an uncomfortable visit, but never in her wildest dreams had she anticipated that she would have to battle him on the implementation of the improvements she'd concocted, since Herr Fischer had promised to see to it. Now she wished she'd asked him to accompany her, so she could find out whether Strobel was lying or Fischer indeed had not forwarded her request.

But she wouldn't leave this place before making sure Uncle Ernst, and with him all the other inmates, were safe from further beatings.

"And you seem not to remember who owns this factory. I don't care what you think, I want these rules implemented, and now!" Margarete was so enraged, she completely forgot to be afraid of the burly man.

"Well, Fräulein Annegret. If this is what you want, leave the list with me, and I'll see to it."

She wasn't fooled by his sudden change of mind. Herr Fischer had said the same, and she realized that he'd played her like the foolish little girl she was. He'd never intended to implement her rules, banking on the fact that she'd never again set foot in the factory. And now Strobel was doing the same. But both of them severely underestimated her if they believed she'd fall for the same ruse twice.

"Thank you, but I'll do it myself. Where's the bulletin board?" She snagged the list from his desk.

He jumped up from his seat, visibly agitated. "You can't do that... it's too dangerous for you out there all on your own. These people are like a pack of wolves, they'll tear you into pieces."

Margarete all but laughed. These people were cowed prisoners, even if there were actual criminals among them, nobody would dare to lay a hand on her, not in the presence of Strobel's whip-cracking cronies. "That's why you will come with me."

"I certainly won't help you commit such madness. Gustav will chop off my head if something happens to you."

For once she was glad about Annegret's reputation as a reckless, stubborn and spoilt brat, because it enabled her to throw a temper tantrum to get what she wanted. "And I'll tell the Reichskriminaldirektor Richter about how little respect you show me, then you can explain yourself to the Gestapo, if you'd rather do that." With satisfaction she observed how the beet-red in his face had turned into limestone-white.

"That won't be necessary."

"Now, where do you think would be the best place to post these rules, so everyone can see them?"

He shrugged uncomfortably. "We do have a bulletin board, but it's only for the information of the civilian workers. Prisoners are not allowed to linger."

This might be the truth, or another ruse to keep her from implementing the improvements. On the spur of the moment, she said, "Follow me," and left his office with the list in her hand. In his outer office sat a plump woman in her fifties in front of a typewriter.

"*Guten Tag*," Margarete said. "I'm Annegret Huber, and I own this factory."

The woman stopped what she was doing and shot up. "Fräulein Annegret. You may not remember me, but we met at church in town. My name is Gerda Klein."

"I'm very pleased to meet you, Frau Klein." A plan formed in Margarete's head, and getting the secretary on her side was the first step. "I've heard only good things about your work and wanted to thank you personally for all you do for the war effort."

The other woman beamed with delight. "I do my very best to please the Führer."

"And you do well. Incidentally, Herr Strobel and I just talked about how we could raise productivity in the factory and agreed on a new set of rules. It might seem counterintuitive at first, but both of us are convinced that less exhausted workers will work more efficiently."

Frau Klein nodded.

"Would you be so kind as to type twenty copies of this list?"

"Certainly, if Herr Strobel wants..." Her eyes darted between Margarete and her boss, apparently unsure whether she was allowed to take direct orders from Annegret.

"Do what Fräulein Annegret says," he groused.

Frau Klein removed the current sheet from her typewriter and got up to fetch several sheets of white paper and carbon paper, meticulously putting them on top of each other, until she had a stack about ten sheets thick that she inserted into the typewriter. Then she typed away, fast as lightning speed.

Margarete stood a few feet away, watching how her fingers flew across the keys, a rhythmic clack-clack filling the room. Within minutes Frau Klein had typed all twenty copies and handed them to Margarete. "Here you go. If there's nothing else I'll return to my other work."

"Thank you so much for your help. I'm amazed at how fast you can type."

"I was best in class at the secretarial school." Frau Klein grinned from ear to ear, but her smile faltered when she looked at her boss. "I'll get to typing your letters right away, Herr Strobel."

"Good."

Margarete didn't like his gruff tone and she hoped Frau Klein wouldn't be on the receiving end of his ire when he returned from the little tour around the premises that she'd planned. "Well, Herr Strobel, let's get going. We need to put up one of these lists in every production bunker."

"You can't be serious. This ridiculous plan will disturb the production process and set us back in reaching the daily quota."

She assumed he was bluffing. "Don't worry. The new rules will raise production a lot more than the little delay it causes pinning the list to the wall."

He glared at her, but kept silent. Apparently the threat to unleash the Gestapo on him had worked and Margarete felt a thrill rushing through her veins. It was an exhilarating feeling to be the one in power.

Bossing Strobel about, she had him post the announcement in

every factory building—and there were many—under the wary eyes of the forced workers. She decided not to chance her luck and kept in the background, albeit observing how the news spread fast.

When they were finished, she asked, "When is dinner time?"

"As soon as the lazy pigs have finished their daily quota, which, thanks to you, will take a lot longer today."

God, that man was annoying. She smiled her sweetest smile. "You're being unreasonable. I had a look at the bulletin boards and it seems most of the production lines already reached their daily goals. What are you doing with the surplus?"

"If we ever have a surplus, we let the Wehrmacht know and sell them more explosives." He almost choked on the answer and Margarete realized there must be more to the theft than simply food. She definitely needed to question Fischer again.

"That is a relief to hear. Now, if you would call all inmates to present themselves in the backyard please."

"How am I supposed to do that? This isn't a kindergarten!"

"Oh, I was under the impression that every well-run factory using camp prisoners has measures in place for exactly this occasion. Roll-calls, I believe they are called." She congratulated herself for the foresight to question Lena about every single detail pertaining to the daily routine at the camps and this factory in particular.

The sun was already setting and she walked over to tell Nils that she'd be ready to return to the manor shortly. Meanwhile, Herr Strobel gathered everyone for roll-call.

Delighting in his discomfort, Margarete read the list of the new rules to the workers. Having learned about the deception of the men working for her she added, "And I'll be visiting regularly to check up on the implementation of the new rules."

A few of the emaciated women and men seemed to smile, while most of the guards showed an angry face. She'd have to do something about them, as well. But for today, she'd done all she could do to help those under her care—even if only in a small way.

26

Gustav was just about to leave his office, when the phone rang.

"Gustav Fischer, Gut Plaun," he answered.

"It's Heinz. You need to keep that woman away from the factory!"

"Hold your horses! What has happened?"

Heinz told him how Annegret had arrived at the factory all haughty and had made him announce her list of unreasonable demands to the workers. If it weren't so awful, Gustav would have laughed out loud at the image of Fräulein Annegret giving Heinz a piece of her mind. He secretly applauded her for taking on a man like Heinz. Although he wondered why on earth she suddenly felt compelled to help those despicable Jews.

"You keep up business as usual and I'll take care of her."

"That brazen hag threatened me with the Gestapo if I didn't do her bidding."

"I'll talk to her. Keep a low profile for a while, will you?" Gustav sighed. He'd never thought having the young woman here would make things so complicated. Why couldn't she follow in the footsteps of her mother and socialize with the ladies in town over coffee and cake? Although, on second thoughts, if he managed to channel her determination to pursue something worthwhile, she could be a powerful ally.

"All right. But can I count on you to get her off my back? There's a new buyer coming next week and the last thing I need is milady snooping around!" Heinz got all worked up about Annegret's interference in his business.

"I have everything under control. Just let me know the date and time of the visit and I'll arrange for my wife to invite her over." Gustav smiled. Beate had been quite impressed with Annegret and would love to invite her over again. It was good for him, too, since socializing with the owner could only continue to solidify his position as the man truly in charge at Gut Plaun.

If Annegret didn't listen to him, she'd succumb to the winning manner of Beate, who'd soon have her attending a myriad of women's activities and afternoon coffee parties, so she wouldn't have time to stick her nose into the factory.

He hung up the phone and looked at the clock. Almost dinner time. Walking into the kitchen he informed Frau Mertens, "I'll be having dinner with Fräulein Annegret."

"I'll set the table for two, she should be down in half an hour."

"Thank you." It gave him just enough time to refresh himself, before he met the insubordinate girl who believed she called the shots around here.

Annegret was already sitting at the table when he arrived. She looked innocent enough with her brown hair slung into an elegant bun and her dark blue woolen outfit. Beate had told him that even at the manor the rationing of material was felt and Fräulein Annegret had asked for a seamstress who could adapt the many costumes the late Frau Huber had left here. This was probably one of them. Chic and timeless. If only the wearer was as classy as the costume.

"Fräulein Annegret, I hope you don't mind me joining you for dinner?" He greeted her with a perfect kiss on the hand and noticed the pleased expression on her face.

"Of course not, Herr Fischer. I wanted to talk to you anyway."

He settled opposite her at the table and waited until the pretty maid had served dinner—roast venison with potato dumplings. He even resisted pinching Dora's ample behind to launch directly into his planned attack.

"My wife was so very delighted by your visit, she barely talks about anything else and wishes to invite you to a coffee party next week, if that would suit you?"

"I would certainly welcome an invitation, and please tell Beate that the seamstress she recommended did fantastic work."

He put a forkful of venison into his mouth. "Please don't think me disrespectful, but since you're now spending a lot of time with my wife, I'd like you to call me Gustav."

She flushed slightly, and he already thought he'd been too bold. "I would be honored."

"We have to drink to this," he said and raised his wine glass. "To our friendship, Annegret."

"To our friendship, Gustav."

"So how was your day? Did you find out something about the thief?" After what Heinz had told him, it was clear she hadn't kept her feet still waiting for him to solve the case.

She grimaced. "First of all I confronted Oliver with my suspicions."

"You did? What did he say?"

"He denied everything and then stormed out on me."

"What a bad-mannered lad. I hate to say this, but his reaction was to be expected."

"Why would that be?"

"He's a coward, always has been. Instead of manning up and bearing the consequences of his deed, he claims to be innocent. Although no innocent man would storm off during a conversation, which clearly shows he's the culprit."

"Do you really think so?" She took a sip from her wine and put down the glass with a frown. "Maybe he was just outraged at the insult? I hear he's quite hot-tempered."

"Not only hot-tempered, he's also violent. Beating the stable hands—"

"He does? Why haven't you told me before?"

"Don't be angry with me, my dear. I only wanted to shield you from the more unpleasant things happening at Gut Plaun."

She sighed. "That is laudable, but not at all necessary. How should we deal with Oliver?"

"A difficult question, since we haven't caught him red-handed. On the other hand, do you really want to wait and give him time to cover his tracks?"

"No... we can't give him another moment to carry on like that here." She paused and he waited patiently for her to make the only correct conclusion. "Fine. You fire him and find a new stud master."

Now that was a command after his liking, and with the very obvious aversion between Annegret and Oliver, he could put all the blame on her. "If that is your wish, I'll do it first thing in the morning. As it happens, I know a man who has returned from the front with only one arm, but extensive experience in horse training. I'm sure he'd jump at the opportunity and will never be disloyal to you."

Annegret nodded her head and took a sip of wine. "I was at the factory."

"But whyever did you have to go there?" He faked surprise.

"Since you're so busy with work, I wanted to do my own investigations into the theft issue."

"And... did you find anything?" Perhaps it was time to make sure Heinz was the one to get blamed for any irregularities.

She stared at him with discomforting determination. "I did."

He all but toppled over, praying that Heinz hadn't accidentally given them away. That fool couldn't be trusted to keep his mouth shut. Somehow, he managed to keep his countenance and asked, "How interesting. What did you find out?"

"That you never forwarded my list of improvements," she hissed the words, barely suppressing her indignation.

He shook his head, frantically thinking. "Are you sure?"

"One hundred percent."

"I'm at a loss for word. Such a callous lie!" He scratched his head. "The very next day after you gave me the list, one of the foremen came to the manor to discuss a shortage of some spare part. I gave the list to him."

She looked at him, suspicion still lingering on her face.

"For some reason, he didn't relay the new rules to Heinz. Perhaps he was afraid, because Heinz can be ill-tempered at times." He looked at her, shaking his head. "I'm so very sorry, I should have done it myself. I'll drive to the factory right after dinner and talk to Heinz."

"There's no need, I already gave him my instructions and made sure copies of the rules have been pasted to every building."

"And that is a relief. Once again, please forgive me for not following up on this, I shouldn't have trusted in the foreman. It was such a stupid thing to do. This is all my fault. I'm heartbroken at all the suffering that could have been prevented." He ran his hand through his hair once more, deliberately leaving it slightly disheveled.

"Please don't feel guilty, we all make mistakes. And now the new rules are in place."

"Thank you for your understanding, it will never happen again." He emptied his plate and put down his cutlery neatly side by side.

"Would you care for a dessert?" Annegret asked.

"Who can resist one of Frau Mertens's delicious sweet buns?"

"I'm afraid she hasn't made buns today, but I believe I saw an apple tart."

"That's even better."

Gustav leaned back, observing Annegret closely. Heinz might not know how to deal with her, but she was certainly putty in Gustav's hands. No need to worry. And as an added bonus, he'd get rid of Oliver and could replace him with a loyal friend. A whole new world of possibilities to profit from the sale of horses opened up. Winning all around.

He ate the apple tart in a wonderful mood and chatted with Annegret about the weather and minor details at the manor like needing material for new curtains in the guest rooms. Women were so easily pleased and as soon as she had her hands full with overseeing the sewing of curtains, she'd forget about the factory workers.

The next morning, he arrived at his office, rubbing his hands in anticipation. He didn't wait for the staff to have their breakfast, but caught Oliver as soon as he walked into the manor. "Would you have a minute, please?" Gustav delighted at Oliver's dismayed face.

"Can't it wait until after breakfast?" Oliver had been up and working for several hours and probably was hungry as a wolf.

"No. It's urgent. Let's go to my office, shall we?"

Oliver followed him with a rather dour face. As soon as Gustav closed the office door behind them, Oliver blurted out, "What's this about?"

"You're fired!"

"What? What are you talking about?"

"That you don't work at Gut Plaun any longer. Pack your bags and leave the premises immediately. I'll send a man to make sure you don't take anything that isn't yours." Gustav barely kept the glee out of his voice.

"Does this have anything to do with the asinine accusations Annegret tossed my way?"

"Exactly so. You've been stealing from the estate and it stops now."

"I haven't stolen anything, and you damn well know it, you vicious snake."

"All of the evidence points to you. If I were you, I'd leave, go out into the forest somewhere, and put a bullet to my head. You are an utter disgrace to the German nation."

Oliver glared at him, but there was nothing he could do, since Gustav had not only the backing of Annegret, but also was a party member in good standing, while Oliver was nothing but a discharged Wehrmacht soldier without influential friends.

Gustav rang a bell and one of his aides came inside. "Please accompany Oliver to his house. He's been fired for stealing from the manor and we need to make sure he only takes what belongs to him before he disappears, hopefully forever."

The aide, a man in his fifties from town, raised an eyebrow. "Will do. Anything else?"

"Yes. Collect his keys, all of them."

"Sure, boss."

Gustav would have to give his aide an extra bonus for being so keen to execute his orders. One thing Gustav had learned was that most people were loyal only to money and greasing palms for small things eased the way for big favors if they became necessary.

"Dirty asshole," Oliver cursed at him, before he stormed out of the office, slamming the door behind him.

"What are you waiting for? Go after him!" Gustav told the aide who looked all dressed up and with nowhere to go.

"Yes, boss."

Gustav waited until he stopped hearing footsteps and then burst into laughter. Today was a good day. No, a fantastic day! With Oliver gone, he'd make another move on Dora. He recited a verse of Goethe's poem "Erlkönig": *I love thee, I'm charm'd by thy beauty, dear girl! And if thou'rt unwilling, then force I'll employ.*

Although she would be willing, if she knew what was good for her. If not, a little blackmail and a few threats always worked wonders on foreign workers like her. Gustav leaned back in his chair, closing his eyes and allowing his imagination to run rampant. A fantastic day, indeed!

The one thing missing from his life being perfect was that they'd never found that Jewish bitch who'd had the audacity to run away. She was probably dead by now from exposure, but catching her and punishing her for her insolence would have been the icing on the cake.

27

"Dora," Margarete stopped the maid as she was about to leave the dining room.

"Yes, Fräulein Annegret?"

"I need you to gather up your cleaning supplies and accompany me to the stud master's house."

"The stud master?"

"Yes. I know you were sweet on him, so this will come as a shock to you, but he's been caught stealing and had to be removed from his position. Herr Fischer has already found a replacement who'll be arriving tomorrow and I want to make sure everything is in perfect condition for him to move in."

"I... yes, Fräulein Annegret. Let me just get the dishes into the kitchen and tell Frau Mertens." Dora curtsied twice, which she always did when she was anxious and Margarete wondered whether the maid had known or at least suspected about Oliver's wiles.

They walked in silence the short distance to the stud master's house and Margarete noticed how the last roses had turned into haws. It was a sure sign that fall was about to turn into winter. Almost without realizing it, the cold season had crept up on them and with it, December and Hanukkah.

Once again, she would not be able to celebrate, except for lighting two simple white candles in the twin candleholders she and Wilhelm had bought in Paris. But she had much bigger problems to think about. One was the question of how to equip several hundred factory workers with blankets, when the market for blankets was emptied. As Gustav had warned her, any and all warm materials were sent eastward to protect the Wehrmacht soldiers from the biting Russian cold.

By sheer luck she had been able to buy several dozen yards of cloth from a house where the Jewish owners had been evicted. Swallowing down her scruples she'd paid the man who'd stolen the house from the rightful owners and had then employed several young women to sew blankets. Not enough to equip all the workers, but it was a start. She couldn't wait to surprise Gustav with her ingenious idea. He'd be overjoyed to hear that she'd found a way to keep the factory workers warm, while not having to spend the money he obviously cared so much about.

"The door is locked," Dora said, bringing Margarete back to the present.

"I have the key." She retrieved a keyring with about a dozen keys from her pocket. "Do you know which one it is?"

"No, Fräulein Annegret, Oliver never locked his door. We have to try them."

Margarete stepped forward and tried to guess which was the correct one. Most of them looked similar, except one which was about double the size and looked to open a barn door, and one that was tiny, possibly for a padlock. She took the first of the middle-sized keys and on the third try, the door opened.

Since she had never been in the small house, she took the time to venture into every room while Dora was cleaning. Downstairs was a living room, kitchen and a bathroom, while upstairs she found a bedroom with a huge, and empty, wardrobe. Simple, but well-kept. As every other house in the country it was equipped with heavy blackout curtains and she had an idea. What if she replaced the blackout curtains with removable cardboard?

She stepped nearer, feeling the heavy material with her fingers. Cut into pieces, each one would make three or four warm blankets for *her* factory workers. She already pictured Uncle Ernst wrapped into one of them during the icy nights that were just around the corner.

"Fräulein Annegret, I'm done down here."

"Good, come up." She waited until the maid climbed the stairs, the heavy bucket in her hand. "I want you to take down the blackout curtains and have them washed."

"We've never done this before... maybe I should tell Frau Mertens first?"

"No need. I'll explain it to her. You just get the curtains to the laundry room."

"Yes, Fräulein Annegret." Another curtsy.

"And stop curtsying."

"I'm sorry, Fräulein Annegret. It won't happen again." Dora was exceptionally shaky and Margarete wondered once more if she might be in cahoots with Oliver and feared her job was on the line, too.

Margarete considered whom to ask for the black cardboard, since she didn't want to spoil the surprise for Gustav. Nils came to her mind. She just had to bind him to secrecy. Satisfied with her new plan, she turned around to observe Dora cleaning the room, work she'd done herself for years at the Huber household.

Memories returned, unpleasant ones of being exploited as a house slave with barely a bite to eat, as well as joyful ones of her keeping Wilhelm's household in Paris. She sighed. Poor, deluded Wilhelm. How she wished she'd been able to save him, make him see the truth and recant his support of the Nazi ideology.

"Please, Fräulein Annegret, can I ask for something?" Dora interrupted her musings.

"Sure."

"It's just... I mean... please... you won't get angry with me?"

Margarete was getting impatient. "That, I can only tell you after I know what you want to ask. Spit it out!"

"It's just... you remember Lena?"

"Of course I do."

"Oliver was hiding her. He never told me where, but I followed him one day. She's hiding in the shed behind the barn." Dora stood like a caught sinner wringing her hands.

"Oliver was hiding Lena? After I told you explicitly not to involve him?"

"Please, don't be angry, but I didn't know who else I could trust. Won't you please consider taking him back? He's a good man. He would never steal from anyone."

"Look, Dora, this is out of my hands now. But just because he's not with us anymore, doesn't change anything for Lena."

"But she'll starve!" Dora cried out.

"Someone else can bring her food."

"No, they can't. He's the only one who had the key to the padlock and he always carried it with him."

Margarete wondered how Dora knew all of this. Was the infatuation between her and this despicable man more than that? Were they actually a couple? For the moment, it didn't matter. "We will find the key." Then she remembered the keyring in her pocket and retrieved it. "Perhaps one of these fits?"

Dora's eyes lit up. "It could be."

"Now listen closely. I'm supposed to return the keyring to Fischer's office, but since the new stud master won't need it before tomorrow, I'll leave it with you. I would do this myself, but I need to leave for a coffee party in town within the hour. After the stable hands have left for the day, you sneak down to that shed and find out if one of the keys fits. If it does, you take it off the ring and keep it yourself. But make sure nobody sees you."

"I will, Fräulein Annegret. I wouldn't want Lena to starve in there."

Several minutes later, Dora finished cleaning and taking down the curtains. "I'll have to go at least twice to carry everything to the laundry room."

"I'll leave it to you," Margarete said. "Make sure you return the keyring to Fischer's office after you are done."

28

Oliver felt like a bull might when someone was waving a red flag in front of his nose. If he could, he'd trample through the grounds at Gut Plaun, charge at Gustav and bury him beneath his body for good. Unfortunately he wasn't a bull.

He shouldered the bundle with his personal belongings and walked into town, where he headed straight for the bar, not caring that it wasn't even lunchtime. "Give me a schnapps!"

Several drinks later his vision was swimming, but the alcohol had still failed to dampen down the rage coursing through his veins. That cursed bastard Gustav! He was pretty sure Gustav was the real culprit, but there was no way to prove it. He slammed his fist on the counter.

"Hey, easy, or I'll throw you out," the bartender warned him.

"Stupid bitch!"

"Grief with your woman?"

"Not my woman, but she's a scheming bitch!" Not a moment too soon he shut his mouth. Annegret and Gustav were the perfect couple and he imagined them laughing at their latest evildoing, since it was all too clear that stupid harridan was smitten with the older man. He'd bet his right arm that they were jumping into the sack together; Gustav's preference for young women to spruce up the boring sex life with his prudish wife was well known. And Annegret... her wild and reckless reputation preceded her. Those two were a match made in heaven, or more accurately, in hell.

When his money ran out, he staggered back to his parents' house. Leaning heavily against the door, he knocked until someone opened.

"What's that noise? Are you trying to smash the door?" his father said.

"Let me in." Deprived of the support of the door, Oliver tottered around like a leaf in the wind.

"Not in your condition. If your mother sees you like this, it'll break her heart." His father stepped into the doorway.

"You're sending me away?" Thinking was difficult and having to decide which of the two men he saw was the real one, even more.

"I do. And don't come back until you're clean and sober."

"But I need a place to sleep."

"Not here." His father slammed the door in his face and Oliver slid down the doorframe until his buttocks bumped on the hard concrete of the doorstep.

"What now?" He was oblivious to how long he'd been sitting there, exposed to the pitying, disdainful, or hate-filled gaze of the townspeople passing by. Not a single one of those rats stretched out his hand to help him up. And all because of that wretch and her accomplice up at the manor.

He couldn't even go and see Dora, because she lived in the lion's den and under Frau Mertens' watchful eye. If he tried to sneak in and was found out, it would get her into trouble, even more than him. No, he wouldn't drag her into this mess. Besides, Gustav had made it very clear that he was no longer welcome on the estate. To hell with the world and everyone in it!

Somehow he managed to stand up, looking aimlessly down the street, when one of the stable lads stepped out of the saddler's workshop.

"Hey, Piet!" he called out.

Piet stared at Oliver in shock. "What you doing here? Fischer said he fired you for stealing."

"I didn't steal a thing!"

"Doesn't matter. You know how fast news travel. And townsfolk will believe Fischer over you. He's a bigwig party member."

Oliver hunched his shoulders some more, stubbornly jutting out his lower lip. "I'm not a thief."

"Boss, I'm sorry, I really am. Nobody will believe you. Even the saddler is shocked that you showed your face in town."

"I need a place for the night."

"Sorry, but my missus wouldn't put up with it. Or Fischer will fire me, too. Can't afford to lose my job."

"Just one night," Oliver begged, but looking at the fear in Piet's face changed his mind. "Forget what I said. Can you give me some money? I'll pay it back."

Piet reached into his pocket and pulled out a few coins. "That's all I have. Payday is still a long way."

"Thanks anyway." Oliver wanted to walk around the other man, but stumbled and fell flat on his face, where he lay for a good while until he mustered the strength to get up again.

With no place to go he staggered out of town and into the forest that was so familiar to him. How many times had he crossed it on the back of a horse? About half an hour later rain drizzled down on him and soon turned into one of those November rains that usually lasted three days before it stopped again.

Within the hour he was wet, cold, and miserable. He huddled into a wooden deer stand that hardly kept the rain away. Even in his alcoholic stupor he realized he had to get out of the elements, or would suffer dire consequences.

He knew the woods like the back of his hand, and there wasn't suitable cover anywhere within reach, except for the stables at Gut Plaun. He'd sneak up to the unused shed and spend the night there. Lena wouldn't mind. He giggled like a madman, the irony of asking a fugitive to give him shelter not lost on him.

Reluctant to use the main gate, he slid through the fence

surrounding the meadow and walked at a crouch from tree to bush until he reached the stud. At this time of day, the stable hands would all be at the manor for dinner. He had about half an hour before they returned to make one last round through the horse boxes.

Shivering, he brushed his sodden hair back from his forehead and ran in a staggering, zigzag pattern toward the quarantine shed, where Lena was hiding. But the moment he reached for the door, the shining padlock reminded him that he no longer carried the key to open it up.

Frustrated, he sank to the ground, not caring that more rain pelted down on him, running in rivulets down his neck and beneath his soaked coat. For all it was worth he could jump into the lake and not get any wetter than he already was.

"Lena, are you there?" he asked, while softly knocking on the door. No answer came. He tried again. "It's me, Oliver."

A shuffling sound came from the inside, but still no answer.

"I'm sorry I couldn't bring you food today, but I'll make sure you get something. You hear me?"

No answer. Fear constricted his throat, but then he realized she was probably too afraid or too cautious to answer him, since this could be a trap.

"You don't need to say anything. I'll go and find the key now." His brain was still in a slight haze, but at least he had gained enough clarity to think straight. The most likely place to find the key was... in Gustav's office. Darkness was settling over the estate, so the risk of being discovered was low, while he sneaked up to the manor. He prayed that Gustav had already left the office for the day.

He heard the clatter of dishes from the kitchen where the servants were eating, slipped quickly past the door and to the end of the hallway where Gustav's office lay. After a perfunctory listen at the door, he cracked it open and slipped inside, feeling for the key rack on the wall. But his keyring wasn't there. He muttered a curse and froze a second later, when he heard soft steps approaching.

Barely breathing, he waited in the pitch-black room with bated breath. If Gustav had returned, his only option was to hide. Just where? The next moment, the ceiling light flared and blinded him. When he could see again, his jaw dropped to the floor.

"Dora? What are you doing here?"

She jumped backwards, her eyes wide. Before she could scream, he put his hand over her mouth. "Don't make a noise, will you?"

"Oliver?" her muffled whisper came and he took his hand away. "I thought you... oh dear, you are soaking wet."

"Shush. Now's not the time. Do you know where my keyring is?"

"Here." She grinned. "I took it to test which one fits into the padlock on the shed."

"But how did you know?" He was incredibly proud of her. "You're such an intelligent woman."

"Actually it was Fräulein Annegret's idea."

Her answer darkened his mood again, but he left it uncommented. Although it was beyond him how Dora could still fall for Annegret's wiles. Did nobody but him realize just how bad a person she was?

"I have to disappear," he whispered.

"You're soaking wet, you'll catch your death if you go out there again." She gazed at him with loving eyes. "You come with me. For tonight I'll hide you in my room."

He wanted to protest, but if he was being honest, he welcomed the offer, because the prospect of sleeping rough all night in that awful rain held little appeal. "All right."

"Follow me. We have to be quick." She switched off the lights and checked whether the coast was clear. When she beckoned him, he followed her and a minute later stood in her room, exhausted but relieved.

"You get out of your dripping clothes and under the bedcovers," she ordered.

"Will you join me to warm my freezing bones?" he said with a smirk.

"Are you even listening to yourself, you drunkard! We're both in serious trouble if someone finds you here. While you get into bed, I'll mop your wet footprints leading into Herr Fischer's office. And then I'll see if I can get food for you and for Lena. After I'm done with all my chores and you're still not warmed up, you can explain this mess to me and only then I might consider joining you in bed."

"If that's the offer, I'll gladly stand wet and freezing by the window until you return to bring the heat back into my limbs."

She slapped him on his behind. "You will do no such thing. You'll be a good boy and slip into bed right now. That is an order!"

"Yes, ma'am!" He'd never thought he could love a woman so much. "I'm sorry."

"Sorry?" She gazed at him.

"Sorry for dragging you into this mess. You must believe me that I wasn't the thief."

"I know," she said, kissed him and turned around to leave.

"I love you. Always will," he muttered, feeling all alone when the door closed behind her.

29

In the afternoon, Margarete was sitting in her favorite armchair in her bedroom, overlooking the garden, although there wasn't much to see except for a gray sky and incessant rain. Her heart ached for the factory workers who had to push the heavy cart back and forth across the factory yard with nothing to protect them from the icy rains.

Especially Uncle Ernst. She had to find a way to get him away from that backbreaking work. Perhaps he could be transferred to the kitchen, or some other light work?

She took a piece of paper and put *raincoats* and *wellingtons* on her list of things to procure for the factory. Not that she was under the delusion that she could simply go into the store and buy what she needed, but her father had always said, "What is not written down doesn't get done." She also believed that by writing things on a list, her mind would subconsciously begin working out a solution on how to get what was on there, like it had done with the curtains converted into blankets.

A smile appeared on her lips. Tomorrow morning, the seamstress would deliver the first three dozen blankets and then she'd show them to Gustav. It would be so rewarding to drive down to the factory with him and give them to the workers—although she wasn't sure yet how to choose whom to give one first. There were five hundred workers, more or less, at any given time, and she had only three dozen blankets to distribute. Perhaps it would be better to wait until she had more, so as not to cause bad blood among the prisoners?

She shook her head. Never once had she anticipated how complicated her mission would turn out to be and nobody had prepared her for the moral dilemmas she would face.

Was it acceptable to exploit slave workers in her factory, if she gave them a blanket to stay warm, and enough food not to starve? Or was she indeed as vile as the Nazis themselves, because she collaborated with them? Produced explosives for their cruel war? Should she have stayed in Paris and helped to kill German soldiers? Was that better or worse than what she was doing now?

She closed her eyes, trying to calm the swirling thoughts in her mind. If there was a solution to this, she had no idea what it was, and she couldn't even talk to anyone about it. For a moment Uncle Ernst appeared in her mind's eye. He had been a philosophy professor and might set her moral compass straight. But how would she even reach out to him without breaking her cover?

Perhaps the priest could help? She'd gotten to know him and he was a very studious and agreeable person, but was he trustworthy? She had no idea. No, she'd have to deal with her doubts all on her own.

A high-pitched scream cut through the air and she jumped to her feet. Peering down she saw a commotion outside, but she couldn't distinguish what was happening and decided to go down and investigate.

At the bottom of the stairs she stopped in her tracks when she saw Gustav dragging a bedraggled creature down the hallway.

He saw her and stopped. "You won't believe what I found!" He yanked on the creature's arm, before he grabbed her chin and thrust it upward, to show her face to Margarete, who all but fainted as she recognized Lena.

"Let this woman go. What has she done?" Margarete somehow managed to keep her wits about her and was incredibly grateful that Lena didn't utter a sound of recognition.

"What has she done? She's only the prisoner who escaped from the factory weeks ago!" The vein in Gustav's temple was pulsating violently, while his voice was hard as steel.

"How do you know? She looks like a farmhand to me." She wondered how he was so sure that Lena was an escaped prisoner.

"Oh, Annegret, there's so many things you have to learn. Even if she weren't a prisoner, I could tell with a single glimpse that she's a dirty Jew."

Margarete bit on her tongue. As much as she wanted, she couldn't defend a Jew, or she risked endangering herself. So she pretended to be aghast that a fugitive had been found, and said, "How awful!"

"I wonder whether she was involved in the thieving as well," Gustav mused.

"Do you think that is even possible?"

"You can be sure that I'll flog the truth out of her."

"Gustav, you know my opinion on physical punishment. Shouldn't we call the police?" Margarete frantically jumped at the hope that Lena could escape while they were waiting for the police to arrive.

"We don't need any police," he growled. "I'll return her to the factory and..." He looked at Margarete and his expression softened. "I know how much you oppose physical punishment, dearest Annegret, but you'll agree that we can't let such a grave offence go unpunished. Remember who this woman is. A traitor to the Reich, an escapee and a Jew. God only knows what other crimes she's committed."

Even Margarete had to accept that an escaped prisoner couldn't simply be welcomed back without consequences, so she suggested, "Perhaps some extra shifts?"

He pursed his lips and she thought he'd laugh her suggestion off as ridiculous, but he said, "That is a very good idea, indeed. I'll see that she's returned to the premises immediately."

"Where did you even find her?"

"I told you, Oliver Gundelmann isn't trustworthy. And as I had feared, he returned last night, possibly to steal more things."

"Oh God! I hope you sent him packing?"

Gustav gloated. "Not immediately. First I followed him, hoping to find the place where he's been hiding the pilfered goods. He had the audacity to break into my office to steal the stud master's keyring."

"How atrocious!" She faked outrage, while at the same time she wondered why Gustav was lying. Oliver couldn't have stolen the keys, because she herself had given them to Dora.

"Well, I followed him to one of the sheds we never use. Still thinking he was hiding the loot there, I confronted him and made sure he'll never set foot on this property again."

"You killed him?" she shrieked. As much as she disliked Oliver, she'd never wished him harm.

"Of course not, do I look like a killer to you?"

Do I look like a killer? Margarete herself had lured a group of SS men into a trap in Paris, knowing full well they'd be blown to smithereens. Instead of an answer, she shook her head.

"Let's just say he's gone for good. But imagine my surprise when I returned to the shed with pincers to break the padlock and I found this bitch there." He yanked at Lena's jaw and she shrieked with pain.

Margarete yelped in horror. "Stop hurting her."

"I'm sorry. It's just, I'm so angry at this pair causing so much suffering to the other factory workers with their thieving." He looked genuinely seized with remorse and eased his grip on Lena.

"You think Oliver has been hiding her?" She knew it was the truth, but not for the reasons Gustav believed. If only she could help him understand that the Jews weren't the depraved creatures Hitler painted them as. That the true enemies of the German nation were the Nazis themselves.

"Definitely. And it makes complete sense. She was his insider at the factory. Together they must have stolen material worth hundreds of thousands of Reichsmark and sold it on the black market."

30

It was a wonderful day for Gustav. The one who'd almost got away stood in front of him shivering with fear. He'd make her pay, both now and later publicly. She'd soon learn what it meant to defy him, and it would be pleasurable only for him.

But first, he'd have to make a few phone calls. He locked Lena into a storage room in the basement and walked into his office with a smug grin on his face. That Jewish bitch wouldn't be the only one to learn a lesson.

First he called Lothar Katze, one of his acquaintances in the SS in the district capital Parchim, whom he knew enjoyed spectacles like public whippings.

"Gustav, I'd love to come, you know, but we're drowning in work here."

He thought quickly. If the SS didn't come, Annegret might be stubborn enough to derail his plans. "That's a shame. I'll have to find someone else to do the honors then."

"You're not doing the whipping yourself?"

"No." Gustav smiled. Lothar had tasted blood and would surely come around, which was essential for his plan to punish the Jewish bitch and stay on good terms with Annegret, while at the same time teaching her a valuable lesson she'd be grateful about for many years to come. "I want to make an example of that bitch nobody will forget."

"What's she done?"

Lothar might be more sadistic than intelligent, but Gustav still had to tread carefully. "She ran away, and managed it because the idiot Heinz decided to save on armed guards. But it didn't last long, because I found her again, hiding in an unused shed."

"Well done." Lothar seemed to think, and Gustav could literally smell the arousal in the other man. "We do need to make sure that nobody follows that example again. How would it look to have escaped prisoners populating our region?"

"Very bad. And the civilians would, wrongly, blame it on the SS, claiming you cannot keep law and order," Gustav said.

"You're right, that can't happen. I'll make time in my schedule and come. Would you mind if I bring a colleague or two?"

"The more the merrier." Not being able to whip that little Jewess to death was a hefty price to pay, but he'd get to punish her tonight. Just the two of them for as long as he wanted.

"Now that's the attitude! I do need to get some practice in, this desk job has me giddy for action. When and where?"

"Tomorrow at noon in the factory yard. As I said, bring some friends."

"I will."

Gustav put the receiver on the cradle and leaned back. His entire life had brightened in the past hours and the only sore spot was that Oliver had gotten away. He'd seen him jiggling at the shed door, and in his eagerness to find out what—or rather who—was hidden in there, he'd been thrown off Oliver's scent and the bugger had got away.

The next call he placed was to his wife. "Beate, darling. I'm so sorry but we have just received a request for a control visit in the morning and I'll have to stay late. Please don't wait for me."

"Oh." She sounded disappointed and he wondered whether she suspected about his sexual escapades. "Dinner is almost ready."

"We can warm it up tomorrow. I promise to be home early and I'll bring a bottle of wine. Then the two of us can make up for the lost time." After raping a woman he always felt invigorated and enjoyed his prim and proper wife so much more.

"We'll do that, Gustav, you really need some time to relax. You work too hard."

He decided to draw out the thrill of anticipation and eat dinner with Annegret, but to his chagrin she had retired claiming a headache. She would be in for a surprise, too.

After eating his dinner in solitude, he chatted a few minutes with Frau Mertens, and wished her a good night, before he climbed down into the basement to enjoy a special session with Lena.

Many hours later, spent but satisfied, he fastened his breeches back up, threw the barely alive woman over his shoulder and dumped her into the back of the truck. He made the detour to the factory on his way home and told the guard, "I found the escapee. Put her into the penal block for the night and arrange a public whipping at noon. Have the camp spick and span, because we'll have visitors from the SS."

"I will inform Herr Strobel, and everything will be done to your satisfaction. Anything else?"

"No, that will be all. Just keep her alive until tomorrow, will you? It would be a shame if we had to pick a replacement who's still able to work."

"No worries, boss." The guard removed Lena's limp body from the back of the truck and dragged her across the courtyard into the penal block. Gustav climbed behind the wheel and headed home, looking forward to his warm and soft mattress and an exciting next day.

In the morning he returned to the manor, giddy with anticipation. He found Annegret in the parlor with the seamstress. What a nice surprise to finally find her attending to the tasks that should occupy a lady. Doing whatever she was with the curtains in the manor would keep her busy and off his heels. But first, he'd teach her a lesson she'd never forgot. If that got her running to Berlin, even better. He surely wouldn't miss her.

"Dearest Annegret, it's refreshing to see you so happy," he greeted her.

"Good morning, Gustav." She looked up. "Have you delivered the prisoner safely back to the factory?"

"I did. Don't worry about her, she's still alive." He chuckled at her horrified mien and added in a more serious tone, "I told the guard to put her in solitary confinement for the time being, but not to lay a finger on her."

"That's good." She seemed genuinely relieved and he wondered what exactly she found in those abhorrent creatures. "I have good news. Do you have a minute?"

"Not very long, but yes." He hoped she wouldn't want to ask his opinion about patterns for the new curtains or any such details.

"That will be all, thank you. Pass by Frau Mertens and she'll pay you," Annegret told the seamstress, before she addressed Gustav again. "You'll be so pleased! I found the perfect solution to the blanket problem."

Which blanket problem? He didn't remember anything of that sort. Fortunately she didn't notice and blabbed on, "Look at what the seamstress did! All these blankets made from the curtains in the stud master's house. And I already gave her more curtains from the rooms in the left wing that we never use. Isn't that fantastic?"

"What do you need all these blankets for?"

"Gustav! Have you forgotten? We talked about sourcing blankets for the factory workers and since there's no cloth to be bought..."

His jaw dropped to the floor. The woman had turned completely insane. She sacrificed perfectly fine curtains at the manor to make blankets for... deplorables? It was high time to rein her in, or she'd start selling the silverware to buy fur coats for them as well. He forced a pleased expression on his face. "That is indeed good news. Such an ingenious idea!"

"Right? I knew you'd be happy."

Enraged might be a better word to describe the emotion forcefully rushing through his veins. Gustav was a master at subterfuge, but nevertheless it got increasingly difficult to pretend liking her. "I'm so proud of you. And you know what? We'll drive down to the factory right away and hand out the blankets."

"You think so?" she wavered. "I thought... maybe we should wait until we had more, because with only three dozen, how will we distribute them between over five hundred workers?"

"We could make a raffle out of it? Or perhaps reward it to those producing the highest quota for a week?" His imagination ran wild. There were endless possibilities to humiliate and torment the inmates, who'd do about anything just to get one of the coveted blankets.

"Hmm... I don't know."

"We can talk about this on the way, my dear. Let me call Nils to load the blankets into the truck meanwhile. I'll meet you at eleven thirty by the car." He left without giving her the opportunity for further objections, since he had other things to prepare.

Exactly at eleven thirty he walked to the truck humming a tune. Not even the blankets on the load bed put a damper on his mood. After today, Annegret would never set foot in the factory again, and he could up the game.

31

Margarete was looking forward to giving the workers the first batch of blankets, although she would have liked to wait until they had more. But maybe Gustav was right, just because they could not help everyone at once, wasn't a reason to hold back until they could.

After what Lena had told her about the conditions in the camp, a blanket might make the difference between life and death for one person. It was inexcusable to wait.

Gustav was such a good man, she'd have to prepare some kind of gift for him. The one drop of bitterness was Lena's recapture and his unnecessary cruelty toward her. But didn't she have to cut him some slack? Even the kindest man would be enraged when confronted with an escaped prisoner whose race he considered the source of all evil.

She'd have to work on sidestepping his indoctrination and make him see that even if he believed the Jews to be his nemesis, they still deserved to be treated like humans. Wilhelm came to her mind. He, too, had been too obstinate to recant the Nazi ideology, but at least he'd accepted that exterminating the Jews was wrong.

Margarete planned to look for Lena at the factory and make sure she was all right. Lena and Uncle Ernst. She might not be able to get him out, but she could surely hold a protecting hand over him. Perhaps even find him a less strenuous work detail?

As they arrived at the factory, the big yard was bursting at the seams with people, lined up in orderly rank and file.

"What's going on?" she asked.

"Must be a roll-call," Gustav said. "Although quite unusual at this time of day."

"Did you tell Herr Strobel that we were coming?"

"I did, but I never imagined he'd arrange a roll-call for us, since that disturbs the production process. There must be something else going on."

"I guess, we'll soon find out." Margarete had a queasy feeling in her stomach.

The sensation intensified when five men in black SS uniforms approached their truck, even before she'd stepped out. One of them opened the door for her and helped her out. "Unterscharführer Katze. And you must be Fräulein Annegret. It's a pleasure to finally meet you, albeit under less than ideal circumstances."

"Herr Unterscharführer, the pleasure is mine. But what brings you here?"

"You don't know?" He cast an inquiring glance toward Gustav.

"Fräulein Annegret rarely concerns herself with the factory, since she's so busy attending to the manor and the household staff," Gustav explained.

And once again, he'd put her in the corner the Nazi ideology had reserved for all women.

"Then we'd better make it good," Katze chuckled jovially. "Come on and let the circus start."

Circus? As in prisoners condemned to be mauled to death by wild animals in Ancient Rome? Margarete's vision swam with dizziness, as she forced herself to follow Katze to the other side of the yard. When she looked up, she saw a temporary stage and a person strung up by her wrists between two poles.

"What's this?" she shrieked.

"The recaptured escapee," Katze said.

Lena. God no! "What are you doing to her?"

That insufferable man grinned like a cat who'd just killed a mouse. "Punishing her, of course."

Margarete somehow managed a nod. As they reached the front row, she turned to Gustav and whispered, "You have to stop this! I thought we agreed..."

"I'm so sorry, but I had no idea. Heinz Strobel must have told them and they've come to make an example of her."

"But can't you do anything?" She asked the question, despite knowing better. There was nothing either of them, both civilians, could do against a bunch of SS men. Not even Annegret Huber, owner of the factory and daughter of the late Standartenführer Wolfgang Huber had a say in this. The SS came to her house, did what they wanted and all she could do was stand by and watch.

Gustav shook his head. "My heart is bleeding as much as yours, but nobody can defy the SS."

With wobbly knees she let him guide her to a chair in the first row, near enough to see the fresh bruises and cuts on Lena's body and the horror in her downcast eyes when Katze took the coiled bullwhip into his hand.

Margarete sat stone-faced through the ordeal, flinching at every whiplash hurtled down on Lena. Never in her life had she felt more helpless than now. With all the money and power she had inherited, and she still could only watch.

When it was finally over, the guard produced a knife and cut the cords holding Lena up. She crumpled to the ground, her eyes open, but the blankness in them a sure sign she'd given up the fight for her life. Her heart might still be beating, but it was just a matter of time until the light in her went out.

Margarete was close to vomiting and for once she was glad that Gustav dismissed her, because the men had business to do. She put on a neutral mien until the moment she reached the truck that was parked next to the administration building.

Nils had been waiting by the vehicle and when he saw her, his face turned into a grimace of sorrow. "You must not let it get to you, there's nothing you could have done."

She knew it was true, but she still was overwhelmed not only with disgust at the SS men and sympathy for Lena, but also with shame and guilt over her inaction. What good was her charade if she couldn't even save one woman from being whipped to death? Another wave of nausea washed over her and she said, "Wait a moment," and rushed into the administration building, where she found the toilet and vomited until there was only bile coming up.

With shaky legs she returned to the hallway, slightly disconcerted. She didn't remember where she'd come from and hesitated for a moment, before turning to her right. As she exited through the door, she realized it had been the wrong way, because instead of the yard with the truck, she stood in front of a bunch of trees.

Still shaking she leaned against the wall and closed her eyes, fighting another wave of nausea, when she heard her name.

"Gretchen," a soft voice said.

She knew who it was, even before she opened her eyes. For a second she even considered keeping them closed, because she hated to look at what Uncle Ernst had become. But then she took a deep breath and scanned the surroundings, before she said, "Uncle Ernst."

"My sweet child."

Frantically she looked around, fearing a whip-swinging SS man to jump forward and make Uncle Ernst the next victim of his bloodthirst.

"It's alright. I was on my way to the latrine." His face contorted painfully as if he experienced stomach cramps.

At a loss for words, she wrapped her arms around him, not caring that he was infested with lice and whatnot. "We believed you dead. Aunt Heidi and I."

His eyes lit up. "My sweet Heidi is alive?"

"Yes, she is. She had to move into another borough in Leipzig and lives in a tiny one-room apartment, but she's fine."

"Thank God! I was so worried about her." It was typical for her uncle to worry about his wife, even when he was the one who'd been deported and was toiling in this horrible place. "But what about you? Why are you here? Posing as a Nazi?"

Hers was a long story, too long to tell in passing, while frantically scanning the area for guards to discover them. "It was my only chance to survive. When a bomb hit the house of my employers and everyone perished, I took on the identity of their daughter and fled Berlin with her papers. Aunt Heidi took me in." Again his eyes shimmered with love at the mention of his wife. "But it wasn't safe for either of us, so I decided to leave Leipzig." She pondered how much to tell him right now. "When Annegret Huber's—that's my new name, by the way—when her brothers died too, she—or better I—inherited the family fortune and I've come here to find a way to do good with all that money."

"That is a very laudable thing to do, my child." He put a skeletal hand on her arm, and she burst into tears.

"I couldn't help Lena. I'm so sorry. I've been hiding her, but then the fumigator came, and Oliver, oh no Oliver, I suspected him, but he hid her. And then when Gustav fired him, he found her and I begged him not to beat her, but the SS came and arranged for this horrible spectacle. And now I've found you and I'm afraid the same will happen to you..."

"Shush, Gretchen." His voice had a soothing effect, and she was transported back into her childhood. At one time she'd scratched her knee falling from a swing and screamed inconsolably, but when Uncle Ernst had put her on his lap, blown on her knee and recited the nursery rhyme, *Holy, Holy blessing, three days of rain, three days of snow, then it doesn't hurt anymore*, the pain had almost instantly ceased and she'd hopped off his knee to jump on the swing again.

"I promise I'll do everything to keep you safe. I'll find a way to get you out of here."

He shook his head with the big brown eyes sunken deep into the shaven skull. "Just because I'm your uncle doesn't mean I'm worth more than anyone else in this factory. Without the help and care of my fellow inmates, I would not be alive today. They deserve your effort as much as I do."

Ashamed by his generosity she nodded. "I already pinned lists with new rules all over the place."

He looked sad. "Herr Strobel took them down the minute you left."

Hot rage coursed through her veins. She had to get a word with Gustav, and urge him to fire Strobel. Although, Gustav had enjoyed the horrid spectacle earlier a bit too much for her liking and she wondered if beneath his charming exterior there might be a dark side to him. His lie about Oliver stealing the keyring came to mind and she decided to keep an eye on him.

"I'll fire Strobel. All of the guards, I'll fire everyone who makes your life so miserable."

"You can't do that. You need to tread carefully."

She shook her head, although she knew he was right. What use would it be if she fired everyone and then the SS came to run the factory themselves? Or worse, arrest her for being a traitor who cared about Jews. "I'll find a way. I swear. But you, you must stay strong until I can get you out of here."

"Don't endanger yourself by helping me escape. But do everything you can to make life more bearable for all of us. You must not have favorites, but try to keep everyone safe."

Her heart melted. "I will, Uncle Ernst, I will. And I'll let Heidi know that you are alive. She'll be over the moon with joy."

"It is my dearest wish to see my Heidi again. Thinking of her was the only thing that kept me fighting to stay alive."

The sound of footsteps caused them both to start and Margarete's soul wept at the sight of the abject fear entering her uncle's eyes.

"I should go," he whispered and shuffled toward the latrines.

Margarete was left behind ashamed, guilty and heartbroken. She hadn't been able to save Lena, but as God was her witness, she would save her uncle, whether he wanted it or not. Obviously, she'd also help the other workers, but he was her first priority.

A person rounded the corner and said, "Here you are, Fräulein Annegret, I was getting worried about you."

She looked up and saw Nils. "I'm sorry, I got lost and couldn't find the proper exit."

"You sure you're alright? You look as if you've seen a ghost."

"Everything is fine," she lied. "Please, just take me back to the manor." As much as she wanted to sob, Annegret Huber would not cry over the plight of a mere Jew.

At the manor, she slid from the truck even before Nils could rush around and open the door for her. She didn't want to see or talk to anyone for the rest of the day, heck, for the rest of her life.

In her room she collapsed on the bed, tears streaming down her face and wetting the quilt. Her soul had been shredded to ribbons, much in the same way Lena's skin had been torn. And she couldn't even return to the factory and see if there was anything she could do for the injured woman, not even to organize a proper burial, because she had to protect her own cover at all costs.

"To hell with my cover! To hell with my undeserving life! What is my existence worth if I'm not a shred better than the Nazis themselves?" She cried some more over the fact that she'd just witnessed a woman being whipped to death and had done nothing to stop it. Lena's blood was as much on her hands as on Unterscharführer Katze's. Plain and simple.

It was already dark outside when she heard a knock on the door. "Come in."

Dora brought a bowl of steaming soup on a tray. "Fräulein Annegret. Frau Mertens sent me up to look after you, since Gustav said you're not feeling well."

"I'm not." Margarete sat up and used her hands to wipe her face dry.

"They told us what happened at the factory. I'm so sorry." She put the tray on the bedside table.

"Is she... did she...?" There was a glimmer of hope that against all odds Lena might have survived.

But Dora shook her head. "She died. The men were boasting about it over lunch."

"Gustav invited them up here?"

"Of course he did, he always does."

A sick feeling crept down Margarete's spine. "This kind of thing has happened before?"

Dora nodded.

"And Gustav never does anything?"

Dora looked confused. "I don't understand. As far as I know he usually does the whipping himself."

"I don't believe you!"

The maid stared at her aghast. "Please, Fräulein Annegret, don't be mad at me, but Herr Fischer is not the kind and caring man he makes you believe he is. Everyone around here lives in fear of him, especially the women."

Margarete stared at her blankly. "Would you please leave me alone?"

As soon as Dora was gone, she threw a pillow at the wall and screamed in frustration. She couldn't believe that she'd been so gullible. That Gustav had deceived her in such a heinous way. That she'd actually helped him in his wiles. No, it just couldn't be true! Gustav couldn't be the cruel sadist Dora painted him as. It was impossible.

She let the soup go cold and sobbed herself to sleep. Everything that had happened today was simply too much to bear and her brain refused to think clearly.

At the crack of dawn she woke, feeling as if she'd been run over by a truck. She climbed from the bed and walked to the window, falling into her favorite armchair overlooking the gardens and the entrance to Gut Plaun.

Hour after hour she sat there and stared out into the approaching day. The employees arrived at the manor for work or their breakfast break and the yard below filled with life. The commotion died down after everyone received coffee and a piece of bread from Frau Mertens and returned to work. After a while the yard lay empty as before with not a soul in sight. Wary to go downstairs and meet Frau Mertens, or any living soul for that matter, Margarete stayed cuddled in her armchair, watching the clouds chase each other across the sky.

A black car with a trailer drove into the yard and a man she'd never seen before stepped out. Gustav rushed out to greet him and the two of them walked around the corner, out of her sight. It was unusual, because Gustav's office lay in the other direction. Margarete wondered where they were going, since the east wing wasn't used for anything. When the two men didn't return, she decided to investigate. Putting on her coat and shawl, she slipped down the back stairs and around the corner.

There was a door ajar she hadn't noticed before. It led into the basement, where she knew Frau Mertens stored the provisions, although she'd never been down there. Voices wafted over and she pressed herself against the brick wall like a thief.

One of the voices was Gustav's, but she couldn't understand what he was saying. She crept nearer to where the sounds came from, until she froze in place, when the other man said, "How many hundredweights do you have?"

"Right now twenty, but we receive supplies for the factory every week. If you need more, I can sell you all you want come Monday." Gustav's voice filled the dark hallway.

"Good. I need fifty."

"It'll be done. Half of the payment now and half on delivery."

Margarete pushed her fist into her mouth and bit down hard on her knuckles to prevent herself from making a scandalized sound.

"And nobody will notice?" the other man asked.

Gustav gave a derisive snort that didn't match up to the image she had of him. "Even if the prisoners complained, who would listen to them?"

"And the new owner, Fräulein Annegret? I heard she's been on a quest for better working conditions."

"After yesterday's whipping I doubt she'll ever set foot in the factory again. I thought she'd puke up right there for everyone to see. Considering her reputation I'd pegged her as someone made of harder wood."

"Women. Hitler is right to keep them in the kitchen."

Margarete had heard enough and retreated out of the basement. She didn't linger outside and raced up the back staircase to her suite, where she pounded her fists against the wall. "I'm such an utter and complete idiot!"

32

Oliver was in the city of Schwerin, about a two-hour train ride from Plau am See, queuing at the labor office. So far he'd only been given temporary work, because without a reference from his past employer, things were slow and tedious. When he stepped out of the building with a list of potential employers in his hands, he bumped into a small person.

"Pardon," he said, even before he looked down and stared into Annegret's hazel eyes.

"Oliver, please can I talk to you?"

Rage spiked up in him. It was her fault he'd had to leave his beloved horses and look for a random job as a factory worker. "For all that is holy! Haven't you done enough damage? Leave me in peace!"

"I came to apologize."

Oliver groused at her statement. "You? Apologize? I didn't think you knew how."

"Oliver, please, I am so very sorry. I was completely wrong, I should never have doubted you. Dora tried to tell me, but I wouldn't listen."

At the mention of Dora's name his heart did a happy dance, but the next second he felt betrayed. How dare she tell Annegret where to find him? "Not listening and making others suffer are two of your biggest talents."

Annegret recoiled and her face took on a hurt expression. "I guess I deserved that. But, please, can you at least hear me out? I have an offer for you."

"An equally enticing offer as when you stole blind Albert's stick and then let me take the blame for it?"

The shock on her face was worth a million marks. If he didn't know better he'd have sworn she had no idea what he was talking about.

"No, not like that. Look, it was all my fault..." She paused and ran a hand through her hair.

"A fault confessed is half redressed."

"The real thief was Gustav. I caught him red-handed and will need to fire him—"

"Why are you even telling me this? You already had *me* fired, remember?"

"I already said I'm sorry. Would you find it in your heart to forgive me?"

"Forgive you?" he hissed. Several passersby had stopped at a safe distance and eyed the two of them suspiciously. He groaned. Making a spectacle of himself wouldn't help to find a job. "Let's go someplace else."

Annegret gave him a confused glance, but as soon as she noticed the audience eagerly watching them, she nodded. "I'll follow you."

They walked several minutes until they reached a park and settled on one of the wooden benches. The walk gave him time to work through his anger and he said, in a much more conciliatory tone, "What is your offer?"

"When I fire Gustav, I'll need someone to replace him. An honest man I can trust. I want you to become the estate manager."

"Me?" He was nonplussed. "Since when do you trust me?"

"Since I realized what an idiot I was. Gustav charmed me with his friendly words, and I never once doubted what he said. But you, you were hostile from the moment I first met you." She slapped a hand across her mouth. "I mean when I returned."

"And you are really wondering why? After all you did to me? The beating your father gave me for the trick you played on Albert wasn't the first one, if you care to remember."

"I am so very sorry. I was a selfish girl. But I have changed, it won't happen again."

"Tell me one reason why I should believe you?"

She stared at him for quite some time and he could tell she was struggling with her answer. "Because I'm not who you think I am."

He shook his head, not buying that flimsy excuse for one minute. "Oh, I know exactly who you are. A false snake only interested in her own benefit."

Annegret nodded, the inner turmoil still visible in her eyes. "I guess I deserve that, although not in the way you believe."

The woman was insufferable. What did she know about him and his beliefs? He stood up and walked away, but she called out to him, "Wait. I'm not Annegret."

He turned on his heels, staring at the madwoman in front of him. If this was another of her vicious tricks... "I don't believe you."

"It's true. Nobody ever knew, except for Wilhelm—"

"How very convenient that he's dead," he said it in a derisive tone, but a doubt was sown in his heart. He'd often thought that she had changed a lot, had even half-jokingly told Dora that she could be a mole for the Gestapo. It could be. All of this could be an elaborate trap. He didn't know what to believe anymore.

"... and Lena."

"Well, then I'll ask her, although I assume she'd swear you're her grandmother if it would save her life."

"I meant, she's dead, too. Gustav found her." Her voice croaked.

His legs became leaden, as if his entire being turned into cold, unfeeling steel. He knew what the factory management did with escaped prisoners, but still asked the question, "What happened?"

"A public whipping. Believe me, it was the most atrocious

thing I've witnessed in all of my life..." She paused, blinking vigorously. When she regained her composure, she continued, "Never in my life did I expect any of the things that happened in the past year. And, you may not understand it, but I believe there's a reason I inherited this estate. When I found Lena I knew that this was my calling, to help those who cannot help themselves."

His jaw dropped to the floor. Annegret didn't have a kind bone in her body and he began to suspect that maybe her scandalous confession might actually be true. "You're positively crazy, you know that?"

"Perhaps."

"First you tell me you're not Annegret, and now you are planning to defy the Nazis by helping the Jews? Who the hell are you? Wait, no, don't tell me. I don't even want to hear."

"My name is Margarete Rosenbaum and I'm a Jew."

His jaw dropped to the floor as the possibility that she was speaking the truth slowly dawned on him. "Why are you even telling me this? Me, of all people? The boy you tormented years ago. The man you fired unjustly weeks ago. The man who harbors so much aversion for you. Why me?"

"I already told you: I want you to come back and take Gustav's position. And for that I need you to trust me. Since you dislike Annegret so much, perhaps you can find it in yourself to work together with her impostor? I need a good man to oversee the estate and the factory, to implement the rules and improvements I make and who won't stab me into the back the moment I turn around."

He was at a loss for words. After a while he shook his head. "You know, I could just go to the local Gestapo and rat you out. Tell them you are a Jew."

For a split-second fear crossed her eyes, but then she answered in a haughty tone, "Go ahead, if you wish. I'll deny every word you say, and whom do you think they will believe, me or the stud master I had to fire for stealing from the Reich?"

Strange as it was, relief flooded his system, because this was the Annegret he knew and hated. "Looks like even if you aren't her, you aren't very different to her. Still willing to walk over bodies to get what you want."

She flinched at his words and her face took on a pensive expression. "I guess you're right. I have become a lot like her during the past year. It was hard learning, but now I won't shy back from tough measures to achieve what I want. The difference between her and me are the things we pursue. I'm determined to do my bit for justice by helping those who would otherwise die. But I cannot do it alone, I need people with a good heart to help me."

"And I have a good heart?" He couldn't wrap his head around her revelations. It was so far-fetched, although... "You don't have an injured back. You can't ride a horse."

"Yes. I was deathly afraid, because it would take only one look for someone to find out."

"And that's why you didn't remember the competition you won." He ran a hand through his hair. "Are you actually telling me the truth?"

"I am."

"Does Dora know?"

"No. She never knew Annegret, so she can't compare. But she surprised me when hiding Lena, so she knows that I'm not the Nazi I pretend to be."

He shook his head. "I can't believe it. How did you even pull it off, under everyone's nose?"

"With luck, acting, and my talent for imitating her voice."

"I don't know what to say."

"Say you'll work for me, please? You took on a great risk to hide Lena, which makes me think you'd be the perfect person to supervise the factory and find a replacement for this awful Heinz Strobel."

"So you're serious about firing Gustav?" He still couldn't quite believe the change of tides.

"Yes. And I don't just want to fire him, I want him behind bars for the rest of his life, so he can never hurt another human being."

"Hmm..." Oliver was wracking his mind. "He has influential friends around here... and he's very vindictive. I'll have to think of a plan. We need to have nailed down proof before we denounce him."

"You said, 'we'. Does that mean you're accepting my job offer?"

"It means I'll think about it. I'll have to talk to Dora first."

"She'll be delighted. She basically begged me to take you back, swearing by God and everything that's holy that you aren't a thief."

"I still need to talk to her," he said. "And tell her the truth."

Annegret—because in his head she still was Annegret—looked shocked. "Is that really necessary? She'd be much safer if she knew nothing."

"I would hate to lie to her, but maybe you're right. I'll have to think about it." He shook his head, since it started to hurt from all the new information.

"Good. Nils is waiting with the car to drive me back home, there's room for another person."

He groaned. The new and improved version of Annegret had thought of everything.

During the drive back to Gut Plaun his head was spinning. He wasn't sure whether he wanted to take over running the estate, including the factory. He'd be forced to deal with the SS on a regular basis and that alone was reason enough to reject her offer. Besides, he'd much rather work with his beloved horses.

Annegret had arranged one of the guest rooms for him and later that night Dora came and stayed with him. As he gazed at her lovely face, he decided not to tell her about her mistress' true identity, at least for now. He didn't want to implicate her, if—God forbid—someone found out.

"I missed you so much," Dora said, after their very passionate lovemaking.

Oliver chuckled. "I wouldn't have guessed."

"Will you accept Fräulein Annegret's offer?"

"Why are you so eager for me to work for her?"

"Because we could be together." She batted her long eyelashes at him.

Kissing her nose, he said, "While that is a very enticing reason, it's not enough to make up my mind."

"I know, you don't trust her, but believe me, she is the kindest person I've ever met. Nothing at all like how you and others from her past have painted her. I believe the loss of her family has taught her a few things. And..." she looked expectantly at him "...she actually helped me to fill in some forms and apply for German naturalization."

"How so?"

"It seems there's some kind of law and when I told her that my maternal great-grandmother came from Germany, she phoned this Gestapo friend of hers and he said I only need a birth certificate of my great-grandmother and he'll see that my naturalization request will be granted."

"This is not a good time for jokes," he said.

"I'm dead serious."

He rolled her on top of him, losing himself in the ponds of her dark eyes. "You know what that means?"

"That Frau Mertens can't have me deported for uncouth behavior?"

He grinned at her. "That, and that we can finally get married, future Mrs. Gundelmann."

"I don't remember saying yes," she said with a mischievous grin and squealed when he tickled her.

"Cheeky girl. Well then, I'll formally ask: Do you want to become my wife?"

"With all my heart."

"I love you, my sweetheart," he said and pressed a hot kiss on her mouth that felt completely different now that she was his fiancée.

33

Gustav rubbed his hands. Everything was falling into place. Lothar Katze and his colleagues had been enthusiastic about the public whipping and had already insinuated that they would love to visit again, no doubt with their arms full of gifts for Gustav and Heinz. And he'd found a new customer for the food that would otherwise be wasted on the prisoners.

Since the whipping, Annegret had mostly stayed in her rooms, except for a shopping trip to Schwerin, and had even dropped the ineffable topic of delivering blankets to the prisoners, which was another outrageous waste of material, since they would do so much more good being sold to valuable Germans than given to useless Jews and other deplorables.

Loathe to give her any ideas, he kept his mouth shut and didn't enquire about the whereabouts of the blankets, that seemed to have vanished. If Oliver was still here, he'd frame him for it, but thank God, that insufferable man was gone for good. He might be a talented stud master, but his incorruptible attitude was beyond annoying.

The only drop of bitterness was that he still hadn't been able to make his move on that busty maid, who seemed to always be in Annegret's presence. Perhaps it was time to talk to Frau Mertens that a change was in order, and they needed a second maid, because Annegret required so much work. He licked his lips, already envisioning himself naked with two buxom girls at his beck and call.

The ringing of the phone interrupted his thoughts. Lothar Katze was on the other end. "What a wonderful surprise. Is there anything I can do for you?"

"Actually, yes." Katze didn't sound jovial in the least. "We've found some irregularities with the supplies to the factory."

Hot shivers ran down Gustav's spine. "I must have forgotten to tell you. We found the thief about two weeks ago. It was the stud master, Oliver Gundelmann."

"I heard. You'll need to come to our office. It was an act of willful default not to inform the authorities and let the traitor go unpunished."

"I felt sorry for the bloke, thought he'd learned his lesson." Gustav's mind whirled trying to come up with a believable excuse. If Oliver had been found by the SS and had talked, Gustav would be in hot water. Even if they didn't believe a word Oliver said, they'd come here and investigate and then they'd find out about the missing copper sheets.

Katze guffawed. "Must be the first time in your life you're showing sympathy for anyone but yourself. Get to my office right now and we'll sort this out."

Cold sweat was pouring down Gustav's neck and forehead. He grabbed a handkerchief to wipe it off. For an instant he considered running away, which was an entirely inappropriate reaction, stupid even. Only guilty people fled. And he was innocent. He'd prove it to them. He'd make a few amends to the books and it would become clear even to the blindest eye that Heinz was the culprit, in cahoots with Oliver. Gustav himself might be charged with being too lenient on the traitors, but he'd repent and subject them to the harshest punishment he could think of—not the easy way out he'd given that Jewish whore who must have welcomed death by the time he was done with her.

He took his coat and hat from the hook by the door and stepped out into the hallway, all but bumping into Annegret. Of all cursed times, now she had to seek him out. Why couldn't she stay in her suite a bit longer? Maybe forever?

"Dearest Annegret, I gather you're feeling better?"

"I was never unwell." She gazed at him with cold eyes, which was a perturbing change in behavior. But he had no time to dwell on this little detail, since he had bigger problems to attend to.

"That is good to hear. You'll have to excuse me though, I need to travel to Parchim, the SS wants my statement on Oliver Gundelmann's crimes."

"You sure they don't suspect anyone else?" Her tone sent chills right through his bones.

"Whyever would they do that? The culprit has been found. In fact," he lowered his voice to a whisper, "they scolded me for having been too lenient with him." He had an idea. "I told them it was your wish, since you're so kind-hearted and couldn't bear the thought of him spending the rest of his life in a concentration camp."

She raised an eyebrow. "That much is true. He doesn't deserve to be sent to a camp for what he did. By the way, Unterscharführer Katze called me, too."

"What did he want?" Gustav's eyes almost popped out of his head.

"Nothing much. My take on things. I told them I didn't know anything, since you're the one to manage estate and factory." He relaxed at her words, because if she backed up what he said, there was no chance in hell they'd believe Oliver, if they had even talked to him.

"That is nice to know, my dearest Annegret."

"I'm glad to help, since all I want is for the true culprit to receive the punishment he deserves. For the stealing and all the other malicious things he has done. I hope you have a good time with the SS."

Did he just imagine it, or was her smile malicious? Either way it sent more chills through his bones. For the first time since Annegret had arrived at Gut Plaun he felt that she was living up to her reputation as a scheming, perfidious manipulator and he didn't like it one bit.

"Have a nice day. I don't think I'll return today. If anything urgent comes up, Frau Mertens or the new stud master should be able to deal with it."

"I'm sure they will." She turned on her heel and walked away, a disconcerting swing in her step.

He shrugged the feeling off and walked outside to the truck. All the way to Parchim, he wondered how much Katze really knew.

Deep in the woods, a military vehicle came toward him and waved him down. Gustav stopped to find out what they wanted, and the last thing he saw before a truncheon slammed down on his head was the fat face of Katze, with the satisfied grin of a cat who'd found a mouse for its cruel play.

34

Margarete waited on tenterhooks. She and Oliver had visited Unterscharführer Katze and given him evidence about Gustav's theft, and now she waited for the SS to arrest him, but nothing happened.

This morning Gustav's wife had called to excuse him from work, since he had come down with the flu. It was a peculiar situation, to say the least, because she couldn't well fire him when he wasn't even there, and she couldn't employ Oliver either without the signature of the estate manager.

So, there was nothing she could do but wait and see. Meanwhile, she located Nils, who was repairing something or the other in the tool shed.

"Nils, would you have a minute, please?"

"Yes, Fräulein Annegret." He put down a set of huge pliers and rubbed his oil-smeared hands with a rag. "What do you need?"

"I was wondering..." She paused. Nils was a good man, but she wasn't entirely sure where his loyalties lay. It was best not to make him privy to anything subversive. "When I last went down to the factory, we were supposed to deliver blankets to the workers there, but totally forgot about it, because the SS..." By now she knew Gustav had orchestrated the whipping and used the SS as cover to hide behind. The sleazy Unterscharführer Katze had taken great pleasure in telling her how much he'd enjoyed Gustav's invitation and the honor to wield the whip himself. Poor man, he'd have to relinquish these joys from now on—at least in her factory.

"Herr Fischer wanted to sell them, so I stacked them in the storage room until further notice. I can get them anytime."

Damn Gustav! She scolded herself for falling into his honey trap and believing he was a good person, when all this time he'd worked against the best interests of the workers and for his own financial benefit. She could slap herself for being a puppet helping him in his sinister ways. But that had ended the moment she'd discovered his deceit and from now on she would call the shots, not trusting anyone, except Oliver, of course.

She'd handed him her life on a silver tray when she'd told him about her true identity. But it had been her only chance to convince him that Annegret wasn't the deplorable girl he'd known.

Despite the grave danger of having a confidant, it had taken a huge burden from her shoulders. She was no longer alone and in danger of losing herself. Even if she would never talk to Oliver about her doubts and fears, the mere knowledge that she could, was enough to keep her sane.

"Fräulein Annegret?" Nils asked. "Do you want me to get the blankets now?"

She smiled. "That would be a great idea. The seamstress is about to deliver another load of two hundred and I'd like to distribute them to the factory workers as soon as possible."

Nils nodded. "I'll get everything done." He seemed to think for a moment. "Won't Herr Fischer need them for his client?"

"He's sold them already?"

Nils ducked his head. "That I wouldn't know. I'm just the handyman and do what I'm told."

"Then there's nothing to worry about. Have everything ready after lunch. Herr Fischer has called in sick, but before that we agreed that we profit more by giving the blankets to the workers." Nils might be the handyman, but she felt compelled to give him an explanation, hoping he'd repeat it to anyone who wanted to hear. Having a financial benefit from the good she did was a reason not even the SS could easily brush off.

She returned to her suite, happy that she'd located the missing blankets and furious at Gustav for wanting to sell them. He really hadn't cared a jot about the well-being of the prisoners. But she was even more furious at herself and how she could have been so dumb to be duped by his friendly façade.

Brushing off all unpleasant thoughts, she settled at her writing desk and took out a postcard she had bought in Schwerin when she'd gone to find Oliver. Dora had agreed to deliver it to the post office on her day off.

She'd written and re-written the text a thousand times in her mind. She and Heidi had agreed on names they would use to write to each other, and Marika meant everything was fine. Dieter was Uncle Ernst's second name, and Margarete hoped, her aunt would be able to decipher the hidden meaning in the message.

Dearest Heidi,

We spent a lovely weekend in this wonderful town. Dieter is still sickly, but recovering well due to the fresh air so near to the sea. Both of us hope to find you in good health and are looking forward to a visit when circumstances permit.

Your friend Marika.

Two days later, a black military vehicle raced into the courtyard, sending everyone scurrying for safety. Three men in black SS uniforms jumped out and stomped up the stairs.

Margarete heard their arrival long before Frau Mertens led them into the parlor. "What can I do for you, *meine Herren*?"

"Are you Annegret Huber?"

"Yes."

"Gustav Fischer is your estate manager?" She didn't know any of the men and wondered if this was a case of the right hand not knowing what the left hand was doing.

"He is, but his wife called in earlier this week to advise us that he has fallen ill with a cold."

"You better start telling us the truth."

Margarete was way past letting a hot-headed, low-ranking SS man intimidate her. "I know nothing about his whereabouts. In fact, my stud master, Herr Gundelmann, and I went all the way to Parchim to denounce him for stealing from the Reich. I believe Unterscharführer Katze is investigating the case. Would you care for refreshment, while I phone him, since I'm not privy to details? I'm sure he can answer all the questions you might have."

The man who'd still not introduced himself, gave a curt nod and strode over to the dinner table to seat himself. It was an exceptionally rude thing to do, but she decided it wasn't worth it to complain.

Once Frau Mertens had delivered coffee and buns to the men, their leader seemed more pliable and said, "There's no need to phone Katze's office. Your estate manager is dead."

"Dead?"

"Executed it seems. In the most gruesome manner."

"How awful." Margarete was genuinely shaken, but she drew herself together and said, "Forgive my sympathy for him. I still grapple to comprehend that my father's long-term estate manager was a thief and traitor to the Reich. I'm sure he deserved what he got, although I would have preferred it if he'd been sent to a camp to repent for his sins. It is never a good idea to take matters into one's own hands when the authorities are so much better equipped for momentous decisions than us normal folks."

The SS man shot her an appreciative glance. "Well said. Would you like to receive his corpse?"

She shook her head. "Perhaps his wife would." Beate had always been kind to her, so she didn't want to cause her additional grief and added, "Although when she finds out what her husband has done, I'm sure she'll be glad to be rid of him."

"Then, there's nothing more for us to do here. Thank you for your hospitality. Unterscharführer Katze will inform you about the outcome." He suddenly seemed to be in a hurry.

"Here at Gut Plaun we're always at the service of the Reich," she said and accompanied them to their vehicle, sighing with relief when they drove out through the gate.

She hadn't wanted Gustav to die, had she? She hadn't realized that she'd become so bloodthirsty, but there wasn't an ounce of remorse in her soul for his premature death. Not after watching what he'd done to Lena. She was glad he was gone for good and she was free to install Oliver as the new estate manager, and hire a trustworthy man to oversee the factory.

Finally, she could put her wealth, albeit not truly hers, to good use and make a difference in the lives of the women and men who found their way to the assembly floor of her factory. She'd make sure they were fed and clothed properly, and treated fairly. And maybe she'd somehow make up for her failures over time.

She knew she had to stay in the shadows though, because she was too afraid to give away herself if she visited her fellow Jews on a regular basis. She especially couldn't face Uncle Ernst again, for so many reasons. How could she casually greet him, when her heart yearned to wrap her arms around his thin body and whisper good news about Aunt Heidi into his ear?

No, it was best for everyone involved that the two of them didn't meet again, for as long as Hitler was in power. But she'd insist Oliver have him transferred to the factory kitchen, because he was such a frail, old man.

35

Directly after the news of Gustav's death had broken, Oliver had been announced as the new estate manager, and his first act had been to dismiss the new stud master, an inept man who couldn't tell a horse's head from its rear, and promote Piet, an able and hard-working man, to the position. Then Oliver had moved back into his old house.

Since he and Dora were now officially engaged, Frau Mertens turned a blind eye when Dora stayed longer at his place than good morals required.

"Do you think I should feel guilty?" Oliver asked Dora as they lay together in his bed.

"Whatever for?" She snuggled up against him.

"So many things..." He hadn't been able to shake the feeling that he had caused Gustav's death by letting the right people know about his betrayal. Maybe he'd overdone it a bit... or maybe not. After what Annegret had told him about Lena's public whipping and subsequent death, Gustav probably deserved what had been done to him.

"You shouldn't feel guilty." Dora stroked his arm.

"But I am... you know, being at the front and shooting other men was bad enough, but this? It was never my intention that they'd kill him."

"It's a good thing he's dead," she said with such a fervor that he rose up on his elbows and scrutinized her face. He'd never seen his sweet and soft Dora so agitated, not even after he'd told her about the false accusations against himself, and she'd been pretty angry back then.

"Why would you say that?"

She squirmed under his scrutiny. "He was a very bad man."

Oliver felt there was more to the story, since Gustav's reputation was well known. "Did he ever... hurt you?"

Her eyes clouded over with fear, but she shook her head. "No... but not for lack of trying. I was lucky that Frau Mertens is so strict. She seems to have a sixth sense and several times came to my rescue..."

Oliver balled his hands into fists. Any man who brought that spark of horror into Dora's beautiful dark eyes deserved to die a painful death. "You should have told me."

"And what would you have done? Knowing that he could hurt both of us would only have made it so much more attractive to him." She cast her eyes downward. "I don't want to talk about him, ever again."

"You don't have to, sweetheart." He kissed her softly, and then made love to her, before he walked her back to her room.

The next morning he got up early and passed by the stables to take his favorite horse Sabrina for a ride, surprised to find Annegret waiting for him.

"Good morning, what can I do for you?"

She looked at him with uncertainty in her eyes. "I was wondering... I mean... the story with my injured back won't fly forever. Perhaps you could teach me to ride a horse?"

He stared at her in disbelief, before he broke out into laughter.

"This will be the second time in our lives that I teach you how to ride."

"Really? You taught Annegret?"

"I did. She was always a handful, but only when she started school did she become the spiteful horrible girl she was."

"So will you teach me?"

He nodded. "We'll have to find a place where nobody can see us, though."

"I'll leave that to you. And thank you so much."

"Whatever for?"

"For everything you do." She smiled. "And for helping me to help these wretched souls."

"I never thought I was made of heroic stuff, but it feels good to resist, if even in a small way. I never liked what Hitler was doing to the Jews, but it never occurred to me to protest."

She cocked her head and looked at him for the longest time. "It may surprise you, but me neither. I always took the harassment and everything for granted, not as something I must oppose. Not until I met people from the French Résistance. They opened my eyes to what it means to fight for your people, your country. But it was Wilhelm, whose last wish it was for me to do good with the Huber money. And here I am."

"Are you happy?" he asked.

"Strange as it sounds, I am. One day, when all of this is over, I'll be glad to shed my skin and become myself again, but for the time being I'll be content to be her and save as many lives as I can."

He continued to watch her when she left, wondering what else this woman had in store. She was a force to be reckoned with and he was grateful that Dora had begged her to employ him again. It was a lot of responsibility, but very fulfilling.

He'd also found a way to be with his horses, because he'd made it a custom not to use the truck, but ride a horse or drive a coach whenever possible. The one thing he enjoyed most, was the long ride to the factory through the winter forest.

It was a time, when he was alone on the back of a horse, where he could sometimes think about problems at Gut Plaun, sometimes merely enjoy the quiet and peace between the trees. He reflected how his life had become so much better since a bullet had shattered his leg, causing his dismissal from the Wehrmacht.

He arrived at the factory, tied Sabrina up to a tree not far from the entrance gate and greeted the guard, "Good morning."

"Good morning, Herr Gundelmann. There's a visitor waiting for you in the manager's office."

Oliver wondered who that might be and walked with long strides across the yard. He still felt a shiver run down his spine every time he came here, but the place was slowly getting less oppressive.

Annegret had made it clear she wanted the forced workers to be treated like humans, and had installed a strict rule of no physical punishment whatsoever. Even some of the hardened guards had soon admitted that the prisoners worked harder and better since then. It was by no means a bed of roses, but perhaps the best someone hauled off to a concentration camp could hope for.

"Herr Gundelmann, I was told you'd be in today," a woman said as Oliver entered the office.

"Frau...?"

"Landgrebe, I'm the block eldest in block eight," she introduced herself, somewhat shy.

"What brings you here, Frau Landgrebe? Is there a problem?"

"No, no problem at all. I came here in the name of all the inmates to thank you. A month ago none of us had believed we could survive the next winter, but with all the changes..." She bit on her lip. "Thank you from the bottom of our hearts."

"It's not only my doing." He and Annegret had agreed that her name or involvement shouldn't be mentioned—to keep up appearances. Everything she did for the benefit of the prisoners working here was supposedly done exclusively for her own financial benefit. If someone suspected her of being a friend of the Jews it would have grave consequences, for everyone involved. "Frau Landgrebe, we both know that I can't change the bigger picture or the rules of our government, but I can at least make lives bearable for everyone under my charge."

"And you do. The blankets alone made a huge difference against the cold, and then we received straw to use as mattresses, protective gear for the dangerous work, regular access to showers, enough fresh water and more food."

He nodded, knowing that the food was a sore point. Annegret always complained that the rations assigned to each prisoner were laughable and she spent a considerable amount of money buying more provisions, supposedly for Gut Plaun, but there was only so much to be had, since rations had been implemented for everyone except the highest brass.

"Thank you again, Herr Gundelmann, you're a true saint and God will surely reward you one day."

"I'm no saint." In fact, he'd known about the deplorable conditions in the factory but had done nothing, until Annegret had basically forced his hand.

36

Six months later, Summer 1943

Margarete sat on the terrace, overlooking the gardens, and enjoyed the wonderful weather. For the first time in ages she felt entirely at peace. Business was thriving, due to the ongoing war effort. She requested more prisoners on a regular basis, not only to work at the factory, but also as stable and farm hands to replace the men who were drafted into the Wehrmacht.

Meanwhile she had doubled the amount of prisoners under her care and close to a thousand Jews and others deemed *undesirables* now worked on the estate, as well fed and clothed as could be expected under rationing, and, most important of all, safe from physical abuse, humiliation and random acts of cruelty.

She took a sip of her coffee coupled with Frau Mertens' heavenly warm buns, thinking about Lena, like she so often did. The horrified look in her big brown eyes was burnt deep into Margarete's soul and she would never forgive herself for not rescuing her from Gustav's cruelty. If only she had seen through him earlier. In hindsight, the warning signs glared at her, decrying her gullibility and stupidity.

It was a burden she would have to live with for the rest of her life. On one occasion she had confided in Oliver about the guilt that was weighing her down. But instead of agreeing with her on how naïve, ignorant and trusting she had been, he'd told her that none of them, not even Oliver himself, who disliked Gustav for his aloof treatment of horses, had been able to see through him.

"Annegret, you have to remember that Gustav was a very skilled manipulator, and you are only a young and innocent woman. You were no match for him." Oliver had paused for a moment and then continued, "We all like to think of ourselves as too astute to be deceived, but unfortunately the contrary is true. Hitler has manipulated an entire nation into hating the Jews and making us believe they are the root of all evil."

"But that's different," she had protested.

"Not at all. Gustav did the same, just on a smaller level. He had everyone in town believe he was a good man. Even the SS men who share his penchant for cruelty were deceived by his charming attitude toward them and would never have guessed that he was the one stealing from them."

"Nevertheless I should have seen through him."

"But how? A Jew who has been persecuted all her life and is living under a false identity, how should you suspect the man who was so kind and generous toward you?"

"Perhaps you are right. But I still feel guilty."

"It's not your fault, but his. If anything, you should use this as a lesson to be wiser in the future and always challenge the motives of a person before fully trusting them."

"Wise words," she had answered, although she still felt the nagging pain that she might have prevented Lena's death, if only... or perhaps not. It was a fine line to tread between caring for the prisoners and appearing to be true to party principles.

Never could she utter even the slightest sympathy for *her* workers, and was always careful to explain their better treatment with efficiency reasons. The same was true when she claimed exemptions for any person in danger of deportation.

It was peculiar how many essential chemical and metal workers were needed to keep the factory running and she only hoped, none of the higher-ups in the SS would take a closer look, for as long as the war effort, and they personally, profited from selling the prisoners to her.

Even Horst Richter had approved of the changes she'd made, as long as they resulted in more or better production for the war effort. Although he'd commented several times that she was overdoing things a bit and the expenses for the maintenance of the workers were too high. But the factory was filling its quota for the Wehrmacht, and, at the end of the day, that was all the Nazis truly cared about.

"Fräulein Annegret, have you been able to go through the list?" Nils approached her.

"Yes. And it's next to impossible to get all of this." She pushed the list of material needed to repair the boathouse down by the water toward him. It was dotted with question marks and scratches. With so many hungry mouths to feed, she was always on the lookout for extra provisions and Nils had suggested buying a proper fishing boat to replace the decrepit rowing boat that hadn't been used since Annegret and her brothers had stopped coming to Gut Plaun.

"I know, Fräulein Annegret, but you asked me to list everything needed. Though, I guess I can improvise one thing or the other." Nils was a magician. He could repair anything at the manor, mostly with cardboard, a few nails and wire.

"Ask Oliver to order the material with a checkmark and for the rest you'll have to find another way."

"Will do."

She looked after him, as he left, a smile appearing on her lips. Living at Gut Plaun was as close as being in paradise as could be under the circumstances. She found so much joy in her version of the mean-spirited girl. The real Annegret would probably turn in her grave if she knew how much good was being done in her name.

"Fräulein Annegret, a letter and a postcard for you," the mailman called out, parking his bicycle in front of the porch.

"Thank you. Would you care for a bun? They are still hot." Since she knew him to read every postcard, it was prudent to stay on his good side.

"I'd love to. The postcard is from a friend in Leipzig," he added as he took the bun from her hand. "Do you still have many friends there?"

Margarete could barely keep a neutral face, such was her excitement. "Three or four maybe."

"I had better go, still have lots to deliver," he said, chewing.

"Please give my regards to your wife."

As soon as he was gone, Margarete took a glimpse at the letter that bore an official stamp and put it aside. She reverently touched the postcard. There was only one person in Leipzig who would write to her.

My dear Annegret,

Our government says that our courageous Wehrmacht will soon have won this war, so I hope we can see each other again in the near future. But tell me, have you met a man who brings you solace after the horrible fate of your family? I often think of my husband and how much I pray for his safe return.

Always your friend,

The signature was scrawled in intelligible letters and Margarete laughed. No doubt, this was Aunt Heidi inquiring about Uncle Ernst's well-being. It would be such a joy to reunite the two of them, but this would have to wait until after the war.

She sometimes saw Uncle Ernst from afar, when he came up to the manor to get supplies for the factory kitchen, but she rarely spoke with him. As much as her heart yearned to wrap her arms around him, it was simply too dangerous—for both of them.

The war looked bad for the Germans after the devastating defeat at Stalingrad earlier this year. She rooted for the Allies and prayed every day that it would be over soon and she could be herself again. Then, finally, she could divulge her true identity to the people around her and they would understand why she cared so much about the Jews. But until that day came, she would continue to be Annegret Huber.

With the factory set on course to be a safe haven for the prisoners she requested, she once again had time on her hands, wondering what else she could do with all the money that she had inherited. Because by now she'd accepted that the windfall profit had been sent to her by God, not to use for her own benefit, but for those who needed it most.

A LETTER FROM MARION

Dear Reader,

Thank you so much for reading *From the Dark We Rise*. If you did enjoy it, and want to keep up to date with all my latest releases, just sign up at the following link. Your email address will never be shared and you can unsubscribe at any time.

www.bookouture.com/marion-kummerow

I fell in love with Margarete writing the first book about her, *A Light in the Window*, which tells the story of how she came to be Annegret. Therefore I wanted to stay with her and see how she evolved and what she did with the legacy left to her.

Initially I planned for her to stay in Paris and join the Résistance, but decided against it, because I know so much more about Germany (being German myself) than France. Berlin was too dangerous, because too many people would know either her or Annegret there, so I searched for a place near Berlin where she could settle down, and I found Plau am See.

As always, when writing I get more ideas and finally the plot about the ammunition factory formed. Perhaps you can guess where I got the inspiration from? From the very famous Oskar Schindler. But apart from the goal to help the Jews in his factory, everything else, and especially all my characters, is fictional. Although I tried to model them after how real people would have behaved back then.

Dora, as an example, is a typical *Ostarbeiter*, worker from the

East, who came to Germany in search of a job and money. The relation between Ukraine and Germany was a checkered one, and depending on the exact date, they were considered friends or foes.

In the beginning of the war against the Soviet Union, Ukrainians welcomed the Germans as saviors from the Russian yoke. Most of them hated their Soviet oppressors and hoped things would improve under German rule. It did, for many, for a while—until it didn't. The details are much too complicated to explain in one paragraph and if you're interested in the Ukrainian history during World War Two, I recommend the book, *The Woman at the Gates*, by my friend Chrystyna Lucyk-Berger, an American of Ukrainian descent.

To get everything right, I undertook a four-day research trip to Plau am See, Malchow and Waren. First of all, the ammunitions factory did really exist, although not in Plau am See, but in Malchow, across the huge lake called Plauer See. Its codename was Albion, and at one time it was the biggest employer in the small town of Malchow. I grappled with the decision to rewrite the book to place Gut Plaun on the other side of the lake, but ultimately decided against it. While researching the actual camp and factory and using the information to make my story as historically correct as possible, I still simplified many details, so felt it was better to put the factory elsewhere.

I had a stroke of luck when the very nice hosts of my vacation apartment in Malchow, who have lived there all their lives, regaled me with many stories and nuggets of wisdom. One of them being that the mother of my host worked in the ammunition factory during the war.

Apparently out of the up to five thousand workers, several hundred were civilian workers from nearby towns and the rest mostly foreign workers from Poland and the Soviet Union (forced and voluntary), plus about twelve hundred camp inmates from Ravensbrück, who had to do the most tedious and dangerous tasks under appalling conditions.

If you are interested in my visit to the remains of the camp and factory, you can read about it here: *https://kummerow.info/munitions-factory-in-malchow*

As for the horses, the Wehrmacht did indeed fall back on horsepower in the Russian winter. After WW1 the animals had been deemed old-fashioned, but when the vehicles got stuck due to mud or cold, horses were suddenly very high in demand.

There will be a third book about Margarete and her adventures hiding with a false identity and I can promise it will be nail-biting

Thanks so much for reading *From the Dark We Rise.* I hope you loved it, and if you did I would be very grateful if you could write a review. I'd love to hear what you think, and it makes such a difference helping new readers to discover one of my books for the first time.

I love hearing from my readers—you can get in touch on my Facebook page, through Twitter, Goodreads or my website.

Thanks,

Marion Kummerow

https://kummerow.info

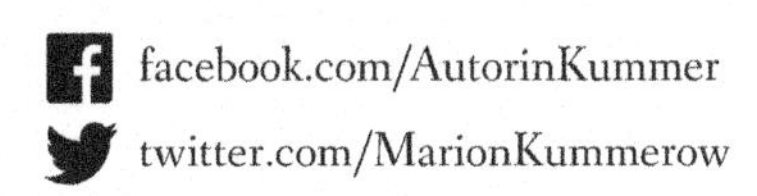